SOUTHERN JUSTICE

A Novel

by

R. W. M.
FLYNN

As I have chosen the non-traditional route of self-publication, all errors, mistakes, typos and similar are my own.

To my parents:

I owe everything I have accomplished and everything I will ever accomplish to you both.

Table of Contents

CHAPTER 1

Summer 2007

The man known as Big Country in a former life took hold of the gold hoop strung through the lion's teeth and let it fall three times. *Knock. Knock. Knock.* Though it was summertime in upstate South Carolina, it was not stifling hot given the sun had set four hours earlier and clouds brought rain just before that. Big Country breathed in the crisp, humid air and loosened his tie. The news he was given earlier that day had troubled him deeply and he knew he had to strike fast. Luckily for him, the Senator was arrogant enough to turn away Secret Service protection in his home, telling the world he would like to see criminals try to reach him before he shot and killed anyone so bold and *reckless* as to try to cross him. *I fought in the Gulf*, the Senator would brag to reporters and in interviews. *I've killed before*, he would go on to state in a braggadocios manner. His constituents would love to hear it. He never specified in these rants *who* he had killed. Little did they know.

The freshly painted white door opened just a crack, revealing the Senator's wrinkled skin and drowsy brown eyes. He was wearing a white undershirt barely peeking out of a black silk robe, cinched at the waist by a gold cloth belt. The Senator recognized the well-dressed man at his door, but it had been years since they had spoken. A gold wristwatch emerged from under a silk sleeve and the Senator squinted to see the dial.

"Do you have any idea what time it is? Why are you here?" It was a pompous sneer that spewed from the Senator's mouth.

Big Country did not utter a word as he shoved a loafer through the door. The kick blew the Senator onto his back and the unwelcome guest strutted in, closing the door behind him. He found a switch behind him and light flooded the grand entryway. A shotgun perched itself in the corner behind the door and Big Country followed the Senator's gaze to it. He shook his head and kicked the man in the groin.

"Fuck! Why are you doing this!" the Senator, now nothing more than a cowardly child, shrieked and squealed, grasping between his legs. He crawled back, pulling himself across the marble floor with one hand as he looked with horror at the intruder. He hit the bottom step of the staircase and sat up. Quickly he was to his feet. He had been at war, remember? He could fight, remember?

"What do you want? Money? I can get you money. Easily. How much? Just give me the number," the Senator begged. "My checkbook's in the office. Come on. I'll go write it out now."

The Senator cautiously limped through an archway under the staircase and motioned for the familiar trespasser to follow. Big Country quietly followed, having no intention of taking any check that evening. He would not let his victim so much as pick up a pen before he would kill him.

Once through the archway, the men turned right, passing between ornate oak doors and into a magnificent office. The walls were mahogany and the floor was a dated, yet opulent green carpet. The room screamed money, despite the fact that the man who commissioned it was set to make only $165,200 of the taxpayer's money that year. Leather books, some appearing to pre-date the existence of the United States itself, lined the shelves housed on the far wall behind a massive mahogany desk. In the center of the room hung a gold chandelier that belonged in Versailles, not Lexington, South Carolina. Oil portraits coated the walls on the left and right. And a wooden staircase led to a balcony just above the desk that offered a spot for even more books and spanned the width of the room. *This space would do just fine*, Big Country thought.

Once he reached the desk, the Senator yanked the chain of a green and gold banker's lamp to illuminate the desk. Papers and legal pads were strewn everywhere. The Senator reached for a pen and a leather booklet on the far end of the bureau. Before his greedy, disgusting fingers managed to ensnare either, a bullet was placed right between his eyes, passing through his brain and coming to rest in the pages of a book on the shelf behind the lifeless body. Less than five seconds after the bullet all but surely ended the Senator's existence, a knife was plunged deep into the man and cut the width of his overweight stomach.

Big Country knelt down and felt for a pulse from Senator, who was slumped low against his desk. There was none. Big Country smiled and left the way he came.

CHAPTER 2

Spring 2025

Robert Remington felt right at home standing in front of the Honorable Judge Jonathan Dickson Grayland IV, in spite of the numerous, self-important names and roman numeral bookending it. Perched high in front of him in his jet-black robe, the overseer of all things criminal in the Fifth Circuit of South Carolina's justice system, Judge Grayland graduated University of South Carolina's Joseph F. Rice School of Law (then just the University of South Carolina Law School) in 1983, a year prior to Robert. Despite the difference in JD class year, the pair shared the stage in 1981 from the *real* USC's undergraduate program where they were fraternity brothers and loose acquaintances. After dozens of appearances in Judge Grayland's courtroom over his esteemed career, the two had a mutual appreciation and respect for each other, despite some heated exchanges in chambers from time to time. Still, this never stopped them from sharing an occasional steak dinner or mingling over a couple of whiskey sours at a State Bar event, colleague's retirement or community baptism celebration.

Judges serving in the Fifth Circuit Court were almost always graduates of SC Law, where the school and Court shared a county. Due to near uniformity in the suit and robe-wearing arbiters of justice, there was rarely a recusal for fraternization amongst defense counsel and judges on the Court; there would hardly be any local attorneys left if that was the practice. The reality was, everybody may not have actually known everybody, but it sure seemed like it in some circumstances; there was no degree of separation and it seemed to bother neither solicitor (South Carolina's version of a prosecuting attorney or district attorney) nor constituent. If it ain't broke—and even if, at times, it is breaking—don't fix it.

Robert slowly and confidently stood up from his old, wooden seat at the defense table, buttoning his sear sucker blazer over his garnet tie in the process and approached the podium. His suspenders felt tighter than usual. Probably from the stress-induced binge eating he often engaged in before trial.

"Thank you, Judge Grayland," Robert said confidently. Having more than once slipped up and referred to his frat brother on the bench by his nickname, "Ole' Gray", an ode to his Confederate general lineage, Robert knew to keep it formal in order to avoid being chewed out in chambers.

"Now DA Hollinsworth and I have gone back and forth for the last week or so *creating* a case. No doubt about it that's what us attorneys do. We create our side of the case and then we *present* it…though these two prongs often overlap significantly. I often like to say the *creating* of the case is lemonade and the *presenting* of the case is the sweet tea: we start with lemonade and often finish the evening with a cool—sometimes spiked—batch of sweet tea." The twelve faces in the jury box grinned. It was fair game to make such a reference in the college town, but in other Circuit Courts within the borders of the Bible Belt, Robert knew such a reference to booze in front of teetotalers would not play. "But regularly, we find ourselves with a spiked Arnold Palmer instead!" The jurors' grins grew and a few let out hardy chuckles. Robert was a master at playing to the jury. He had made a fine career of it and thought he deserved an Oscar nomination for some of his performances.

Robert's southern twang was soothing to the jury. It was slow, pronounced and bordered on more of a Savannah *drawl.* Once, Robert had gone toe to toe with a DA born and raised in the Bronx, New York in this same courtroom. And if looks could kill. These southerners do not like outsiders. The twangy-drawl, which he often played up in court, ingratiated him with the folks in the box.

"Now, now, I digress. I say this all to you so you know that I—that we—" Robert pointed to the table for the prosecution. District Attorney, or as he preferred, Circuit Solicitor Darren Hollinsworth, sat upright, staring at his legal pad, seemingly ignoring Robert. He pretended to take notes, but it was obvious he was rehearsing his own closing. He too, was a Gamecock lifer. "We, ladies and gentlemen, know and understand that you think one of us is full of crap. My job is to make sure you think Mr. Hollinsworth and his witnesses are full of crap and his job is to do the same to me and mine.

"Now this 'full of crap' thought process is unfortunate, but this is one of those cases where the *facts* are firmly on my side. The case—or lack thereof—was already created in full by the time I saw the facts of which I am referring to. I merely had to present these facts to y'all and yet you fine, smart Carolinians use your common sense. Because guess what? The ball of yarn the prosecution has strung just doesn't add up. My client," Robert pointed to a young woman seated at the defense table, "could not be responsible for the untimely demise and tragic death of her young Johnny because she was not there. Who was there? Who was there the entire time as evidenced by cell phone tower records and one Dominoes delivery driver? The boy's grandfather, Harold Clark III; Betty's ex-fling's father. And who—has it been established beyond a reasonable doubt by cell phone tower records, not one, not two, but three store attendants and, albeit grainy, CCTV footage—was at the grocery store, Circle K and Chick-Fil-A during the time Johnny lost his life?"

Robert did not take his eyes from the jury box as he pointed at Betty. A couple jurors mouthed his client's name. This was a great sign for the defense. "My client. That is the answer. My client.

"Ladies and gentlemen, how we even got to a trial is beyond me. When I was given this case, of course I knew all about it. Betty Stevenson was deemed the Casey Marie Anthony of the Palmetto State. She was plastered over the front page of the *Post and Courier* down in Charleston. Then I was up from the Low Country on the Grand Strand and it was plastered there on the.*Sun News*. Every day of my mini-vacation I allow my wife to bring me on once a year, I couldn't get away from Miss Betty's beautiful, innocent face. Heck! I even ventured to New York, New York on some business during that time and they had her plastered all over the *New York Post*. People are to think that just because a young, single mother goes on dates and may from time to time post provocative pictures of herself online that she is somehow capable of such cruel negligence of her only child?"

With this last line, a couple of the middle-aged men in the front of the jury box blushed beet red. They had done the same when the prosecution—over Robert's vehement objections both in chambers and in the courtroom—brought out an ancient, tube television on wheels to go through a slideshow of both Betty's Instagram account and portions of her OnlyFans page. Luckily for Betty, the prosecution had to subscribe and pay to have access to show the photos in court. Another subscription to pay for Robert's hefty fee.

"The evidence clearly shows that the drugs found in Betty's house were Harold's. Despite the police letting Harold leave the premises without questioning him, without any drug or alcohol testing, eye witnesses told of Harold driving erratically and—I'm quoting Mr. Mitchell here—" Robert walked to the defense table, picked up a yellow notepad with his firm name plastered across the top and read a line from a key witness, "'as if Mr. Harold Clark was a handle of Southern Comfort deep and two sheets to the wind.'

"Mr. Clark has a minor history of substance abuse. As does his son, the father of little Johnny, whose history is quite more robust." Hollinsworth started to get up to object before thinking better of it. It was thought to be bad form to object during closing arguments for petty matters. Bringing up Harold Clark IV's addiction issue was bait Hollinsworth almost took.

Robert had made so many closing arguments in his career it was like second nature. He often let his mind wander while delivering these artful orations. He was so relaxed. An actor reprising his beloved role. Decades of trials will do that to a man. What also helped was Robert knew that unseasoned, rookie trial lawyers like Hollinsworth tried too much to play to the jury during their first few trials, often to the neglect of the judge, who may not make the final ruling but held sway over what the arbiters of justice got to hear. Then, after a few reprimands and dirty looks, rookie trial lawyers become befuddled and, in turn, play too much to the judge at times when they should focus on the jury, becoming altogether lost when it comes to who they should cater to. Closing arguments, for example, should always be for the jury. Unfortunately for Hollinsworth, he had been turned around so much in this trial that Robert was sure he would try to play at least a little to Judge Grayland to save face. The trial was all but lost, though that wasn't Hollinsworth's fault. It was his boss's.

The higher ups in the attorney general's office marked this case as an easy win way too early on and that's why they gave it to the rook. Young Johnny Stevenson, just six months old, was found face down in the bathtub, lungs filled with water in his mother's Elgin, South Carolina apartment. Johnny's parents were Betty Stevenson and Harold Clark IV, neither of whom claimed to be home watching Johnny that night. Early on in the discovery phase—and even earlier thanks to national media attention—it was established that Clark IV was at a fish fry for the local Baptist church and Betty was on a date. Because the boy was at his mother's apartment; because his mother was on a date and at another man's apartment for part of the evening when, in the eyes of the southern Bible Belt public, should be abstinent and dedicated only to Johnny; and because his father was being a Godly man at his local church's fish fry, the court of public opinion had spoken and Betty was guilty early on. Oh, but the people love a comeback story. An underdog. And this case—more specifically, this defendant—was not like others Robert had. He believed in this young lady and that was part of the reason why he decided to take it as his swan song. Robert's usual clients were those who deserved swift justice, so this was a nice change of pace to go out on.

What Robert and his team of crack investigators were able to dig up and hold until trial (not exactly ethical, yet common and "inadvertent", the defense would claim), was that, to the "surprise" of Clark IV, the babysitter that evening was none other than his father. Further "confusing" Clark IV was the fact that Clark III had volunteered to babysit the grandson he all but ignored the first six months of his life. Naïve Betty happily took him up on the offer to go on a date with a man she met through her OnlyFans account. Robert was able to link her date—Samuel Jones Jr.—to Clark III. Robert was also able to prove through a thousand dollar an hour medical expert that the boy, Johnny, more likely than not was held under the bathwater and drowned. The final nail in the coffin were secret recordings of Clark III and Clark IV seemingly discussing an early demise for the "unwanted", the "mistake of a bastard" and the "stain on the bloodline" child. The prosecution, of course, somehow spun a web to explain this conversation away as a mere discussion of the young boy's pneumonia he had contracted just before the conversation.

The trial—sensationalized throughout the South given the attractiveness of Miss Betty and the C-List celebrity status of Clark III as a former state congressman turned gameshow host—was broadcast live on CNN, Fox News and every local channel in between. A good murder trial known no political leaning; all are welcome to consume the public spectacle.

DA Hollinsworth and his superiors had made several offers during the trial to Robert and his client, each one more favorable than the last. At the outset, Betty was charged with homicide by child abuse and could see anywhere from twenty years in prison to life in prison, though the death penalty became a real possibility during evidentiary hearings when a man was put to death by firing squad in the Palmetto State. After day two, the DA offered ten years with the likely result being freedom after six. Then, a day later, five years. Just before closing arguments, they knocked it down to some kind of child negligence (Robert was not even listening as he ate a tuna sandwich in the cafeteria, gazing at Hollinsworth with a smug grin) that would mean a year in prison. Robert convinced Betty she would get off and have a great civil suit on her hands. No dice, Hollinsworth. It was crystal clear that Clark III and Clark IV conspired to kill the boy, yet the prosecution pridefully held onto the idea that Clark III was drunk and asleep and Betty, not Clark IV, conspired to get Clark III drunk and then have Johnny killed. This theory, by the way, was formed on day three of the trial after their original story fell apart on the witness stand. A complete Hail Mary. An about-face for the losing prosecution.

"Ladies and gentlemen, the great State of South Carolina asked you to do one thing here. One simple thing and that is to use your God-given common sense on this one. Don't let the prosecution use big words and confuse the darn hell out of you with some wild conspiracies. It's clear what happened. Miss Betty is suffering enough from the loss of her only son. Don't make her suffer further. Thank you."

Robert nodded to the jury and Judge Grayland and returned to his seat next to Betty. He put a consoling hand on her shoulder as she fought back tears, moist tissues in each hand.

CHAPTER 3

The Remington Family had three homes, each in South Carolina and two-thirds of them with a rich history of its own. The first and most historic was the Shelby home, inherited through Robert's wife, Caroline Shelby Remington. From 1985 until 2000, Robert and his wife counted the structure as their main residence just north of Broad Street in Charleston. The Shelby-turned-Remington compound had sparkling views of the sun dancing off the Ashely River in the distance, beyond Colonial Lake Park, a pineapple water fountain that her grandfather built from scratch and a stunning green lawn that would give a fairway at Augusta National a run for its money. That particular area of Charleston was deemed to be only for "SNOBs" since it was "Slightly North of Broad" and tended to be inhabited by rich, entitled, well, *snobs*. This moniker was mostly accurate as a good portion of Charlestonians inherited their historic homes from old money, slaveholding families, but, by all accounts, the Remingtons did not fit the snob mold and were generally liked slightly north of Broad, south of Broad and even as far north as Park Circle.

The Shelby home was built by Caroline's great-great grandfather upon his return from near exile in 1870. The self-imposed exile of Sean Shelby and his family was due to the fact that they had committed the deadly sin of being staunch abolitionists in a city that saw the first shots of the Civil War; better yet, in the state that seceded *first*. As such, trying to avoid any and all squabbles, he relocated his family to a cousin's estate in rural Virginia during the bloody war and managed to avoid most of the action.

The house he managed to construct upon his return was a white Charleston single with a faded red brick wall surrounding it. The hospitality door, a fake front door that led only to a "piazza" as the Charlestonians called their porches, was a distressed teal with gold embellishments. The home itself was three stories with uneven flooring (Caroline recounted many stories to her children of errant marble racing from one side of the house to the other, with nothing but gravity and the lopsided framing doing all the work) and historic charm. The four small bedrooms were just enough for the Remington clan and an old carriage house out back was renovated into a garage with studio apartment/guest quarters above. Though it was dilapidated in areas, half falling apart and haphazardly updated in others, it could easily fetch close to five million dollars on the open market. But Caroline was not selling. Ever. It was essentially her only tie to the Shelby family history, for better or for worse.

While Caroline loved the house's history, she loathed living there given haunting childhood memories of alcoholism, fighting and death. Robert, on the other hand, preferred living in the Shelby house given its proximity to the Remington Law office during the '80s, a period when he was trying to get his struggling practice off the ground. He wanted to be as close to his downtown office as possible, was what he told others. The truth was, he liked the proximity to the jail (though he still was not remarkably close) since there were plenty of late-night calls regarding shootings, drug deals, rapes, beatings. Each one helped pay for the Remington's life. Besides, they could not afford to buy anywhere else on the peninsula or even close to it with the struggles Robert faced early on in his practice and Caroline accepted that fact.

In 2000, after twenty years of marriage, three kids and a successful practice taking off, bringing in bigger cases, Caroline successfully convinced the workaholic to slow down at least a pinch. Robert was making a name for himself as a go to criminal defense attorney, charging $250 an hour ($325 an hour for trial work) and had decided he could hire a partner to help his growing caseload. (Ironically, his bigger breaks came from befriending law enforcement officers and getting tips and work from them.) Robert, his two secretaries and his rotating cast of young law clerks and associates could use the help. Having at last gotten more time with her husband, Caroline did would any loving wife would do—sent him off to get more work. That is, she had him down on Sullivan's Island overseeing the renovations of their pride and joy: the Sullivan's Island house they creatively named "Sully's".

Sully's was a little, 1,300 square foot, first row bungalow with 3 tiny bedrooms and one bathroom. Robert and Caroline scraped enough together to purchase it in 1990—after Hurricane Hugo had decimated the island, flooding the entire house. The previous owners were an older couple who could not afford the renovations—cash or time-wise—and chose to move to a modest condo farther north on Pawley's Island, leaving Sully's to be grabbed up on the cheap by the Remingtons. (Robert had secretly gotten the husband out of a DUI and managed to keep it all quiet around town, endearing himself to the elderly couple to the tune of a pocket listing twenty-five percent under market.) Over the next decade, Robert and Caroline spruced it up to the best of their ability—both financial ability and handiwork ability, that is—and shortly after beginning operation spruce up in Summer of '99, Hurricane Floyd came and flooded the entire thing again. After picking up the pieces, Caroline was set on getting the mini fortress built and fortified stronger than Fort Sumter before next hurricane season.

Fast-forward twenty-plus years later and Sully's sits at just under a couple thousand square feet with a pool, a fourth bedroom, another full bath and—Robert's favorite—a sauna that worked about half the time.

Unfortunately, Robert was not fiddling with his cedar barrel sauna at Sully's tonight. He was not tinkering in the carriage-turned-garage off the Ashley River either. He was alone at their third house—the Lexington house. Less historic, more practical and purchased to make *future* memories for the Remington's. The Lexington house had been purchased in 2010 when Robert got sick of spending weeks on end either commuting from Charleston to the courts in Columbia or staying in hotels. As the cases and clientele became more lucrative, he began expensing more and more of his hotel suites and Uber Blacks (and, before Uber Blacks became an option car services), but it was exhausting, nevertheless, for the reluctantly aging attorney to live out of a suitcase half his life. Given this relative wealth and success, Robert discussed it with Caroline and they bought the suburban Columbia home a short drive from the Fifth Circuit, but secluded enough to make him feel like a rugged outdoorsman in the backwoods. The Lexington abode became even more useful when the first, followed by second and third, of the Remington children all became Gamecocks. Having a home-away-from-home for the garnet and black family made it an easy selling point. No more missed home football games.

At the Lexington compound that evening, Robert was sitting in his weathered brown recliner, flipping through various newspapers on his iPad. The Braves-Mets game was faintly audible from the television in front of him as Atlanta's first baseman hit his league-leading thirtieth homerun of the season to put them up by one over New York in the fifth, but Robert had not noticed. His hearing was not what it used to be and for all intents and purposes the television was muted so he could catch up on the news.

During trial of any magnitude—let alone a trial for murder—Robert had tunnel vision. He was pathological and methodical with how he spent his time. He woke up on trial days at 4:30 A.M. and went to the gym. His physique and strength were not what they once had been, but for 65 Robert still cut a commanding presence. Standing just over six feet and around two hundred and thirty pounds, he made sure to make his trainer push him during his daily 5 AM sessions during trial. Robert felt the testosterone from lifting helped keep him mentally sharp and competitive in the courtroom. He needed to be in tip top shape to stay alive in his profession.

After the early morning gym session, Robert's pre-trial routine included wolfing down eggs and oatmeal, reviewing court documents that he would need that day or the next and, by late morning, a light jog (though lately, it was more of a brisk walk) to focus up for trial before a shower and a shave. He would clean the salt and pepper beard trimmings from the sink, throw on his suit of the day and head to meet his paralegals and, if he had any at the time, his associates or law clerks. They would sip coffee and meticulously run through the day. His routine was a far cry from the earlier days of his career when he ran around, hair afire on days of trial, little to no sleep, filled with cheap coffee and fast food, or no food at all, and secluded from his family. Just like his appearance, Robert Remington aged like fine wine in his trial preparation skills.

With his closing argument finished and nothing left but a verdict, all Robert had to do was wait for the jury: young Miss Betty's fate fell to the twelve South Carolinians in the jury box and all Robert could do was show back up to court tomorrow, see jury instructions get delivered and then wait for the phone call. Half of his profession amounted to a full-blown waiting game.

With the trial all but behind him, Robert let himself catch back up on the world via his beloved news. First on his slate were a few articles on the usual political drama and congressional infighting that made the political arena so infuriating to Robert. He could only take two articles about two different corruption investigations into sitting Senators and the lead sentence of a third article about a White House bribery scandal before he needed to move on, his blood boiling. Next, he read a handful of articles and op-eds on the various wars and proxy wars and almost-wars and cold wars going on overseas. These always interested Robert. He was a sucker for what drove humans to kill en masse, whether it be religion, politics, geography or some sort of desire for world domination. After about an hour of world wars, Robert turned to catch up on the news around his Palmetto State. He read up about new bridges, roads and general infrastructure improvements set to begin around the state, with the caveat that permits were still needed and funding not fully committed. He read about a former client languishing on death row, in limbo after his last appeal was denied. After making a mental note to see that ex-client soon and half an article about a young girl in Fort Mill who had just lost both her parents in a murder-suicide, prompting Robert to think about taking on some pro bono cases in retirement, his phone rang.

"Hello?" Robert said on speaker phone, holding the phone close to his ear. He was not great with technology and never looked at the caller ID. He was becoming an old man, hence, retirement.

"Hi, Dear. How'd today go?" Caroline's sweet voice asked.

"Oh hello, Honey. Today went as well as I could've hoped. As I'm sure I've told you half a dozen times already, it's odd how they had the defense deliver closing first, then the prosecution, but I'm allowed a rebuttal if needed. I know what I'll say if I feel a rebuttal is needed. Short and sweet. But I doubt the prosecutor will have anything other than a negative impact on his own case. He's been stumbling over himself this entire trial. I can't blame him—he was given a loser of a case loosely disguised as a winner. Too good to be true and it was."

"Well, that's good. So, you think you'll win your last ever trial? Go out on top?" Caroline inquired with a twinkle in her voice.

"Barring anything unforeseen, this will be a big win. Jury probably won't even take more than a few hours of deliberations," Robert bragged. "I've already got Katz & Stiller on standby with a civil suit for the girl. But I'm not sure. This win may make me want to keep going...."

"Robert Henry!" Caroline snapped.

"You know I kid. The firm will be in good hands with cousin Morrison taking over. That son of a bitch just better not try to change the name on me. Remington Law is now an institution in the Low Country, dammit." Robert stated, only half kidding. He erratically slammed a closed fist on the side table for emphasis and took in the rippling veins in his forearms with glee. *Still got it.*

"I'm so gullible. You get me riled up with that ruse every time. Retirement will do you good."

"How're the boys? Have you heard from them?" Robert asked, chuckling at how naïve and innocent his wife could be at times. Robert asked every night he was away from home about the boys because, as any good sons, they called their mother almost every day. The three boys were the couple's pride and joy, the Remington legacy. Bobby was the oldest at thirty-four and had moved to Atlanta to pursue a career in advertising for a brief period after college, before quickly moved back to the Palmetto State and currently lived in Summerville where he opened up his own advertising firm in Summerville. Liam, thirty, was the middle child and after a short stint in the Minor League Baseball—which included a stop at the Charleston Riverdogs for a month—accepted that he would never make it past High A ball let alone sniff the Majors and was in his second year of law school at SC. The baby was Ben. He was twenty-five, had opened one coffee shop in downtown Charleston with his wife, was about to open a second in Hilton Head and already eyed a third on Daniel Island.

"You know Ben stopped by and brought his old mother coffee from *Peninsula Coffee*. He started chewing my ear off about whether or not *Heady Coffee* would be a good name for the new shop and then turned to bouncing *Island Coffee* ideas off me for D.I.. At least he loves what he does, but I secretly think he just figured I may be lonely and need a male presence around. I told him Max is doing just a fine job and Louie ain't half bad either." The family dogs made sure Caroline was never truly alone, especially on Robert's somewhat frequent road trips when they got to take his side of the bed. "He started explaining this new roasting technique he's trying for the Hilton Head shop. I can't even explain it, but to me it tasted exactly the same, if not worse, than the normal drip." They both chuckled.

"But hey, I did get another call," Caroline's tone changed from lax to staid. "It was Jenny. Sounds like there's trouble. Derrick's going to need a good lawyer. Know any?" Robert put the phone down for a moment to sigh; Caroline almost certainly heard it anyway. And expected it.

Jenny was Caroline's only sister who lived about halfway between Columbia and Charleston in an old town named Florence. Jenny had been cut off from her and Caroline's parents decades earlier and rarely spoke to the family. And there were many, many reasons for that. Caroline, however, always had a soft spot for her troubled sister and continuously answered the phone when she called, especially since she was the only Shelby family she had left. It was Caroline's version of survivor's guilt, Robert had surmised. Caroline was doing well while her baby sister rotted in the middle of nowhere with only God knows who.

"What is it this time?" Robert asked as patiently as he could without sounding sarcastic.

CHAPTER 4

Flying down the interstate had always been one of Robert's favorite pastimes. If it was up to him, he would never fly anywhere in North America. Though he did not fear flying or become cost-conscious when traveling, as so many increasingly do, he simply enjoyed taking in the scenery afforded one on an extended drive; it made him introspective in a way few other activities did. It was almost as if such drives reignited appreciation for life and the creations around him. Caroline, however, got a bit bored on such drives and as the boys came along it became more and more of a chore to entertain three young children for such protracted periods of time—especially in a time *before* iPads. But with the boys having all grown up, Caroline being back at Sully's and Robert calling the shots, he took the long way home from Lexington. His only wish was that he still had his 1969 Mustang to feel the American muscle as he churned up the miles to home.

It had been four days since Robert delivered his closing arguments, breaming with confidence. Both a lot and nothing at all had happened in the interim. The following day, Judge Grayland delivered jury instructions which, boiled down to its simplest form, were whether the facts presented were sufficient enough to convince them beyond a reasonable doubt that Johnny was in the custody of his mother and his mother was negligent in letting a six-month-old play in a bathtub by himself, then Betty should be found guilty. In the alternative, if such negligence was not proven to the jury beyond a reasonable doubt, the defendant should be found innocent. There were other confusing and convoluted explanations offered by the Judge Grayland, almost willing for the jury to have something to talk about or debate, but these two options were the heart of the case. Simple enough, right?

Wrong. In what Robert assumed would be quick deliberations turned into a day and a half of waiting around paired with almost a dozen questions from the jury. They wanted to hear Harold Clark III's testimony again. They wanted to see the written definition of negligence. They wanted to hear the cell phone tower expert's testimony again coupled with another review of Betty's cell phone record. They wanted to hear more about Samuel Jones Jr.'s background. In what Robert believed was the most clear-cut example of an innocent defendant he had in his career, a miscarriage of justice was percolating and potentially bubbling to the surface. Robert's confidence was dwindling by the hour as he began to wonder whether his own past misgivings were creeping back to haunt him on that jury.

As Robert waited around the courthouse on the second morning of deliberations, Hollinsworth approached Robert with two cups of coffee. As the young solicitor trudged forward, Robert noted one was a cup of decaf and the other was a cup regular, both black. The prosecutor stood in front of Robert, gleefully holding up both local coffeehouse labels as some sort of peace offering. Robert peered up from the rickety wooden bench he was spread out on reading and smirked.

"Goll-*lee*, Hollinsworth. This a *bribe*?" Robert said with a chuckle as he took the regular coffee. "I find it offensive you even offered a decaf. Undoubtedly due to my advanced age, huh?"

"Well, Ole Bobby I wasn't quite sure. Figured rather be safe than sorry. I may be half your age but I think you're in better shape than I've ever been. Heck, I'm not even thirty and I already take blood pressure meds and a handful of others. The missus has me going to get a full blood panel tomorrow, so maybe it's for the better here. Besides, I drink half-caf quite often. A decaf won't hurt in taming my thick blood. The missus will be happy when I tell her." Once trial was over, prosecutors and "Ole Bobby" got along quite well. And why wouldn't they; in Robert's opinion, both sides were merely doing their jobs and once closing arguments were delivered, all artillery had been fired and the case was out of the lawyer's hands. Due to this, Robert was a staple in both the prosecution and law enforcement community. If they had to deal with a defense attorney, better be Ole Bobby.

"Keep doing high profile, high stress trials like this and you're gonna run yourself to an early grave, youngin'." Robert had been chairman of the SC Bar Association's mental health arm for a decade and took the mental health issues in his profession very seriously. He had seen plenty of his fellow Bar members trade the uppercase "Bar" for the lowercase "bar", lose everything drinking to excess under the stress of trials and the billable hours and meet the good Lord earlier than they should. Some self-inflicted.

"I know, Bobby. I was at your last speech down in Savannah about mental health. That former prosecutor scared me straight." Robert had asked a friend of his, a law professor named Dr. John Carol, to speak at an annual conference that most trial lawyers in the southeast attended every year. There was networking, some fun activities, mostly boring activities and a few sobering undertakings, such as the speech Hollinsworth was referring to. Dr. Carol taught numerous courses which included Arbitration, Tort Law I and II, and Client Advocation I, but his specialty was Morals and Ethics in the Field of Law; he had written several books on it. Early on in his career as a prosecutor, Dr. Carol began toeing the line of what was ethical and what was unethical in terms of what was zealous advocacy and what was over the line. He began flouting the *Brady* rule by routinely "forgetting" to turn over key pieces of evidence to the defense in discovery. He began writing witness testimony that they, the witnesses, would recite under oath. And worst of all, he began putting innocent men and women on trial, playing ball with certain corrupt detectives and police, planting evidence and putting the innocent behind bars. By year five of this in rural Georgia, having progressively gotten bolder and more unscrupulous, Dr. Carol's transgressions finally caught up to him. A cop Carol routinely worked with was busted for selling drugs stolen from evidence and agreed to flip on Dr. Carol, singing like a canary on the scheme. As a result, all twenty cases Dr. Carol had a hand in were vacated.

After being presented with numerous witnesses to Dr. Carol's behavior, some of which were undercover cops and federal agents, Dr. Carol avoided a lengthy, circus of a trial by pleading guilty and serving five and a half years in prison. Upon release at age thirty-five, Dr. Carol, having been disbarred, had no job but still had a mountain of debt from student loans for a degree he could no longer use. He spiraled upon release from incarceration: drinking, drugs and a few half-hearted suicide attempts, all of which he spoke about at the conference and in one of his books. There was no great awakening or moment of reversal, but gradually, after finding his current wife and Christianity, Dr. Carol managed to get a Ph.D. in Ethics by age fifty. A real one-eighty that kept the attorneys on the edge of their seats, hanging on every word. It also helped that it followed an hour-long speech on the advances in the Internal Revenue Code's interpretations.

"So, what do you say, Hollinsworth? Why're they taking so long in there?"

"Bobby, I ain't got no clue. This case was a stinker from the get-go. Can't imagine what's going on back there. I did my best, but I couldn't have convinced an Eskimo to build an igloo with the facts I was given," Hollinsworth said, shaking his head and sipping his coffee.

"Well, I'm glad you at least admit it. 'Nough attorneys never know when to be straight and own up on a case. 'Specially youngins like yourself."

After twenty more minutes of amicable chit chat, the doors to the courtroom burst open and the bailiff, all three hundred pounds of him, sauntered out. He looked up the hall opposite Hollinsworth and Robert, then turned and made eye contact with Robert. He gave a prolonged nod and a wave accompanied by labored breathing. The jury had a decision after just over a day. Quick for a jury in a trial involving the death of an infant, but long for the facts of this particular case.

Robert patted Hollinsworth on the arm as he rose from the wobbly bench. "The moment of truth is upon us, my friend. No hard feelins either way," Robert stated with a twangy smile.

Hollinsworth nodded and gave a pained smirk. He had a bad feeling about the verdict. After holding the door open for his elder statesman, Hollinsworth took his seat at the prosecution's table and Robert took his for the defense. Robert had let his associate drive back to Charleston the day prior for a family baptism, so he sat alone until a door opened behind the juror's box. Betty was led in by a wrinkled and grey policeman. She was in handcuffs, but no ankle bracelets. As the trial unfolded, it became more and more clear to all paying attention (except Hollinsworth's boss, apparently) that Betty had been set up and the bailiff, Grayland, the police and all involved had a silent understanding to act with more sympathy toward Betty. She had lost the ankle bracelets about a week before, but explained that, for optics, they needed the handcuffs to remain. They were, however, as Grayland put it to the bailiff, "to be looser than a two-dollar whore."

Betty was in a wrinkled, lowcut blouse with lint-covered dress pants and matching flats. Robert's associate had been in charge of clothing. Given that Robert did not think a second day of deliberations was possible, the team was out of clean outfits. This outfit was the same as yesterday's, when Betty had spent the whole day in the court's holding cell known as the "tank". It had no air conditioning, was rarely cleaned, wreaked of body odor and was, per Robert's opinion, cruel and unusual punishment. Most of Robert's clientele deserved time in the tank. Not Betty.

Betty and Robert exchanged smiles—Betty's a tortured, anxious one and Robert's jovial and reassuring—and she took her place at the table next to Robert. The officer removed Betty's handcuffs and signaled to the bailiff that they could bring Grayland and the jury in.

As the Judge Grayland and the jury took their respective seats, Robert could not help but notice that neither of the Harold Clarks were in the courtroom. There were a handful of reporters and that was all. Most of the benches were empty.

After some standard preliminaries and other formalities, the foreman of the jury handed a note to the bailiff. The bailiff walked it over to the Grayland who opened it, squinting through reading glasses that were much too small for his face. He reviewed for a moment or two, confirmed with the foreman—a rather portly young woman who was still out of breath from standing and handing the note to the bailiff—that the decision was unanimous and that the note represented the verdict of the entire jury, and Judge Grayland read aloud what they already knew: Betty Stevenson was not guilty. On all counts.

***

Jurors are not required to stick around after the verdict had already been delivered. After their job is done, judges thank jurors for their service with a standard, half-hearted civics spiel and give them the option to leave. Some attorneys like to question the jurors on what worked, what did not, why they came to the verdict they did and so on. This was usually to help them be better attorneys in future cases, so, in theory, Robert had no reason to stick around. But he did anyway out of habit. And out of curiosity.

All but one juror opted to stick around after hearing the news that Robert bought them all sandwiches and barbecue from his favorite local place—Dee's Sweet Sauces. He was always appreciative of those who stayed and wanted to show it. Sticking around after being forced onto a jury with no way out was not people's favorite thing to do and Robert knew it. Plus, Robert was starving and wanted one last brisket sandwich from Dee's before he went back to the Low Country. He had no idea when he would be back to this part of the state.

Robert noticed something different about these jurors. Usually, if a juror stuck around, they appeared jovial and relaxed, like a weight had been lifted now that their job was done. Not this bunch, though. As Robert placed the box of sandwiches on the unsteady deliberation room table, he noticed a sense of irritation on at least a few of the faces.

Once he closed the door and before he had a chance to turn to face his class, a middle-aged woman blurted out, "That bitch, Charlene. Of course she left." There were head nods and looks of disgust all around the table. The woman who spoke looked ashamed at having cursed, but nodded with her fellow jurors as reassurance she was right.

"Mr. Remington," a young male juror spoke up while grabbing a BLT on rye. "We would've been back with a verdict in about a half of an hour if it wasn't for Charlene. She's the one that just stormed out. She refused to acquit."

"Why's that?" Robert inquired as he took a seat and unwrapped his brisket, mouthwatering. He usually had standard questions and a bedside manner in these post-verdict meetings, but that's because jurors were usually hesitant to talk. His genuine curiosity led him to allow the room lead.

"She claimed that any young lady who posted pictures of herself like Miss Betty did deserve to be in jail," a thirty-five-year-old banker-turned-juror said.

Robert could not help but to chuckle to himself thinking back on the interaction during the drive from Lexington. After about fifteen minutes with the jurors, most of them took the sandwiches to go and everyone dispersed;

they all just wanted to make sure Robert knew about Charlene's stubbornness. Robert checked his notes before beginning the drive to refresh his memory. During jury selection, he always kept notes and saved them all for his library. Charlene was a staunch Baptist who, ironically, had been divorced twice already and was in the midst of a separation from her third husband. Robert had no objections to her during selection and, given her divorce, thought she would be an asset on the jury. OnlyFans, however, was a bridge too far for the angel Charlene. Miss Charlene was just another disgruntled juror whose opinions were misguided. Robert had seen his fair share, but he could not help but wonder whether his jury had been tampered with. Probably not, but he made a mental note to find out for certain. Covington would work it out, he thought.

Another trial in the books and another set of war stories to swap with fellow attorneys. It was bittersweet to be done with this last trial and his practice, but he knew he would be back in some capacity. Maybe for pro bono cases; maybe as a mediator or judge; and definitely just to linger around Remington Law from time to time when Caroline let him. He had chosen to fully retire from dealing with bigger client issues, though he would loiter. He needed the adrenaline.

A few days after the verdict, Robert had finally managed to tidy up the Lexington house, clean out his files and tie up some loose ends. After dropping Betty off in Florence with some distant cousins to start fresh, a promise Robert had made to her once he was fully convinced she was innocent, Robert merged South onto Interstate 95, passing Buc-cee's, and let his mind wander.

What to do about Jenny?

CHAPTER 5

Jenny Shelby-Diamond was watching the eleven o'clock news when she saw the flash of headlights flood the short gravel road. The ancient air conditioning unit in the living room had been broken for some time now, so to all outsiders, the windows all remained ajar in the evenings for a cooling breeze, but the real reason was for safety from what lived inside the house. Having that extra moment to know when Derrick got home on nights like this one could very well save Jenny's life.

Jenny and Derrick married in a Vegas wedding years back. She was there on a bachelorette trip, he, on a bachelor trip. Both of them were avid users of any substance they could find back in the day, but in Vegas, cocaine was their drug of choice. *When in Rome.* They bonded over being cut off from the rest of their families, the idea of not being lonely and, most importantly, a couple bottles of Patron stolen from a motel mini-mart. The final pieces in their wedding puzzle—other than a little white chapel off the main Strip and a subpar Elvis Presley impersonator who looked more like a decrepit George

Bush with black hair and emphysema—were a few tabs of Molly. *When in Rome.* After both drugged out, drunken fools ditched their parties for the third day in a row, severing friendships for life, they tied the knot and started thinking of where to move. When reality and partial sobriety set in on their last day, they decided Florence, South Carolina would be their home for five reasons: Jenny had four kids all within an hour's drive, one of whom even lived with her and, fifth, Derrick was homeless at the time and had no options to offer. As for parenthood, Derrick, played no part in the lives of the two children he brought into the world.

Fast forward five years and not much had changed. Both still used on and off, though Jenny had been on an "off" streak for about twenty-seven months now, her personal best. Both remained mostly estranged from their families, Derrick's somewhere in Louisiana and Jenny's remaining family, Caroline's Remington crew, in Charleston. And both were terrible parents. Despite this last commonality, they both wanted another child, this time with each other, thinking that somehow a child with each other would change their lacking affinity for children. Jenny, however, had had one too many abortions paired with some rough encounters and it seemed had a hostile womb. Derrick loathed her for this fact ("defective goods" was what he had called her often) and wanted a "male heir", though such an heir had nothing to inherit besides a mountain of debt, a mortgage that was underwater and little-to-no shot at happiness or success.

After the first few months of marriage spent pretending to tolerate Jenny's children, Derrick forced her to cut the eldest grown children out of her life. This was not a problem for Jenny, whose maternal instincts were ravaged by years of heavy drug use and drinking. Plus, three of her children were grown up and had mostly given up on their "mother" years earlier. Their father was Jenny's first husband, Sergeant Doug Bradley of the United States Army who fell for Jenny's good looks when she was young and still unaffected by drug use. He was fifteen years her elder and met her at a local honky tonk she technically was not old enough to be in at the time. After their first passionate meeting, Jenny became pregnant and Doug, an honorable, pious man, decided to make an honest woman out of her, proposing and walking down the aisle with her before she began showing. That marriage, however, fell apart after five years when he came home early from deployment to another man in his bed—for the third time. The couple managed to co-parent during and, at least for a bit, after the divorce, with much help from Doug's mother and father during the periods he was deployed overseas or across the country.

All three children of Doug and, at the time, Jenny Shelby-Bradley (Jenny refused to fully drop her maiden name, despite estrangement from the family; she thought it was a status symbol of some sort, though the Shelby name had long been forgotten around those parts) were boys, born in consecutive years when Jenny was only nineteen, twenty and twenty-one. So now, in her forties, all were in their twenties, idolized their father, respected and loved their paternal grandparents and detested their mother. They each were just as happy as Derrick when Jenny severed ties. No more forced visits, faked smiles.

Always wanting a girl, Jenny made it her duty to find another husband after the divorce from Doug. (Doug, however, always made the snide remark that she made it her duty to find another husband *before* the divorce too.) Her inheritance was running out, so she could use steady income, too. After a few years of co-parenting, unable to find another man given her local reputation as a philanderer, Jenny spiraled into a life of hard partying; likely a depression brought on by isolation and declining a beauty that paired with diminishing marriage prospects. Until that time, she did not drink much and never touched a drug, but that all changed during this period of her life. She started with heavy drinking and quickly upgraded to drug use. A Tuesday late-morning blackout was not uncommon when it all came to a head.

One day when Doug was deployed in the Middle East, Doug's parents arrived on a Saturday morning to drop the boys off for a weekend with their mother. They had each reached the teenage phase of not being affectionate nor wanting to spend time with their old, uncool mother, but went anyway because their grandparents and father told them to. They were becoming decent young gentlemen despite a broken home. After a series of knocks and rings went unanswered, Doug's father used his key, found Jenny passed out in the living room with a needle in her hand, another on the ground and hurried the boys back in the car. Heroin was growing in popularity in the area and had apparently found another customer.

After a judge refused visitation rights due to pictures Doug's father had snapped of Jenny's drug-induced coma, Jenny checked herself into rehab for the first time with the help of some friends. She still cared for her boys and wanted to see them. Unfortunately, this was short lived and after a week of withdrawal, she escaped out and went on a bender. She was plowing through the remainder of the Shelby family money she inherited at age eighteen and at thirty, found herself pregnant again. This time, she had no clue who the father was and, chances were, it was not a decent man like her ex-husband. It could have been any number of the dozen or so men in her rotation, most of whom were junkies themselves. She could not remember them all, the encounters or even their names. She did not even have a way to contact half of them.

That baby, Rose Lillian Shelby, sobered Jenny up—to a degree. That is, after she tried and failed to find an abortion clinic in rural, ultra-Baptist South Carolina. With a baby girl at home, Jenny only occasionally used, got a job as a receptionist at a dentist office, hired a nanny with the little Shelby money that remained and raised Rose. She was awarded limited, supervised visitation of her boys and appeared to be on the straight and narrow. Until she met Derrick.

Derrick had a steady job doing menial labor at a local paper mill and had tried—and failed—rehab half a dozen times in his life. He was in his mid-fifties, had been to jail more times than he could remember—possession, assault, battery, grand theft auto, larceny, public intoxication—and had no savings account, a credit score lower than a batting average and was a dastardly, violent drunk. He got high less and less, but that was because Jenny would not give him the cash for it and a few bad batches of fentanyl had plagued the areas, killing most of the dealers he would get his supply from.

Tonight was one of the nights Jenny wished a bad batch had gotten her husband.

Jenny slugged another glass of Jim Beam and turned up the volume on the television. She wanted the news on the war in Ukraine to drown out whatever war might break out downstairs. *Please sleep through this, babygirl.*

Jenny steadied her breathing, covered herself with a blanket and braced for what was to come. She had been with Derrick five years and four and a half of them he had been violent with her. She had learned to more or less tolerate it, but she knew she would never get used to it. What kind of example was she setting for that girl upstairs? The first few times she fought back, thinking about her daughter and how she hoped to stand up for herself one day, but that only made him angrier and more violent. She had called the cops three times, but every time refused to press charges because the officers that showed up were drinking buddies with Derrick. She never tried to run because she did not know where to go. She never told anyone because he said he would kill Rose if she did. She was trapped in a nightmare of her own making.

And that nightmare was lumbering up the front steps of their picturesque porch right then.

"Unlock the fuckin' door, bitch!" A chill went down Jenny's spine as Derrick yelled out before he had even finished ascending the steps. She hurried to her feet to comply before he could get to the handle. She silently prayed Rose did not hear and was still fast asleep. She figured the girl had heard at least a handful of her beatings, though she could not be certain as they had never discussed it. Her black eyes and bruises were always "accidents" of her own doing. Rose was not naïve. She had to have known.

"It's open, babe," Jenny said in a whisper as she opened the door. She undid her frayed, timeworn robe as she went in for a kiss. She wanted him to appreciate the ample cleavage she still had practically falling out of her tank top. Maybe it would take his mind out of fight mode as it had in the past.

Not this time. All six-foot-five, three hundred pounds of hulking drunk stretched out a meaty hand, shoving Jenny violently to the dusty hardwood. It was more of a hard shove than a violent initiation of a beating, so Jenny remained hopeful. *Maybe this is a good sign*, she thought from her lowly spot on the floor. Again, thoughts wavered to fighting back if needed, but she quickly filed those away. The few times she fought back were early on in their marriage when Derrick relied more on drugs and was a hundred pounds lighter. Even if she wanted to fight back, five-foot-three, one-hundred-pound Jenny would not have stood a chance against the three-hundred-pound mammoth.

"If you ate the pizza in the fridge, I'm gonna be pissed, Jenny." He did not even look at her as he kept through the living room to the kitchen. Now it struck her that a fight was brewing. She saw the look in his eye. He was drunk. *Drunk*, drunk. His knuckles were already bloody and matched his eyebrow which was split from a fresh encounter. He must've warmed up at the bar. And he was not going to like her response to his statement.

"Baby, I told you to grab something out with the boys. I gave you cash, baby. I let Rose have the pizza. It's all that was left in the house," Jenny said timidly. Even though she was not using and barely drank, she recalled how sobering the realization that she was about to be beaten by her own husband always was. Her adrenaline pumped, she sweat cold salt from every pore and her senses heightened. The air left her lungs and a lightheaded sensation overcame her. *Fight or flight.* She clambered from her spot on the floor to her feet as the drunken giant stopped, numb in his tracks. He whirled around, led by his right fist, without so much as a word or breath. He connected with her rib cage and she could feel the crunching of bones as she returned to the frigid ground.

"Are you fucking kidding me? You and that stupid little bitch! That was *my* pizza. You and that *whore* probably gave it to the neighbors again!" She knew better than to argue back at the accusations of infidelity. Maybe in a past life, but not now. She had no energy for it. She had welcomed the neighborhood boys from Rose's class over once a few months back and Derrick went berserk on her, just as he was now, calling Rose and her whores, sluts, you name it. Going after her child with such insults made Jenny want to leave even more, but no safe harbor seemed available to the women. And, tonight, Jenny knew it was not about the pizza. Derrick was a nasty drunk and he would fight if he wanted to fight. Regardless of what she said or did not say, it only added fuel to his drunken rage. Tonight, was one of those nights.

She kept her spot on the floor, attempting to avoid eye contact, hoping he would go sleep it off. He was not much nicer when he was sober, but at least he was not violent.

After a couple of minutes that felt like hours, Jenny thought the coast was clear. She slowly got up and walked back to the couch, thinking about the conversation she had with her sister earlier that day. She silently said a prayer that her brother-in-law would help Derrick with his latest DUI. Here she was, scared half to death of the man, but still praying for him to stay out of trouble.

She climbed back under a blanket, laid down, lowered the television and put on some reality tv to fall asleep. She would sleep out on the couch tonight. It was safer.

***

Around one in the morning, Jenny was startled awake by glass shattering in the kitchen. She jumped to her feet and grabbed the ceramic pan she had placed under the couch as protection.

She would not fight her husband, but if anyone else was in the house, she was prepared to kill. She had seen death before.

She peered into the pitch-black galley kitchen from the tiny living room, straining her sleepy eyes to see anything. She heard humming from the table and saw glass at her feet as she approached. She approached cautiously, pan raised like a baseball bat. As she reached the middle of the kitchen, feet soaked with some kind of liquid, she flipped on the light.

"Agghhhh. Wha da fuck. Turn off, whore." A man's voice slurred from the table. When Jenny's eyes adjusted, she saw Derrick slumped in boxer shorts and a stained, white undershirt that was two sizes too small. She looked at the glass and fluid around her and quickly realized he had smashed her grandfather's decanter along with a bottle of Red Stripe. The decanter was one of the few possessions she still had from her Shelby roots and she protected it the best she could, by locking it in a safe with a bottle of Pappy Van Winkle her grandfather left her for her eighteenth birthday. Derrick was apparently slugging the bourbon as if it was generic brand, cheap liquor and chasing it with beer.

As furious as she was, she attempted to de-escalate. "Derrick. Please go to bed. You could've woke Rose and scared her like you did to me. I'll clean this up." Jenny had plenty of experience trying to talk the drunk down in these situations. She could have been a hostage negotiator for the FBI at this point. She put down the pan and reached for a broom in the corner. Before she could start sweeping, she felt a sharp pain on the back of her head and the sensation of liquid pouring down her back. She stumbled, turning around to see Derrick, through blurred vision, who was laughing but faltering himself, with the stumpy neck of a broken Red Stripe in his hand. He had apparently just smashed the beer over her head. His level of intoxication was apparent by the fact that the blow did not have the knockout force it usually did and Jenny remained up for a moment. Still, the room was spinning and she eventually crumpled to the soaked, glassy floor.

"I don't give fuck 'bout you nor that bastard up da stair! I'll kill ya boff!" Derrick's boisterous laugh turned to a scowl as he steadied himself on the kitchen counter with his left hand, opened a drawer and pulled out a handgun. He had a habit of leaving loaded guns all around the house, possibly as reminders to the ladies in his home, but Jenny swore she had gotten them all and put them in the safe too.

"Put that away, Derrick. Come on," Jenny reasoned with a broken voice as he cocked it and pointed it between her eyes. His hand wobbled as his thousand-yard stare bored into her. Innumerable thoughts rushed into Jenny's mind at once, first and foremost was Rose. Who would raise her? She could not do this to her. Leave her alone. Derrick would surely abandon her. Maybe kill her. If Jenny survived this, she was leaving him. He had never pulled a gun like this. This was the last straw.

She let her fury take over and dove at his feet, hoping she would knock him to the ground. Instead, she was met with a swift kick in the jaw paired with a few cracks and the taste of blood. Two yellowed teeth fell to the floor, along with some blood, but she was determined to survive. The gun had triggered something in her.

The kick had left Derrick swaying on the wet floor, trying to balance himself on the counter. Through hazy vision, Jenny grabbed the broom and in one fluid motion swung it at her husband with all her might. At the same time, she heard the pop of the gun shot and fell hard. She slipped into unconsciousness, Red Strip, blood and glass keeping her company on the kitchen floor.

CHAPTER 6

Rose was seventeen and had decided to move out and leave Florence in her rearview the day she turned eighteen. She would give her mother the option to come with her because this was no life for either of the women, but she had told herself a hundred time she would leave without her. She had heard some beatings her mother had taken from Derrick, but never did anything about it. She always stiffened, unable to decide what exactly to do. She was a kid; how could she help? Especially when the cops did not even do their job. She had listened from the top of the stairs when the police came on previous occasions, ignoring her mother's blood and bruising while smoking cigarettes and talking pleasantly about SEC football with Derrick.

Gamecocks look injured again coming into the year, but still better than your wife right about now, Derrick.

She sat at the head of her bed; knees held tightly to her chest as she listened to the events unfold below her. She had managed to doze back off after round one, when she assumed Derrick had drunkenly passed out and left her poor mother alone. That was usually when these one-sided brawls stopped.

Round two had woken her back up with the smashing of glass. She had heard it all before.

Despite her young age, Rose was not enrolled in high school, looking forward to prom, graduation or college. She had become a truant years earlier, when Derrick and her mother were frequently too high to drive her to school and the school district refused to send a bus to their rural plot of land in the backwoods. She enjoyed school and loved learning, especially English, literature and generally anything to do with books, but at this point, she was too embarrassed to go back and have to pick back up in eighth or ninth grade. Because she rode her bike to the local library and spent most of her time there, she did manage to keep strong reading and writing skills for her age and remained quite intelligent despite her circumstances.

She had a cell phone, but it was an old, hand-me-down blackberry with no internet, apps or fun extras for a teen. Besides brick breaker. It did not matter, though. Rose did not have any close friends and mainly used it to talk to her mom when she was at her job as a grocery store checkout clerk in town. She fumbled with it in her hand as she sat in bed, deciding whether tonight would be the night she called the police on Derrick. She knew nothing would really happen, but her mother would know she knew. So would Derrick.

Suddenly, Rose jumped from her bed, dropping her phone. She heard what sounded like a firecracker go off in the kitchen below her. She grabbed her phone and dialed 9-11 as she unlocked her door, rushed down the stairs and saw her mother lying in a pool of her own blood on the kitchen floor. She could not find the source of the blood but stopped dead in her tracks at the sight of a belligerent, half naked Derrick steadying himself on the kitchen counter, gun in one hand, what looked to be half a beer bottle in another. Their eyes met, but neither of them moved.

"Hello? Hello? What's the emergency?" A muffled voice yelled. Rose and Derrick's joint gazes turned to the phone in her hand. Rose was too petrified to speak and stood still, hoping the man five feet from her somehow could not hear or see her. "Is any-" Just as the operator continued on, the hulking drunk lunged for the phone, but slipped and fell. This gave Rose enough time to run back upstairs and slam her door shut. Once she made sure it was deadbolted, she yelled into the phone, "Hello? Hello!"

"Yes, what is your emergency? Are you okay? Please state your address," the operator said, sounding irritated.

Rose screamed the address into the phone, telling the operator to hurry and hung up the phone. She began crying, realizing she left her bleeding mother downstairs. Was she conscious? Had she been shot? Was she dead? Rose had no clue, but she had no time to think. She heard Derrick lurching up the steps, mumbling incoherently to himself and pinballing from wall to wall in his drunken stupor. Did he have the gun? Was he going to shoot her?

An answer to her question rang out on the stairway. She had no clue where the bullet went, just that it was not in her; she was not even sure it was shot into her room. Then another bullet rang out, closer, this time bursting through the top of her bedroom door with a fragmented hole. She ran to the opposite side of her room and ducked down in a closet, closing the door behind her. Just as she did, she thought better of the plan and climbed out. He would find her and she would be a sitting duck. She opened the old, single pane window above her cluttered dresser, smashing a lamp to the ground in the process and climbed onto the roof of the front porch. She heard Derrick pounding at her bedroom door. She looked back and saw the frame starting to splinter. Rose knew she needed to jump but could not bring herself to act. Before she had a chance to, she heard the door break free of the hinges, was deafened by the fire of the gun and felt a shooting pain in the back of her thigh. She tumbled down the slanted roof to the cement sidewalk below, the very one Derrick had blindly stumbled up a few hours earlier.

This time, two police officers were there and watched in horror as the young girl cascaded down with a bullet in her leg. This was going to be a tough house call to cover up.

CHAPTER 7

Most lawyers in the military use their *juris doctor* to some degree. Otherwise, what's the point of incurring the obligatory mountain of debt that comes with law school? Young attorneys would enlist shortly after graduation as "JAGs", serving in the Judge Advocate General's Corps. Each branch has its own JAG Corps, because, of course, each has its own issues requiring legal expertise of some kind. A JAG can handle anything from the legality of a specific military operation abroad to particular legal queries the United States government had about international law all the way down to drafting wills for other service members. Most, however, end up managing standard court martial-type, military-specific cases ("*you can't handle the truth!*"). Some defend their troubled colleagues while others enjoy prosecuting them with the swift hammer of justice. All the while, they are setting down a path toward student loan forgiveness, courtesy of Uncle Sam.

"Big Country" and "Sweet Carolina" were the rare, card-carrying attorneys who decided to enlist as lowly Privates in the United States Army. Neither wanted the hassle of the legal world any longer, as their dreams of fortune and fame in the courtroom diminished with age and wisdom. Big Country was tall, broad shouldered and gruff in demeanor with a bit of a southern accent while Sweet Carolina had a matching southern accent, but was gangly and built more like a stout NFL wide receiver. They were both from one of the Carolinas, but no one bothered to remember North or South. The other privates and lowly recruits did not even know their real names, they just knew their favorite country boys as Big Country and Sweet Carolina, or simply Country and Carolina. That's how it generally was: never bother learning true, full names when nicknames would suffice in the service. Country and Carolina did not mind it after a while, but, at first, both were irritated at being grouped together with the other simply due to their accents. Each was afraid that his reputation would hinge and forever be intertwined with that of his counterpart and each attorney-turned-recruit, ever the Type-A, did not like that one bit. What if the other man was an asshole? What if he sucked at his job? Wasn't fit enough? Couldn't run? Couldn't shoot? That would somehow reflect poorly on both of them.

Despite the initial wariness, the two quickly dispelled these frights and became fast friends due to all of their similarities.

Prior to enlisting, Country had been a struggling attorney in private practice for a number of years, barely scraping by before her decided to pack it all in and sign up to protect and serve his country. Carolina, on the other hand, took his J.D., passed his state Bar exam and hauled right to the recruiting office after doing so. Both could not stand the "professionals" in their given field and rejected their pompous workforce altogether. Why not make a life-altering decision and join the military? Soviet Russia was on the brink of collapse, Reagan had planted the flag of American domination and the testosterone of the U.S. was going to bring rock 'n' roll abroad by kicking down the Iron Curtain. Plus, *Rocky IV* convinced hot-blooded American men everywhere to go kick some Soviet ass.

Not so fast.

Before any hopes of deployment to the Eastern Bloc could come to fruition, Carolina and Country first had to struggle through basic training and get screamed at through their time at Fort McCoy. And by the time Bush Sr. won the election, they were warriors in the making without a war to fight.

That all changed with Operation Desert Shield in 1990.

"Attention! Listen up, shitbags," Sergeant Spellman screeched at his unit as he dramatically kicked in the door to their barracks. The men all stood at attention, butts two inches from the foot of their respective bunk beds, ready for another round of useless physical training (PT). They had been at Fort McCoy in the middle of nowhere Wisconsin for over half a year at this point, and did nothing but train. They were turning into Sylvester Stallone and Arnold Schwarzenegger with rippling muscles and tight six packs, just nowhere to go and use their newfound physiques. The men were all itching for action. "The day you sorry sacks of useless shit have been waiting for is finally here!"

Carolina and Country shot each other a quick glance, hoping Sergeant Spellman was not screwing with his lackies as he liked to do. Neither of the men particularly liked the vulgar, overaggressive and macho Sergeant. Other Sergeants were not nearly as aggressive and demeaning to their respective units and the men envied their peers for it. Being cooped up with Spellman for so long practically in Canada did not help the situation, either. If Spellman had good news for the men, though, it would all be worth it.

"At ease, men. I'm finally not fucking with you for once in my God-forsaken life," Spellman confirmed before explaining. "The fucking sand gnats in Iraq and Iran have quit whipping on each other long enough to let Iraq—full of *our* weapons and *our* money—start threatening their other neighbors. Apparently, the money they got from every other fucking country isn't enough and they're in debt. Now threatening every country on the Arabian Peninsula—I'll show you dumb fucks a map later so you know where I'm talking about—with war if they don't chip in on their debts. Our intelligence indicates that this sonuvabitch Hussein is gathering his troops to swing them from Iran to one of its other lucky neighbors. Now, I know none of you can think the way I do, but my thinking is they ain't dumb enough to try to swing their weight at the Saudis to the South because of their sheer size. That leaves Jordan or Kuwait as likely targets. My money—*if* I was a gambling man, *which I am*—would be on Kuwait. They're smaller and Jordan backs right up to Israel who, of course, is one of our biggest allies."

The men in the room had relaxed a bit and a few had switched to sitting on the edge of their beds. They were mesmerized by Spellman's words. The training was over and they were going to see action.

"Nevertheless, we've gotten orders to round up ten thousand of you *scallywags* and ship out tomorrow. To where? That is, in fact, classified. I do not know. My boss does not know. My boss's boss does not know. So, you pieces of shit sure as shit will not be hearing anytime soon. From what I've heard, Bush knows, fucking Dick probably knows and my money says Colin Powell, too. Below that, probably only a select few. Now, I want all of you packed and bedded by twenty-one hundred hours. We'll be up for standard PT before departure at oh-five hundred. Over and out!"

Spellman lingered for a moment, giving a relaxed smile and nod to all the men. He looked like a proud father, seeing his child off to college. Without saying anything more, he gave a thumbs up, turned about-face and lumbered back out the door.

"I was beginning to doubt I made the right choice here, Country," Carolina practically shouted from his side of their bunks. "I don't mind being shouted at and running around all day, but I at least want to be rewarded with a gun and an all-expense paid trip from Uncle Sam to some other place besides the states."

"Or bum-fuck Wisconsin," Country fired back with a chuckle. "Trust me, Carolina. You are missing *nothing* in the field of law. I'd scrape for clients, get shit cases, lose and make no money. Looks like it's all turning up roses for us now. Heading to the Middle East to pop our cherries!"

CHAPTER 8

For the stretch of drive back to the Low Country, Robert's mind jumped back and forth between Jenny Shelby-Diamond (or whatever hyphenated name she was calling herself these days) and Betty Stevenson. Two women who came from entirely different backgrounds, had different starting points in life, had different skin colors and different socioeconomic status yet two women who seemingly ended up in the same place.

Jenny had grown up with a silver spoon in her mouth and was given every opportunity to succeed. She started life on third base, as Robert liked to say to Caroline, thanks to the business acumen and good fortune of the generations before them. Upon returning from Civil War exile, Sean Shelby opened a pharmacy just off Market Street in downtown Charleston. It sputtered along at first, Sean barely making ends meet, but as more and more opportunistic carpetbaggers arrived from the North, the secessionist-led boycott of abolitionists' businesses died down and impacted the pharmacy less and less. With the opportunism came a new crop of customers, a crop with no hard feelings on secession or slavery and they arrived to rebuild the South, make money in the process and, just like everyone else, needed their pharmaceutical needs met in the process. With that, Shelby Family Pharmacy took off. By the turn of the century, they had opened five more locations and held a monopoly on the medicinal needs of the Low Country. Fast-forward to the mid-eighties and Jenny and Caroline's father, also named Sean Shelby, managed to sell the chain to a national pharmacy for well into the eight figures. As the sole owner, Sean Shelby found himself a very, *very* rich man, in turn, investing most of his windfall in real estate, stashing a good chunk in trust funds for his two girls and predicting his family would have it made for decades.

Two major occurrences happened to dash this optimistic prophecy: first, Sean Shelby's wife became terminally ill and, second, Jenny hit puberty.

Barbara Shelby was diagnosed at a relatively young age with amyotrophic lateral sclerosis, or ALS, more commonly known as Lou Gehrig's Disease. ALS can turn a perfectly healthy person—even a world class athlete like Lou Gehrig—into a wheelchair-bound, helpless individual in the blink of an eye. The nervous system turns on the body and starts breaking down nerve cells resulting in a body that slowly becomes unable to control its own muscles, eventually making the patient immobile. The root cause was unknown, but Sean Shelby was determined to change that. Barbara and Sean's relationship went back to the fifth grade and Sean did not want to think of a world without his Barbara. Sean was smitten with Barbara more and more every day of their life together, in good times and bad, and seeing her slowly rot away broke the man.

Rationalization and business capability gave way for an unbridled, shotgun spray of misguided enthusiasm. Sean sold most of his real estate, cashed out some of the girl's trust funds and plowed it all into research for ALS. He refused to lose his best friend and made the decision to abandon the world and moonlight as an ALS researcher, spending most of his waking hours reading scientific journals and calling hospitals, universities and research centers around the world. He flew around the globe, studied stem cells in Mexico, sampled herbal remedies from the Amazon Rainforest and prayed at the couple's church daily. In the end, no progress was made and Barbara succumbed to her illness at age forty-two. The broken man puttered along for another decade, long enough to see both his girls into young adulthood, but he was not the jovial, pious, affectionately domineering father they once knew. He was a shell of himself, a recluse and an alcoholic until he died when Jenny was eighteen and Caroline was twenty-nine.

When Mr. Shelby died, Caroline was off and married to Robert with a life of her own. Jenny, on the other hand, had begun her foray into hard partying and entertaining the opposite sex. Caroline, ever the mother Jenny needed, fought with her younger sister often over everything from her taste in men to her much too frequent states of *over*-intoxication. Robert, who detested drunks from first-hand experience as a child, tried to help Jenny as much as he could at first. His assistance, seen as nothing more than nosiness by his sister-in-law, slowly gave way to altogether absenteeism: he downright refused to try with Jenny until she tried with herself. In Robert's mind, she was a lost cause, but he would not persuade his wife or come between her and family so he let Caroline come to the same conclusion on her own. Caroline did eventually agree with her husband, slowly distancing herself from her sister as drinking and, ultimately, drugs took over her life.

By the time Caroline had cut Jenny out of her life, she estimated that Jenny had maybe a few grand of their modest inheritance remaining. This was even *after* Caroline and Robert bought Jenny out of her half of the Shelby Charleston house. Despite the tens of millions Sean managed to receive decades earlier, a fraction of a small percentage of that saw its way to Caroline and Jenny. What was left was tied up in practically-defunct medical company stocks, leaving little in comparison to the original windfall. By the time Jenny, Rose and Derrick lived under one roof, Caroline's estimates were right and most of Jenny's share was gone, as was any relationship with her only relative.

Even with the turbulence of her youth, a lost mother and the self-inflicted issues during early adulthood, Jenny was still far better off than his last client and the South's newest exoneree from the get-go. Betty was born in a small village near San Juan, Puerto Rico, but she had very few memories of her early childhood in the U.S. Territory, moving with her grandfather when she was very young and barely knew any English. San Juan was a place where she was surrounded by *primos*, *tios*, friends and a community of support and familiarity that she had grown up in. When she arrived in rural South Carolina, it was a drastic change and shock to the little girl's system. She never knew who her father was and her mother died before she could even walk, so Betty relied on her community and her *Abuelo* to raise her. Now, it was just her *Abuelo*, one single bilingual teacher from Teach for America that spent schooldays with her, members of her new Hispanic Catholic church and some stray neighborhood cats to keep her company. All of this while still unable to understand most of the people around her every day.

Her *Abuelo*, feeling a religious obligation to raise Betty since she was his only grandchild, had moved them to South Carolina for a job opportunity at a plant assembling vehicles. Unfortunately for the both of them, the job never materialized, the move was for naught and Betty's *Abuelo* did not have enough money to move them back to Puerto Rico. In other words, they were stuck. To top it all off, by the time Betty got her first period, her "family first" *Abuelo* had begun molesting her. This went on unchallenged for a few years, Betty not understanding what was happening at first, soon graduated to seeing no alternative or way out.

It had been a few years since their move to the continent when Betty came home one blistering afternoon to an empty home. They were renting a small two-bedroom home with a leaky roof on the property of a local farmer named Dennis McNaught. It was all her *Abuelo* could afford as he worked early mornings on the farm in exchange for a place to stay. It was not at all unusual for Betty to walk into an empty home after school since her *Abuelo* found other odd jobs as a laborer around town and worked off hours when not on the farm, often leaving before she woke up and getting in after she fell asleep. Betty certainly did not mind her abuser being gone for as long as possible.

What was unusual was that this trend happened for a week straight, then two and then a third. By the fourth week, moldy food in the fridge and a severe lack of Modelos led her to the conclusion that her *Abuelo* was gone. For good? Perhaps. Where though? Did he head back to Puerto Rico without her? Did someone, somehow find out about the sexual abuse and arrest him? This was unlikely since she told no one, but what should she do now? She was a fifteen-year-old who barely knew the language, had no family or friends nearby and was suffering the trauma of intrafamilial sexual assault.

For a couple of months, Betty carried on without telling a soul about her newfound independence. Why should she tell anyone? After all, the abuse had stopped and she felt she could start healing. If healing from such trauma was possible, she was determined to achieve it. Plus, if she told an adult, maybe her *Abuelo* would come back and continue with his demonic acts. She was not going to risk that.

By the second month, Betty began resorting to thievery at the local convenience store for survival. At first, it was easy: she would just steal candy bars, toothpaste, cookies—anything she could easily fit in her pocket. Eventually, she started trying for larger items like soap, bread, chicken and other articles she could not fit in her tiny little pockets. One day, when she was trying to put a whole jar of Extra Crunchy Jif peanut butter in a hoodie on a ninety-degree, day, an employee caught the thief in the act. The police arrived, brought her to an abandoned home and Betty found herself in the foster care system. For the next three years, she bounced around from home to home, finding nothing but more abuse.

Robert had gotten her whole story in trial preparation after hearing about the case from an old friend, who had also filled in some of the gaps Betty was less than forthcoming about. If he was going to put Betty on the stand, as she insisted, opening her up to cross-examination by a hostile prosecution, he needed to know it all. Every last detail as if he lived it. And that was perfectly fine with Betty, as she was up front with *almost* every detail, down to the way she was molested by her *Abuelo* and by one of her foster parents; her recounting was nothing but matter of fact, cold and devoid of emotion. She was used to it. It broke Robert's heart, but as his vintage Ford Bronco rolled into Charleston County, he wondered how Betty became a positive, happy woman despite terrible circumstances. Yet Jenny became—Jenny.

After a scenic drive through the Low Country over some bridges and through some marshes, Robert pulled into the seashell-covered, gravel driveway of Sully's and decided to put both women out of his mind. It was early afternoon and all of his boys' cars were in the driveway. A pleasant surprise for a weekday. He eased the Bronco (despite being a defense attorney, no it was not O.J. Simpson-white, but instead a *"Sea-Breeze"* blue befitting of the sea-shelled driveway) in between Liam and Ben's matching Jeep Gladiators, one fire-engine red and one olive green, and settled behind Bobby's sleek silver BMW. He had given his boys a good starting point, he just hoped they would end up like their mother, not like him. Especially not like their good-for-nothing aunt. Robert had done all he could—and all he would—for the boy's aunt, many of his actions wholly unbeknownst to anyone but himself.

As Robert stepped from the Bronco and grabbed his suitcase, he felt his phone buzz from inside his blazer pocket.

Thanks, counselor. You'll have the cash by the end of the day. Maybe a normal life lies ahead for the girl after this. Cheers.

Robert smiled, deleted the message and walked toward his front door. Another happy customer. Hopefully his last.

CHAPTER 9

Coral Sands knew her name sounded like a luxury resort in the Caribbean. That or a stripper's alias. Or perhaps even a porn star's film name. She had been told all of these things since she was too young to hear or understand them. She caught them nonetheless and preferred to dream of owning a luxury resort rather than fantasize she danced naked for old, overweight men and dollar bills. Or performed private, unspeakable things on camera under a giant stage light in a room full of other people. Besides, she had no boobs, no ass and was pushing two hundred pounds and she knew it all, even embraced it. She had been reminded of these facts, verbatim, her whole life too, so thoughts of a white sandy beach were a good escape.

Coral would often lay awake at night, imagining what her five-star complex, "Coral Sands", would look like. Where would it be? Would it be a standalone, or a chain? Would it be its own private island or would it be surrounded by other luxury resorts? How much would she charge? Would the rich and famous love it? Would it have tragedies like the White Lotus?

Coral usually imagined "Coral Sands Beach Getaway" (*by Coral Sands*) as a standalone resort on a remote island off the coast of South America. It would be just far enough from Venezuela and Brazil that fishermen or drug smugglers would not bother the island, but close enough that she could set up South American excursions for the guests who wanted to be adventurous. Those would be far and few between since the focus was rejuvenation, but the option was there. The beaches would be private, with chickee-style structures covered by palm fronds hovering over her guests as a barrier between their fair European and North American skin and the blistering sun. There would be a golf course—no, two golf courses. Designed by Arnold Palmer or Tiger Woods. Or maybe by Mike Trout and Tiger Woods. She had heard they did some sort of collaboration like that before. They would do it for her. Definitely Tiger, though. Afterall, they were all frequent guests in the Presidential Suite at her imaginary resort.

There would be multiple pools. One would have a water slide. Another would be for toddlers and young kids. Or maybe not? Maybe this was an adult only hotel? Yes. It would be adult only. The second pool would have a DJ set up in the middle of cascading waterfalls, playing only EDM with occasional foam parties. The last pool would be on the other side of the resort, overlooking one of the golf courses and the ocean. It would be quiet and mainly for reading and napping. Booze at all the pools, though, of course. Yes, yes. That's a good mix.

Coral snapped out of it when she saw the Bronco's headlights skate down Ben Sawyer Boulevard. She could spot that chrome Atlanta Braves front license plate from anywhere. She had strategically parked on Rifle Range Road, the most redneck sounding of roads, but actually a nice area in Mount Pleasant; her favorite restaurant was just down the street. So was her favorite coffee truck. Those cardboard/plastic disposable cups sure came in handy.

Rifle Range was her standard stakeout spot for this subject. Specifically, a gas station parking lot on the corner of

Ben Sawyer and Rifle Range. She swore she would stay off Sullivan's until he got there because she was convinced his family caught her stalking once. It was a close call at least. So Rifle Range with the gas station near here favorite coffee stuck with the good disposable cups (doused in Smirnoff) was good enough. She would sip her spiked coffee, to calm her down, and watch. The subject could only get to his home from the route she was currently watching or a circuitous route that led from Mount Pleasant to Isle of Palms to Sullivan's Island. That route would not make sense unless he was actively avoiding her. So this was always her spot.

She took a swig from her to-go coffee cup, let out a burp that wreaked like a Russian hockey player and pulled onto Ben Sawyer towards Sullivan's Island. She did not know what she would find, but it was better than nothing. Besides, she had to get close enough for her software to work.

Coral was in her mid-thirties, twice divorced (due to her taste in men and, in turn, those men's taste in women that were not her) and had been on her current slow spiral downward in life for a few years. She had three cats and a one-bedroom apartment on Daniel Island just on the other side of Mount Pleasant; a really nice, wealthy area, in which she clearly did not belong in. Though she owned the apartment, she owed almost three hundred thousand on the mortgage while the shanty was probably worth just under two hundred thousand.

She had moved to the Low Country from Springfield, Illinois just after college. Both her parents were dead and she wanted to live out the Coral Sands dream on a beach somewhere, a commodity for which Springfield, Illinois was not known. Her major in college was Communications and she managed to parlay that into a menial paying job as a journalist for the *Low Country Ledger*, a poorly selling newspaper based in McClellanville. In exchange for her meager salary, she could travel about the Low Country (in exchange for ten cents a mile) and write whatever stories interested her. In the beginning, she was given strict instructions, overbearing guidance and practically had stories written for her by her editor. When she was finally given a chance, she was actually a decent sober writer—and an excellent writer when she drank. She once wrote a story about the butterflies at Boone Hall Farms—after a night of drinking three bottles of subpar red wine sold at that very farm—that was republished in every major newspaper in the country, earning her notoriety, awards and even a small bonus. So, she stayed loaded.

Her silver Honda Civic turned right across a few lanes of traffic, catching some honks and dirty looks as it stayed a few car lengths behind the Bronco. She knew where he was going, so she did not need to get too close. That is, until she needed the software to work. It had worked in the past, but she had to be quick. And close.

Once past the Cove on her right, with the cemetery visible ahead, she leaned to her passenger seat and flipped open her laptop, placing it on the center console.

"Let's see what you've been up to, Mr. Remington," Coral mumbled, keeping an eye on the road and one on her ancient computer, booting up slowly. She caught herself swerving into oncoming traffic and jerked the wheel back to center. It did not faze her. The sober drivers would dodge as they always did. She was not drunk anyway. Just buzzed. Her constant state.

The Bronco eased passed a few new builds and a few old builds, planting itself in the tacky, shell-covered driveway. The Civic followed until it did not, easing into a driveway across the street. From some earlier research, Coral had learned that the owners were seasonal and would not be back for a few months. And they were too rich to even think about renting it out. Others in their third or fourth or fifth home? Disgusting. They were not poor.

The Bronco was put into park and the Civic did the same. Coral typed away as her computer beeped and pinged. Messages from her editor could wait. She knew she would get Remington on something one day. She was close.

"I'm in!" She yelled to no one.

Remington was just getting out of his car and the message disappeared.

"No!" She exclaimed. Why did the message disappear? It looked important. Something about "cash" and a girl. That's all she saw. Shit. She wished she was sober for once. The software could show her texts on any phone in about a hundred-foot radius. The only catches: she needed to know the number and she could not search the phone. She could only see what the user was looking at. If the user deleted something or closed something out, she was SOL.

She got out a yellow legal pad and scribbled what she knew. She would figure it out. Sober her would. She knew it.

"Cash for a girl. What're you up to this time, Remington?"

CHAPTER 10

After a pre-dinner bourbon or two by the pool, swapping law school stories with Liam and listening to the waves crash in the distance, Caroline wrangled her four men up for a dinner of shrimp and grits, hush puppies and fried okra. Caroline had an accounting degree from South Carolina and, as such, had adorned many hats for Remington Law during her tenured career including bookkeeper, secretary, paralegal and more than once, quasi-lawyer before the children came along. None of these roles stopped her from her most important role: chef for the Remington men. Mrs. Remington's she-crab soup, deviled crabs and oysters Rockefeller were unbeatable in Robert's eyes. And her hush puppies? There were never any left over for poor Louie or Max. Anytime the Remington's had parties at Sully's, their neighbors were smart enough to offer a large supply of ingredients beforehand and booze the day of in lieu of having to make their own dishes, which never matched up to Caroline's. Half the recipes came from Caroline's mother and the other half came from Miss Julip, the black nanny Caroline had as a girl in the Shelby house.

Thanks to Miss Julip, Caroline's food knew no color and pleased black and white alike.

"Alright, Dad," Bobby said with a sigh, eyeballing both his brothers and his mother. "We've gotta discuss something as a family. Can't be ignored anymore." Caroline handed out dessert plates to everyone for the colossal, steaming peach cobbler she had just set in the middle of the table. She turned quickly to the China cabinet in the corner of the dining room, not wanting to miss Robert's reaction and retrieved a bottle of Bailey's for the coffee Ben was pouring out in Waterford glasses.

Without removing his gaze from the peach cobbler, Robert took a whopping slice and admired as mist rolled out of it. After rescuing a couple extra slices of peach and a large chunk of crust stuck to the Pyrex, he poured a mug of coffee, taking his time. He had become a master of letting others speak in awkward situations, never breaking first, seeming to relish the long pauses. Decades of trial work made him a ruler of maneuvering conversations ranging from the birds and the bees to the boys asking for money. He would sit in silence all night if he had to. Silence was his superpower.

"It's Aunt Jenny," Ben said, pouring a swig of Bailey's in his coffee. Robert was surprised but did not show it; he had thought a lecture on staying out of the office in retirement was coming, not an inquisition into his low-life sister-in-law. Masking his slight shock, Robert was reminded that he had a bad habit of treating his family like witnesses on the stand, one Caroline had scolded him for a time or two. He made a mental note to calmly challenge, diffuse and disengage methodically. When it came to Jenny, though, he wanted to wholly disengage every time. Especially around the boys.

"She's called all of us, Dad," Liam spoke up, clearing lying. "Well, I doubt she called you, but she's called Ma, Bobby, Ben and me. Ain't none—"

"Liam, 'ain't none' will work if you're a trial lawyer down here in front of a jury but not in Federal court nor in any sort of corporate law setting. Strike it from your vernacular,"

Robert said. He had a habit of being box condescending sarcastic toward Liam now that the boy was entering into one of Robert's fields of work.

"Robert, now's not the time. Listen to them, please," Caroline said, taking a seat at the opposite head of the table from her husband. She took a sip of white wine from a Waterford crystal glass that Robert always thought was comically small.

"Now me, Bobby and Ben didn't answer. Let it go to voicemail. Didn't even recognize the number if we're being honest. We know she hasn't made the best decisions in her life and we know you'll say 'You boys don't know the half of it' and 'We're not discussing her in front of your mother', but Ma agrees we've gotta at least talk about it," Liam kept on. "Ma talked to her and it sounds like she's sober and has her act together. So I don't know…."

"She needs help, Robert," Caroline jumped in as Liam trailed off, losing steam. They had only spoken briefly of Caroline's call with her sister, agreeing to discuss after Robert's trial. Robert did not think it would (nor should) become a Remington family affair.

Without giving anyone a chance to interject further, Robert snapped, "Jenny needs help, or is it Dennis that needs help? That was my understanding." Robert knew it was Derrick, but he was getting a trial lawyer's rage in him thinking about that man. He only met him once, bailing him out of jail for a DUI years back, but in Robert's eyes he was the one who sullied Jenny for good. Put her past the point of no return after Robert had all but saved her. Over time, Robert had done some digging with P.I.s of his own and found out Derrick was prone to slapping around women. He was almost certain Derrick beat Jenny, but anytime the topic was broached by a P.I. or Caroline, Jenny became angry and denied it. You can only help someone so much that refuses to help themselves.

"I don't see that it matters. Family is family. Isn't it?" Ben said. Robert couldn't help Ben from thinking like that, being optimistic as he always was. And the saying was true,

Robert had always instilled family as the foundation of a joyful, successful life in the Remington household. But then again, he was young, naïve and without the facts. Bobby grimaced when Ben said this. He was the oldest and knew the most about his estranged aunt, as was the case in most families.

"You're right, son. Family is family. But that's only until they get hooked on the needle and the pills. Then they're nothing more than—" Robert began before Caroline cut him off.

"Robert! We don't know that. Jenny said she's been clean for three years and I believe her. And so what if it's for *Derrick*?" she said, emphasizing the correct name for her brother-in-law. "If it's for Derrick, then it's for Jenny, too. She's the one who called."

"Dad, I was thinking maybe I could help you with it. Shadow you, make filings and anything I can do as a law clerk, ya know?" Liam said. He was eager to begin practicing law, but was leaning toward transactional work. White shoe, Northern, big city mergers and acquisitions. Where the money was unbeatable and the hours unbreathable. Robert knew the offer was a bluff. Liam would maybe help for an hour or two of billable time just to get Robert stuck alone with his deadbeat brother-in-law.

"First off, how very kind, but I see right through that, younin'. That's a good'n. You'd never go down to a filthy prison. It'd take the shine off your wingtips, city boy," Robert said playfully with a touch of sternness. Then he stiffened up and looked around the table. No one was bothering their world-famous cobbler. They were too focused on backing up their mother. He turned to his best Broadway voice and went on, not budging. "Now seeing as how we have a few surprise *witnesses* today," Robert said, waving his fork at his three boys as he slipped into a theatrical demeanor, "who were not made known to the court prior to this, it seems I have been ambushed. In my own home! This is clearly improper discovery practice and abhorrent and I'd like to object…*however*, I know the honorable, presiding justice of one

Sully's is Caroline *Shelby* and my objection will merely be for the record and, as we all know from experience, the record is useless since *this…This!* is the court of final appeal and without remand."

"Here we go," Bobby said under his breath, just loud enough to make sure the rest of the table heard it. Caroline held back a smirk and Liam chuckled. Deflection at its finest.

"In other words—Justice *Shelby* has final say and will do whatever she wishes. I am without recourse." Robert stopped, stood up abruptly and walked down to Caroline during his oral argument. He picked up her miniature glass, swirled its contents and downed it like a shot. He was putting on a show, attempting to distract his family from the matter at hand on his way to disengaging and a date with his deck chair to listen to the ocean. Perhaps he could even inject some humor and levity into the conversation before he would abruptly get off the topic and disappear. "However! What is being asked is something only one with admission to the South Carolina State Bar can accomplish and, correct me if I am wrong, but I certainly believe I am the only one capable of such acts as I am the only one who has *passed* the Bar examination, correct?"

Robert looked around eagerly before returning to his seat. He polished off the last bite of cobbler before scooping a second. He could not resist. "Now, frankly," Robert returned to a normal voice and met eyes with his wife, "I don't want to talk about it anymore. I may think about it over the next day or so, but that's for me and your mother to discuss, boys. Thank you for having the interests of your mother in mind, but I'd like to at least talk to the police myself before we even think about getting Derrick out of jail for yet another DUI. He is nothing but a low life and I'm sorry to say I don't want to aid someone like that in this family."

The Remington's finished their dessert without another word on Jenny or Derrick before watching the last few innings of the Braves on the deck television. When it was clear the Braves were not mounting a ninth inning comeback, the boys retired to various bedrooms around the house, each deciding they had drank a bit too much to venture home.

CHAPTER 11

Five o'clock. Pitch black. Robert emerged from his slumber at his usual working time, but now without an alarm. It was his first day as a retired man, though his sleep schedule did not get the memo. To make matters worse, he had heartburn most of the night from overindulgence in cobbler and tossed around the bed until about one in the morning. He checked his sleep on his smart watch and learned his recovery was a measly fifteen percent. Sounded about right.

What to do about Jenny remained front of his mind.

After sitting on the edge of their California king-sized bed for a moment, a purchase only made possible by additions made on the bungalow resulting in a larger Master, Robert crammed his feet into moccasin slippers, stood at attention and stretched. Feeling a few good cracks and no bad ones, he gazed at his slumbering wife while slipping into a robe that hung on his bedpost. He smiled to himself before leaning in to kiss her forehead. He was still just as in love with her today as he was back in high school. He had aged considerably since then, sporting silver hair and some wrinkles but she looked just over thirty-five now, if that; Father Time seemed to have spared his lovely wife.

Coffee needed to be made and his iPad located. His eyes resisted adjustment to the darkness of early morning and his body shivered from meat locker conditions at nighttime—temperatures sixty-two degrees or lower were common for Caroline. Lexington was his domain; Sully's would always be Caroline's. The Shelby house was fifty-fifty for some reason, but slight edge to the blood beneficiary on that one. What Robert's sweet bride wanted, she got. In retirement, he would be at her beckon call. She had always had him wrapped around her dainty finger. She knew it, too.

Having located his trusty, half-charged iPad—undoubtedly unplugged in the middle of the night by one of his sons as a sacrifice for their own device's battery life—and a steeping cup of Black Rifle, he ventured to the patio. He slid his slick-bottomed and worn moccasins across the pavers carefully once out on the deck, grains of sand skating with them, as nothing but a crescent moon over the Atlantic lit his way. With the sea turtles hatching any day now, Sully's and the surrounding homes remained on a strict no-light protocol. If any outdoor or even bright indoor lights were left on in the evening, residents ran the risk of attracting new hatchlings their way instead of letting the baby turtles follow the moon to the great Atlantic. Only once had Robert found a broken baby sea turtle shell on his property, undoubtedly a casualty of a seagull, crab or some other wildlife. Such is the circle of life. Things die. A criminal defense attorney knew it all too well.

Nestled in an Adirondack chair overlooking his pool, set back from crashing waves, Robert clicked on his iPad. He had an extra kick in his step in search of the news today. Maybe it was retirement elation, maybe something else. He moved to the *Post and Courier*, refreshed to get today's edition and smiled at the cover story. He devoured it with pleasure and checked a few other papers. *The Sun News, The Herald-Sun, The State,* and *The Island Packet* all ran similar versions of the same story on the front page. *The Atlanta Journal-Constitution, Charlotte Observer,*

Daily News and *New York Post* had the story with pictures on the back pages. Half a dozen of the big boys in Washington, LA, New York and D.C. ran similar articles somewhere in the first two pages as well. Even the *Associated Press* ran a short blurb. Robert lowered the brightness on his screen as he consumed every exposé with delight.

APPARENT MURDER-SUICIDE AS SPECIAL GRAND JURY SUMMONED IN S.C. CASE.

Less than twenty-four hours after a jury acquitted Betty Stevenson, 25, of all charges stemming from the death of her infant son, John Stevenson, 2024, the boy's father and grandfather were found dead of an apparent murder-suicide at the former's Spartanburg, South Carolina home. A neighbor of Harold Clark III, (67 and grandfather of John Stevenson) told reporters on scene that they had plans to play poker and watch the NBA playoffs the evening of May 10. When the neighbor, who wishes to remain anonymous, rang the doorbell and received no answer, he peered through a window to see if he could locate his friend.

"I knew he ain't in that trial no more, cause I seen the jury decide something in the paper. Can't remember what cause I don't read gossipy-like. So figured what the

hell? Is he okay? Not the type to stand me up." the neighbor said.

He saw what appeared to be Clark III on the floor and decided to take action. After breaking down the door with a rock from a nearby flowerbed, the neighbor was shocked to find Clark III and his son, Harold Clark IV, both lying in what he described as "pools" of blood in the living room of the Clark III's Spartanburg estate.

"The stench and flies already got to 'em. Must've been a good bit since it happened, but I ain't never seen nothing like that so I ain't too sure or trustworthy a source, I guess," the neighbor said.

The neighbor went on to describe a bloody scene in which it appeared from his self-described untrained eye that Clark IV had shot his father multiple times through the chest and head before turning the gun on himself. Clark IV, the neighbor said, was only recognizable from a courthouse nametag, covered in blood, still hanging onto his shirt.

According to sources close to the matter, a special grand jury had been called the morning of May 10 and heard just a few hours of testimony before voting to "true-bill", or indict,

Clark III and Clark IV for crimes not yet announced or confirmed. As the indictment is mere speculation at this point, we reached out to contacts in the South Carolina judicial system and received no comment on the matter. It is believed, based on a source connected to the case, that the indictment is for charges as severe as Clark IV's murder of son, John Stevenson.

Vehicles and personnel from South Carolina Law Enforcement Division, more commonly known as "SLED" and similar to the State's FBI, were seen at Clark III's home shortly after the neighbor discovered the bodies. When approached for comment, Chief John Mosby of SLED provided none.

This is a developing story. Check back for updates.

CHAPTER 12

Bobby put the car in reverse and began the short drive from Sully's to Charleston. Robert sat upright in the passenger seat while Caroline and Liam reclined in opposite bucket seats of the middle row of the new Cadillac Escalade. It was a recent birthday present from Robert to Caroline, who swore up and down she did not want or need a new car. Robert agreed, but figured it was time to retire the decade old Tahoe she was tooling around town in and bring his wife into the 2020s. Caroline did not drive much so it was just as much a gift for Robert. Caroline knew the ulterior motives of her hubby but was elated nonetheless. The silver paint glistened in the Southern sun and the tan leather smelled like a Rawlings baseball mitt. Robert lived for the ventilated seats, while Caroline fancied the heated seats. Everyone enjoyed the sunroofs (plural) while no one enjoyed the television that dropped from the ceiling and rendered useless with the advent of iPads and smart phones. Robert figured maybe the screen would nevertheless prod Ben and Portia, Ben's wife, into giving them their first grandchild, but he would never say that out loud. It was easy to envision a little car seat or two watching a Pixar movie on a long summer drive.

"This backup display is insane, Ma. Should buy me one next, huh," Bobby said, pointing to the center screen followed by a backhand slap to his father's chest. The center dash had an aerial view of the Cadillac backing up, picking up the entire roof of the car, Sully's mailbox at the end of the driveway and a palm tree opposite it. "It must be some sort of satellite. Never seen something like this. Insane."

"It's too much," Caroline said, flipping her hands in disgust. "What kind of an old woman like me drives such a high-tech rig like this? I told your father to take it back, but he claims he '*lost the receipt, so we're stuck*.' Ha. Ha."

"I'll take it off your hands, Ma. Ten K. Cash. What do ya say?" Bobby grins, looking in the rearview mirror at his mother as the rig glides over Ben Sawyer Boulevard, easing into Mount Pleasant. Caroline pretends to spit in her palm and reached a hand out to shake on the deal, prompting Robert to playfully push her hand back into her lap.

"Now, now. No one is taking this beautiful beast from their mother," Robert stated. "She claims she's too lowly and simplistic for a car like this, but you know she's eating this up. She loves it. Maybe when I'm six feet under you'll even find a sugar baby in this bad boy." Caroline slapped her husband's shoulder in actual disgust before simply replying with a wry smile, "Maybe."

The family, minus Ben, Portia and the dogs, rolled passed Shem's Creek, envying the craft beers and margaritas being consumed by local college kids and a smattering of tourists. The silver bullet veered left with the road, passing by Patriot's Point. A few golfers smoked cigars in the distance and a baseball team was probably practicing on the field of the College of Charleston Cougars, but that was too far in the distance to know for certain. They careened up the Arthur Ravenel Jr. Bridge, a now famous emblem of the Low Country, each occupant of the car immune to the hoopla made over the structure. The modern marvel was a cable-stayed bridge with two monstrous, twin spears that shot five-hundred-seventy-five feet into the sky. The Cooper River below was an almost two-hundred-foot drop. Joggers, bicyclists and daring walkers shot by as Robert thought about the fear he had as a young man trying to navigate the current bridge's predecessor, a structurally unsound, petite thing.

Once about halfway over the bridge, Liam spoke up, "Dad, wasn't this your case?" Robert knew it was coming, but hoped it would be after a few drinks. He always lied better with a buzz. Funny, though, most of his clients told the truth drunk.

"What case?" Robert asked, playing dumb as he peered out the driver's side window at the U.S.S. Yorktown perched in the waters off Patriot's Point.

"That drowned infant. Well, this is related to that and mentions it. Looks like the new suspects killed themselves," Liam offered Robert his phone for a look at the article. "Thought they were about to be indicted and bam. Murder-suicide. If it's true, then the world is probably better off. Right? Do you know these two?"

"Oh wow. When did this happen?" Robert asked, as he pulled minuscule reading glasses from his blazer pocket and grabbed the phone.

"Says they found them last night, but think they'd been dead a day or two. The one guy was still wearing his nametag from court. He was a witness or family, I guess? Do you recognize either of them?" Liam asks, clearly elated by the idea his father could be so close to the action. Liam may want to draft purchase agreements and shake hands with the ultra-rich for a living, but any lawyer worth his or her salt finds murder cases to be a novelty. Lawyers consume murder trials, filings, reports and shows like oxygen. Nine times out of ten, a defense team or prosecutor cannot make much money from such a case, but it is always the talk by the proverbial watercooler of any type of law office.

Robert, pretending to meander through one of the numerous articles he had already read, scrolled with his finger slowly through the article. He could feel his wife's eyes boring a hole through the back of his head. "I'm not sure. I see so many faces in trials, but I try to block all of them out besides the judge, jury and my client," Robert stated coolly, before handing the phone back to his middle son with a joke. "Write that down. That was good advice. Ha!"

"Wait so what happened? Explain it to me, Lee," Bobby said, peering from the rearview mirror to the road and back as they pulled off the bridge and stopped at a light on the Charleston side of the Cooper River.

"So, it looks like dad got this woman—" Liam paused, scrolling for a name. "Betty Stevenson off at this trial a few days ago. Article says 'Mr. Remington, clear as day, convinced everyone in the courtroom by the end of day one of trial that Betty was innocent. By day two, it was clear that the infant most likely died at the hands of the Clark men.' The dad and grandad. Then they killed themselves."

The car went eerily silent. All eyes were on Robert, he could feel it as they pulled passed the dilapidated, old houses on the northern section of Meeting Street. Robert needed to say something. "I think I read something about it this morning. I don't know. Haven't checked email, voicemail or texts. I'm trying to stay disconnected and actually *enjoy* retirement like your mother's asked me to. If it's the men I'm thinking of, all signs pointed to them. But you know the drill. Innocent until proven guilty and I believe that. Sad way to go, though. No justice for anyone."

"I'm proud of you. Disconnecting like that," Caroline said, reaching up, rubbing her man's shoulder. "Now, no more work, death, murder or dark talk. In fact," Caroline looked at Liam next to her and said firmly, "no law-talk at the dinner table. We want a *relaxing*, carefree evening." Caroline patted her husband, saying "Ooo, Robert, that's the new gin place I was telling you about. On the right. We've gotta try it one day. Maybe this weekend."

"Sure, honey," Robert nodded, patting his wife's hand. His heart was beating rapidly under his Brooks Brothers button down. He did not want to think about those two men. They were in his past now.

CHAPTER 13

Coral sat on her faded green couch and sipped Tito's straight from the bottle. She fancied herself a professional drinker and knew not to overdo it. Instead, she would steadily graze on the bottle most of the night until she passed out, never getting too drunk, but never leaving her comfortable, *heavy* buzz.

She turned up the volume on her television to hear the episode of Perry Mason she was watching for the fourteenth time. With the volume up high enough, she could almost drown out the sound of the Jason Aldean concert playing at Credit One Arena down the road. It was loud and sounded fun, but she did not have the money to join in. She needed another big story to bring in some extra cash. Her salary was not cutting it on the expensive island and she needed to pay off her mortgage. And her outstanding vet bills. And pay for groceries. And a hospital bill from when she got her stomach pumped last year. And more liquor.

Her mind stayed percolating on what she briefly read earlier that day on Sullivan's Island. Remington got a text from an unsaved number and all she could remember was "girl" and "cash". He was not running girls now was he? She had run a story years back on a prostitute smuggling ring out of Columbia and it was nasty, intense stuff. Some of the guys went to jail. Others got off on technicalities. Others disappeared. It was a breaking report on her part, but she never got the satisfaction of seeing all the thugs jailed.

She would never let that sort of thing happen at *Coral Sands: A Coral Sands Exclusive Resort*, she thought, drunken thoughts wandering.

Remington did not strike her as the type to run girls, although, she did not put it past anyone. Cash was cash to certain criminals regardless of the harm caused at the source. Most of the guys she investigated in the Columbia ring were normal family men with office jobs just like Remington.

She flipped the channel to the news and took another sip of Tito's. It tasted like water to her, so she sucked down another. *Ahh.*

The reporter was somewhere near Kiawah Island in front of a flooded street. A water line had broken somewhere. Exciting stuff.

Coral drained the rest of the Tito's as she walked to the kitchen. The two fatter of her three cats followed, thinking they were getting a third dinner. Their drunk, forgetful mother tended to do that. Hence the obesity. She threw the empty bottle into the liquor cabinet to accompany the other liquor corpses, trophies of the conquered strewn about. In the fridge she found an old bottle of Corona behind a bowl of three eggs and some expired milk. She popped the top off the beer and took a swig. Refreshing, but not strong enough. She threw on a hoodie, grabbed her keys and walked toward the front door. She would grab another bottle at the liquor store on the corner. Her credit card had at least fifty bucks left before the limit and she would get paid in a day or two. She could not remember which. She would make it work.

Coral's attention was caught by a news correspondent on the television just as she went to turn off the television. She recognized the reporter; one she had spoken to during the

Columbia prostitution ring story. The reporter was from the upstate and was outside a massive colonial-style house with blue and red lights reverberating off the old brick.

"…the Spartanburg home of local celebrity Harold Clark III. The home has been a crime scene for much of the day as you can see by the caution tape stopping me from getting any closer. It was reported by a neighbor that he found Clark III and his son, Clark IV, dead in the home of an apparent murder-suicide…."

Coral sat back on the couch, swigging her Corona without taking her eyes from the television. Liquor could wait.

"…recognize the elder Clark from his former occupation as a South Carolina state congressman for more than two decades, before trading in his career for a new one hosting the popular gameshow *Who Got The Mail?* on our sister station More recently, though, the Clarks were tied to the prosecution of the lover and mother of the younger Clark's now deceased son."

Coral pulled out her laptop and started pecking away at the keyboard. She pieced the text together. The cash. The girl. She had him.

CHAPTER 14

Bobby pulled up to a small building in downtown Charleston and followed the tight, brick-laden loop around to a valet's table. The valet stand—clearly new, but made to look vintage—was covered by a slanted overhang that matched the antique building. The building the Remington's pulled up to was a light, faded-red-grey mix and could not have stood taller than ten feet above the tan, cobblestone drive. The brick stacked up each side looked as if they were a couple centuries old and once could have been a vibrant red, but had now faded from the weathering of seasons over time. As the Remington's disembarked from the Cadillac, a valet snatched the keys from Bobby and took his place in the driver's seat. Robert could not help but notice that the man was in his sixties, much older than most valets who tended to be young men enrolled in one of the numerous nearby colleges. Robert made a mental note then silently chuckled at the standard valet outfit at Charleston establishments such as this one: a short-sleeve button down concealed by a tight vest that belonged under a suit jacket, which was nowhere to be found; a bowtie tied the ensemble together, but the most comical parts were the shorts, high socks and wingtip-style, leather loafers. The outfit screamed Charleston class—it wanted to be fancy, but was at the mercy of the humid Low Country weather. Even the cruelest of employers would not dare force pants upon employees in the spring, summer and fall months.

Henry's Steakhouse had been Remington and Shelby staples for decades. It was a staple of any well-to-do Charlestonian for important life events, standing strong since 1771. Robert and Caroline had their rehearsal dinner here as well as graduation parties for each of the boys—high school and college. Family and friends reserved at least one of the three, modestly-sized private rooms for all types of celebrations and Caroline told Robert it would be ideal for a nice, quiet family dinner to celebrate his retirement from the practice of law. Nothing big, she had said, just an easy, quiet night with the family at a table in the main dining area.

As long as he could get a sizzling, well marbled, medium-rare steak, he had informed Caroline, he was in.

Robert buttoned the ivory buttons of his sear sucker blazer and motioned for his wife and children to enter the steakhouse first. Always the gentleman. After following, he entered through the right side of the massive, oak double doors, held open by a second, much younger valet. Robert remembered from his early days as a valet at this very establishment that the two or three on duty at any given time would have an agreement: the eldest or longest tenured (rock, paper, scissors sometimes being the ultimate determinant) would drive the nicer cars and the other(s) would tend to the less expensive, "regular" cars. He emitted a childlike smirk thinking his wife's new ride would be categorized as nice enough for the eldest of the men; how far they had come, he thought silently.

After giving the Remington name to a cute hostess just inside, Bobby nudged Liam with a firm elbow to the ribs as she turned her back. Liam shot Bobby a sharp look of disapproval in return, obviously still broken-hearted from a high school flame re-emblazed during his first year of law school only to be doused once again. Young love, Robert thought as he watched his sons rib each other (literally) like they were still boys. Ben had his love life figured out, but, ironically, Robert's two eldest were still struggling and bouncing around in search of a "forever".

After grabbing large, leather-bound menus, the hostess launched a longing smile at Liam and waved for the family to follow her. Robert wondered if they already knew each other, but thought better than to pry into his sons' lives. That was Caroline's job.

Following his family, Robert stepped down into the main dining room, whose floor had been essentially excavated in the sixties to leave the structural integrity of the building intact, but allow for people taller than six feet to easily maneuver the restaurant. Many older restaurants had lower ceilings, mirroring the population's smaller stature decades ago. After walking between numerous tables, three-quarters of which sat individuals Robert or his family knew, they turned right toward a white door with its original gold adornments. The young hostess turned the doorknob, opened the door and stood back as three loud *bangs!* came from within.

Robert flinched and took a step toward his wife, instinctively reaching to protect Caroline. Simultaneously, he shoved his hand into his pocket, fingering the brass knife handed down through the generations of Remingtons. He had used it before and would not hesitate to use it again. His only regret was leaving his pistol at home.

Everything had finally caught up with him, he thought, but he refused to let his family suffer for his indiscretions.

Just before he was able to remove the knife from his pocket, Robert noticed pistols protruding from each side of the white molding attached to the door frame. These were not ordinary pistols, however, as they were long and bulky, reminding Robert of something from a *Looney Tunes* episode. Hanging out of each were metal sticks, white flags on the end with blue, bold lettering. "GUILTY" said one, while the other commanded "OF RETIREMENT!". Robert released his grip from the knife, took a deep breath and smiled at the confetti falling from the ceiling. Three bangs: two fake guns and confetti gun.

"You sons of bitches," Robert said, taking a hand from his pocketed knife to cover his fast-beating heart, nervously chuckling. He looked around at his family and grabbed the two closest into a bear hug, Caroline and Bobby. "And you! You guys knew and wanted to let your old man spend his first day as a retiree in the E.R. My own heart near 'tacked me!" Caroline smacked her husband with a nearby menu for his swearing, which Robert gladly accepted. It still was not proper to swear in old, Southern families such as the Shelbies and Remingtons, especially in a public setting. Robert thought a fake shooting with corny flags warranted saying every word in the book.

Robert released his grip on his wife and his eldest. He sauntered his way into the private dining room which, apparently, had been reserved for his very own retirement party. The new retiree shook hands with everyone present, all fifty or so lined up, sipping champagne and ready to greet the man of the hour. First were the gun wielders: Ben and SLED Chief John Mosby, the former, he hugged and the latter, he shook hands with firmly and gave him a look as if to say, "We'll talk later." Next was Ben's wife, Portia, who gave her father-in-law a big hug and a gift bag that clearly contained alcohol of some kind. After Portia, the faces began to mesh together as he gleefully thanked everyone for coming: local politicians, his staff, current and former alike, as well as Ralph Morrison, the Remington cousin taking over the firm, local police, distant relatives, friends and neighbors. Everyone Robert knew was crammed into that tiny room. All for him. Tears welled up in his eyes by the time he was done greeting each and every guest. It meant a lot that he could put his successful careers in the rearview and still have a retirement left to enjoy.

***

Caroline had reserved all three private dining rooms for the evening. Two of the rooms were next to each other on one side of the main dining area and one, a dining room that was formerly for blacks only, on the opposite side, adjacent to the kitchen. This dining room near the kitchen would serve as the main bar this evening for the drinkers too onery and impatient to wait for one of the numerous servers. It would also act as the dessert bar for later in the evening, while the connecting two rooms would keep their doors ajar and housed a dozen tables for the guests to eat and mingle.

After some initial drinks to get everyone—except the teetotalers in attendance, of course—good and liquored up, Caroline tapped her glass and asked everyone to take their seat for the courses to begin. Before taking a seat with his wife, Robert's eyes darted around the rooms looking for two people: Chief Mosby and Detective Joseph Covington. Robert wanted to ensure both sat at the table with Caroline and himself. This maneuver was not necessarily so he could schmooze with the officers over a meal, but so he could keep them from talking too much to others. Mosby was two decades sober, let everyone know it, then still drank. Robert spied the Chief standing in line across the restaurant while sipping from a crystal whiskey glass. Before hurrying off to gather the Chief, Robert snatched his youngest son and told him to reserve two seats at their table for the officers. After doing so, he tapped Covington on the shoulder and pointed to Ben. The commanding black Detective nodded and Robert hurried to Mosby.

"We'll get you another at the table, Chief. Come with me," Robert scolded, grabbing Mosby by the elbow. Mosby nodded obediently and followed Robert without a word of debate. The officer looked more like a child being led to timeout—somber-faced paired with sunken, defeated eyes—than the Chief of South Carolina's most serious armed force. Robert only hoped that by the time he sat the man down—a man who stood Napoleonic at five-foot five and a hundred and fifty pounds—he would forget his desire to drink. The seeming second-hand embarrassment bestowed on him by the man of the night may have done the trick as Mosby took his seat next to Ben with only a handshake and a humble nod.

Robert grabbed the chair in between Covington and Mosby just as the she-crab soups and Caesar salads were being served by white-gloved waiters and waitresses. Caroline sat opposite him without so much as a look, knowing that there must be business to attend to. It was, after all, his night. She understood there would need to be a transition period into retirement in order to wind down Robert's affairs. Caroline knew this, but no details and she wanted to keep it that way.

For as small in stature and sheepish Chief Mosby was, Detective Covington was considerable in build and breaming with confidence. Covington was six feet, seven inches and carried about three hundred pounds on his portly frame, but supported it well. He was just as suave to those who did not know him as he was intimidating. For Mosby's milky-white complexion, there was Covington's dark, mocha skin. Where Mosby was "sober", Covington probably should at least try to be given his affinity for the drink; instead, Detective Covington was a heavy drinker who managed to hold his whiskey well. A former guard for the Bucs basketball team of Charleston Southern University, Covington played overseas for two years before returning to the Low Country and joining the force. Early on in his career, Robert and the then-junior officer at his table had met numerous times, each encounter featuring Robert cross-examining the defiant officer, at least two of which when Covington was deemed by the presiding judge a "hostile witness." After a cold start to the professional relationship, Covington and Robert grew to find their interests aligned more often than not and a mutually beneficial partnership formed.

"I'll take another, miss," Covington said to the waitress, holding up his empty glass. Before Mosby had a chance to raise his barren glass, Robert placed a calming hand on his wrist and shot the Chief a frown. Mosby nodded and reached for his water glass, taking a swig.

"You need to stay by me tonight. Why are you drinking?" Robert mumbled so only Mosby could hear, smiling so all appeared well.

"I'm fine, Rob. I've only had a few. I'll stop for the night if it'll make you feel more comfortable, Boss. Seen a lot, lately, okay, *Boss*?" He returned Robert's frown. Robert ignored the jab and looked away.

"How are things? Everything good?"

"Yes. It's all taken care of. Clean. You seen it all."

"Good," Robert said before turning to the menacing presence on his other side. He took a sip of his soup and said to Covington, "Any word on the other thing? Inland?"

Covington took a new whiskey neat from the waitress, holding her eyes for just long enough to get a blush out of her. Covington was married, but never wore his ring. He claimed it was for her safety in his line of work, but Robert knew better.

"I checked around. Sounds like this mutt slaps her around quite a bit. Kind of a known thing up there, but no one gives a shit since she's a pill fiend and he's friends with the locals on duty," Covington was sure to speak low and switched from behind a menu to his glass. He was always discreet, that's why Robert liked him. "Last week the kid got involved, though, so everyone's on edge. They've been covering for the mutt so long with the lady. Never thought he'd touch the kid. Everyone turned out wrong."

"Wait, what?" Robert was afraid of this. He had no love lost for the pill fiend, but her daughter was another story. She was young and innocent. "I thought it was drinking and driving or something? What happened to the child?"

"The DUI was a few days ago. This is new. The kid managed to mumble to cops the scumbag was beating up her mother pretty bad that night. Came home in the bottle. Was standard OP, but this night was different because he stayed in the bottle when he got home. Usually, he'd call it a night by the time he got back and smacked the lady around a few times, according to the girl," Covington suddenly looked at Robert, startled. "No disrespect, Boss, I know she's your sister-in-law.

I don't mean to minimize what happened here. Just giving it to you straight as I hear it."

Robert lifted one hand a few inches off the table. *Proceed.*

"Well, the kid mumbled something about this being the first time she'd heard shots during one of these. Said the beating and yelling started earlier in the night, died down and then all of sudden some gun shots. She calls 9-11, runs downstairs, thinks better of it and hides back in her room. I think the mom got shot, but nothing life threatening. The drunken POS breaks down the kid's door and shoots her as she's escaping out the window. In the leg. Mainly a flesh wound, but still. She's a kid for Chrissakes. Falls out the window and everything right in front of the cops. No covering this one up."

"So where does it stand now?" Robert asked, happy to see the rest of those at his table lost in their own conversations.

"Apparently, before this incident, it was easy for the thug. Every other time, the kid's mother refused to press charges and the cops calmed things down. This time, the kid said she wants the book thrown at the guy. She's cooperating. Good for her. Only string Derrick's friends were able to pull was to get a low bail and get him out." Covington scanned the room as he spoke through his glass. Robert was not sure if he was scanning for women or threats. Probably both. "The issue, though," he continued, "is that the girl keeps going in and out of consciousness so far. Memory's in and out. Sometimes she remembers it and wants the book thrown, others she does not remember any of it. I spoke to a doctor on her floor who said she thinks because of the trauma and loss of blood, she may end up forgetting a lot of it one of these days she comes into consciousness."

"So he's out? Any restraining order or anything?" Robert asked, ignoring the girl for the time being. He was beginning to fear for his niece.

"Nothing, Boss. My guys can get up there and stand protection around the girl, but she lives with him. Still in the hospital from what I hear, though. Might be awkward and—"

"No. I don't want them knowing I—or anyone else—is involved. Sounds like we can't trust the friendlies up there anyhow," Robert interrupted. Mosby craned his neck to hear every word. Even for a semi-drunk, he was usually a great cop, eager to work a case. "I'll probably head up tomorrow. C's on me to help the sister. The sister wants me to defend the 'mutt'. Sounds like I need to go up and help the girl, though? Do you agree? C's only heard the mother's side of it all."

Covington nodded zealously. "That's what I'd do, Boss. Poor girl needs a glimmer of hope if her own ma hanging her out to dry for some dick."

"Watch it," Robert snapped. He knew Covington was right, though.

Robert had enough of this kind of talk. He was concerned about his niece, but nothing that could be done about it now. He did not want to talk to only these two men about dark topics the whole night when so many others came to celebrate his retirement. The irony was not lost on Robert that this was his retirement party and yet he was discussing work. Robert put an arm around Mosby and patted Covington's thick arm.

"I appreciate you both. Thanks for coming. We're certainly not done working together, but just want to let you both know I'm appreciative." Robert mostly meant it, but he knew he needed to keep both in his corner.

"Thanks, Boss," both said in unison.

"Now, Covington," Robert said, looking back and forth between the two. "Feel free to order Mosby another one if he so chooses, but if you do, you're in charge of him. Make sure he doesn't stray too far."

Without another word to Robert, Covington held up two meaty fingers to the waitress. He loved a drinking buddy. "Loose lips sink ships, Chief. Remember that tonight."

CHAPTER 15

As the night carried on, the drinks steadily turned from mint juleps, champagne and beer to shots of every variety for all. The few truly sober folks began trickling out with hardy handshakes, thanks and congrats around ten thirty, eleven. Around midnight, a brave soul confirmed the humidity toned down, a slight breeze cooled the air and suits were breathable outside so the party made its way to the patio out back. The perky, young hostess joined the group as the night wound down, giggling with Bobby and indulging in champagne, obviously having missed the memo that champagne was so three hours ago. Her name was Addie and she was currently studying interior design at College of Charleston. Robert pegged her around twenty-two, a bit young for thirty-four-year-old Bobby, but Robert was not one to judge. Love is love, if that's what Bobby was after. Besides, Caroline would judge on his behalf.

Chief Mosby had snuck out with Covington about an hour earlier, too embarrassed (or oblivious) to say goodbye in his inebriated state. He would undoubtedly apologize—albeit, unnecessarily—in the next day or two with a call disguised as business. Tonight, though, he was likely headed for a local strip joint with Covington. Not the best influence for an AA member, but again, Robert was not one to judge and Mosby seemed to be in a good stretch of handling his liquor. If he ever stepped over the line, Robert would be the first to ring him in—as he had a few times before. So long as he kept his mouth shut tonight, he would be just fine. No harm, no foul.

By one in the morning, no one who made it to the patio was budging, an age-old sign the party was a hit. As everyone got drunker and the booze mixed with repressed lethargy, a former secretary at Remington Law began getting handsy with a childhood friend of Bobby's and things looked to be getting sensual. Robert, having witnessed firsthand what alcohol abuse can do to a family, sipped casually all evening, keeping an even buzz but never reaching a drunken stupor. Caroline was much the same, though young Ben and Portia were two sheets to the wind, as was Liam who managed to hide it much better than his baby bro. Bobby, not much of a drinker, was smoking a cigar and swapping it back and forth with Addie, his new *pal.* Robert could not help but to give his wife a wry smile from across the room, both admiring what they had managed to achieve. The friends, family and relative wealth was just what they had hoped, but never thought they would actually achieve with their family histories. Names can only do so much when it comes to fattening a bank account.

By a quarter after one, Robert found himself speaking with his cousin, successor and, as of that day, Remington Law LLP managing partner Ralph Morrison. Ralph was a cousin on Robert's mother's side, eldest son of an aunt and uncle who raised Ralph and his siblings near D.C. Ralph graduated middle of his class at George Washington School of Law before managing to lock down a Federal District Court clerkship thanks to his parent's political connections. Ralph Sr. was fairly high up in the FBI and had thirty years on the job, while his mother worked in a clerical capacity in the CIA for nearly just as long. Needless to say, Ralph had connections; D.C. connections, not small town, Low Country connections. D.C.

was the big leagues when it came to money, the legal profession and, most of all, *power*.

After the clerkship gave his resume a much needed shot in the arm, Ralph was able to secure an associate position at a white shoe law firm on Pennsylvania Ave specializing in all types of litigation. Every day he would march past the White House, kick his Gucci shoes up on his desk and stare out his window at Capitol Hill. By year five, he was bringing in big time clients equating to a big book of business, nearly half a million a year in income and little-to-no free time for Liz, his high school sweetheart-turned-neglected spouse. By this time, the couple had been together a dozen years, married seven and had no children to show for it. Robert knew children were no savior for nor scorecard of a marriage, but his inkling was Liz was antsy and his suspicion was proven correct when Caroline confirmed Liz was livid and thinking of leaving workaholic Ralph. By year six at the firm, Ralph was rewarded with a very early "Partner" beside his name—and divorce papers.

During a messy, contentious divorce, Ralph fell apart. He was politely asked to leave his partnership after a few drunken outbursts and he sat unemployed, determined to win Liz back, for about a year. With plenty in the bank, unemployment did not matter to the broken man.

Fast-forward to Robert's retirement party and Liz had cancelled her divorce plans, Ralph had opened a small, but relatively profitable defense firm outside of Charlotte, North Carolina and the couple was in a state of constant bliss for the last five years.

Robert had helped Ralph out of numerous jams in his career, both in D.C. and Charlotte, thanks to his own connections. As such, he had grown fond of the once troubled young cousin of his. Robert had offered him partnership at his own firm numerous times, but was always turned down with a pat on the back and the same response, "When you hang it up and I can run it all my way, give me a call." So Robert did. After a lucrative buyout, some signed contracts, airtight NDAs and an un-ceremonial passing of the torch, Remington Law LLP was Ralph's. In the contract was a strict do-not-rename-clause that Robert took five percent off the buyout price for. What also did not hurt was Robert had a few secrets over Ralph that he could always use to his advantage if need be.

"Thing was you, right? The father and son." Ralph asked Robert after twenty minutes of prolonged pleasantries, sports talk and staffing discussions. He was in the bottle too much and had some liquid courage.

"Don't you worry about that, Ralphy. You're told what you need to be told," Robert said as he smiled and pulled out his phone. Two missed called from Joey Covington. He did not need to know what strip clubs they were at and hear that he needed to come or he was a "whipped pussy" as Covington liked to say.

As he started to slip his phone back in his jacket pocket, it vibrated again. A text from Covington this time: "News. U need to call me. Ur niece needs help. Confirming that the guy we talked about is after her and the mother is refusing to cooperate."

Robert's heart sank as he walked into the now-deserted restaurant and made the call.

CHAPTER 16

Rose woke up to a hand on hers, gently shaking it. Just over the beeping and pulsing that surrounded her head, she heard her mother's voice calling to her in a moaning whisper.

"Hey, Rose. How're you doing, baby?" Her mother's voice strained softly. The girl could not see anything but the glare of bright lights. Her head was pounding and her eyes were having trouble adjusting. She lifted a hand to each eyelid and rubbed as if trying to force them into an alert state. Once the rheum, built up around each eye, was brushed away, she let her eyes blink into focus once more. A flood of light rushed in like water through a broken levee. As her pupils regulated to her surroundings, Rose noticed her mother's bruised face near her own. The mother smiled sympathetically at her only daughter, portraying a look of guilt deep behind pained eyes.

"Mom? Are you okay? What happened to you face?" Rose began to sit up in bed and reach for her mother's bruised face, but was immediately stopped by pain shooting through her entire body. She could not pinpoint the source because it was everywhere, so she eased back to a lying position, eyes clenched and face scrunched in pain.

"Easy, Rose. You're in the hospital. Everything's okay. You've had a few surgeries so you're a bit out of it and sore. Everything's okay now, though. Momma's here," Jenny said in a soothing, hushed tone, gently rubbing the girl's hand. As the pain dulled from a ten out of ten to an eight out of ten, she studied her mother. Her chin and one side of her cheek were heavily bandaged, the swelling and bruising still visible, pushing through the bindings. She was sitting in a wheelchair next to Rose's hospital bed, arm in a sling and something pushing through her clothing. Her mother was draped in a hospital gown that matched Rose's—white with off-green flourishes and an ugly purple set of interlacing dots all over. Upon closer inspection, it appeared as though the protrusion in her mother's abdomen was a stack of thick gauze held in place by dressings that wrapped around her torso.

"Mom, what happened to you? Your stomach...," Rose lifted the hand closest to her mother cautiously. Trembling, she pointed at the injured woman. Rose grimaced and dropped her hand back down in pain.

"Nothing, nothing, sweetheart. I'm worried about you. You feel okay?" Her mother asked, gently playing with the girl's hair, her own pain obvious with each stroke.

"I feel out of it. Like I'm in a cloud. We're at the hospital? What happened?" Rose asked, unable to recall anything at all. She remembered spending a day at the library, reading, writing, doodling and doing anything she could to avoid being home on her day off from the convenience store. Even with severe physical trauma and obvious mental trauma, she knew she despised being around her stepfather. "Did we get in a car wreck or something? I'm hurting everywhere and you look just as bad as I feel, Momma."

"We're fine, honey. You've gotta get some rest. I'll tell you everything that happened in a bit, after you catch up on rest and recover, darling," her mother assured her as Rose's eyelids began to betray her. "You keep waking up with some memories, then drifting back off. The doctor said after the last surgery you'll probably forget everything so all the blood and oxygen can focus on your wounds. We'll talk when you're better. You're going to be okay, though, babygirl."

Rose remained at least somewhat aware of what was going on around her as she drifted in and out of sleep, reassured by her mother's presence. She heard what must've been a nurse or doctor reprimand her mother, demanding she return to her own bed which, from the sounds of it, was in the same room as Rose's. At some point later on, she also heard an investigator—*from one of her mystery novels*? —asking Jenny questions, most of which her mother refused to answer. The questioning went on for what seemed to be an hour, but Rose was not sure as she continued drifting, never reopening her eyes, but continuing to hear her surroundings and feel her heartbeat in every corner of her aching body, the pain emanating.

"Ma'am, this is a child endangerment case at this point. If you don't cooperate there's a chance we take you in too. Just look at your poor girl, ma'am. Don't make us take her mother, too," a deep baritone barked at her mother.

"Officer…I…I just don't know what you're talking about," her mother forced back at the officer, a few sniffles sounding like Jenny was talking through tears.

"Ma'am, your husband shot both you and your daughter. Your daughter fell out of a window while trying to escape your *heavily* intoxicated husband. She fell right in front of our officers. And you were beaten within inches of your life before being shot. You need to get real, ma'am. Your doctor and the nurses say you suffered zero memory loss. You know *damned* well what happened."

"I told you…I don't know anything. I don't remember anything. None of… Nothing you just described sounds like my husband. We have our lawyer, Robert Remington on retainer if necessary," her mother lied, only stopping to sob briefly. Her tone was unsure and unconvincing, even in Rose's delirious state she did not believe her mother's argument.

Eyes still shut, migrating in and out of consciousness, the officer's description of what happened all sounded vaguely familiar to Rose. She remembered gun shots. Derrick shouting. Chasing her. *Or was that a dream?* She could not remember.

CHAPTER 17

Rose opened her eyes without prodding this time. It was dark in the hospital room and she felt much more coherent than she did last speaking with her mother. With coherence, the price paid was pain. The drugs in her system must have worn off as she felt blood agonizingly pumping through her with each heartbeat. The monitors that surrounded her all beeped at a steady rate. The labored breathing of her numerous hospital wing roommates cut in and out over the beeping. Some of her senses felt keen, while others, absent as she sweat profusely in silent agony.

Searching the wing, she made out two shapes at the foot of her bed. The visitors had certainly been watching her sleep and their presence woke the ailing girl. One was broader and slightly taller than the other who was lean and petite. They turned to each other, lips moving but no sound coming out. Rose thought they were talking, but could not be sure. Fighting through the pain, she reached for her ears in an attempt to rub them awake as she did her eyes earlier that day. She was met with resistance as each ear was stuffed with cotton balls. She pulled them out gradually, each one sticking with dried blood to her eardrum.

"Rose Shelby?" One of the voices whispered. Rose nodded and they both approached the right side of her hospital bed. One of the figures, which Rose could now make out as a nurse not much older than herself, pressed a button on the side of her hospital bed, raising Rose's torso and allowing her to sit up.

"Easy now," the nurse whispered, noticing Rose's face wrinkle in discomfort. She brought the bed to a stop and motioned to the man, now visible, beside her. "Rose, honey, this is Officer Johnson. He's a nice man who just wants to help you and has some questions. I'll be right her if you need anything. I'm not leaving you."

"Where's my mom?" Rose asked immediately. She did not want to answer questions while she still needed her own questions answered.

"Hi there, Rose," the officer whispered as he knelt down beside her bed. Through her tearful eyes, she noticed the stature of the man was squat and unassuming. He had broad shoulders but was about the same height as the nurse. "I'm talking low so we don't wake the other patients here, but I'd just like a few minutes of your time if you're feeling up to it. Does that sound alright?"

Rose studied the officer's face as it came into focus. He looked to be in his forties, with thinning black and white hair and a matching mustache, neatly trimmed. He was in uniform pants, a short sleeve button down and black shoes that Rose assumed shined in the daylight. What drew her attention the most was the holstered gun on his hip. This sent a shiver up Rose's spine as her memories flooded back. Officer Johnson must have noticed her eyeline and raised a calming hand to the bed.

"If you'd like, I can put the gun somewhere else. I promise I'm here to help, not hurt you, Rose."

"No, it's okay, Officer," Rose said, shaking her head. She prided herself in maturity. She could be with a gun. "Where's my mom?"

Officer Johnson glanced at the nurse, who was standing behind him. Trying to be as sensitive as he could in an often-insensitive profession, Officer Johnson seemed at a loss for words. Quickly, the nurse filled the silence, "Rose, she's resting. She's very hurt herself, but will be just fine. There weren't any beds next to each other," she lied, "but once there are we'll be sure to have you two close. Right now, she needs to heal. So do you, but now is a good time to talk to us."

"Do you remember what happened a few nights ago?" Back to Officer Johnson.

"Were you the man asking my mom questions earlier today?" Rose countered with another question of her own. The girl did not know how to feel about cops, fully aware that they had so often turned a cheek when her mother called following a beating. The cops in her mystery novels, however, were usually helpful and genuine.

"Yes, I was. We thought you were asleep. I'm sorry if I disturbed you," Officer Johnson shot the nurse a look of uneasiness, as if they were losing a potential ally.

"I was, kind of, but I heard it. It reminded me about the other night. Jogged my memory. Derrick shot my mom."

"Start at the beginning of what you remember, Rose. If you can."

"You've had a concussion, so just take your time," the nurse chimed in.

The girl took a moment to think and focused on the night she heard the gunshots downstairs. As she concentrated, blocking out the pain enflaming her body, a flicker of rage replaced the discomfort. The day and night flooded back to her. She detailed to the officer and nurse how it was a regular day. She spent most of it at the library, avoiding Derrick who she disliked for numerous reasons, first and foremost the way he treated her mother. She ate dinner with her mom in the den while watching *Jurassic Park*, which was based on a book by a doctor she read earlier this year, she told her audience of two. After the movie, her mother hurried her up to bed because she must've known Derrick was drinking and would come home looking for a fight. Her mother, she said, of course didn't tell Rose this when sending her upstairs. Rose knew anyway; it had happened numerous times before. She went on to describe the beating and verbal abuse she heard earlier in the night when Derrick first got home. Again, this was expected and normal. What was not normal was the sound of gunshots, which prompted Rose to call the police.

"I was petrified," she whispered, fighting back tears. "I was afraid I'd come downstairs to a dead mom and just Derrick's stupid, drunk smile. I came down and couldn't tell if my mom was dead. Sure looked like she could've been. Lying in a puddle of blood. I ran back upstairs, thinking I'd barricade myself in the room. I read about it in a book. Some girl was able to blockade her room off when some assassins came in. They couldn't get the door down before the cops came. I was thinking maybe I'd have the same luck.

"After realizing Derrick was too big to let a door stand in his way, I tried climbing on the roof," tears now streamed down the girl's face. The young nurse wiped them gently with tissues as she too teared up. "Last thing I remember was falling off the roof after hearing a gunshot. I'm guessing I'm here and in pain because of that?"

"That's right, Rose. Some officers arrived, heard a gunshot and saw you take a nasty tumble off the roof with a bullet in your leg. You lost consciousness," Officer Johnson confirmed. "Are you willing to testify to what you just said? In a courtroom in front of everyone, including Derrick and potentially your mother?"

"Calm down, Officer," the young nurse crinkled her face. "She's been through enough and—"

"Of course," Rose said without hesitation, cutting the nurse off. Something inside her burst with joy thinking of Derrick going to prison. She and her mother could move far away and start over. Without a maniacal abuser.

"That's great, Rose. You're doing the right thing. This will help you and your mother and potentially others out there who are victims of abuse."

"I don't consider myself a victim, Officer," Rose stated plainly after a moment of contemplation. "My mother is the real victim. And I'm happy she can finally go through with pressing charges and getting us away from that man." Rose allowed herself a smile. "He's not my real dad anyway," she added, making sure they knew.

Officer Johnson craned his neck back to the nurse. Rose assumed he was smiling at the thought of a "cooperating witness", a term she had read many times. When he turned back to her, his brow was furrowed and the nurse took charge. "Sweetie, it seems that—at this point at least—your mother won't go through with pressing charges," the nurse warily stated. "But the bright spot is, you can on your own for your own injuries. You can also cooperate and tell the court and officers and all of 'em about what you heard and saw that night. You can kinda testify on her behalf. Be the witness she won't be."

Rose was taken aback; a rage bubbled within her. "You're wrong. My mother wouldn't get shot at, let me get shot and let the shooter get away with it," Rose offered up, trying to convince herself more than the nurse or officer.

"I'm afraid we spoke to her a few times and this is her position: 'nothing happened.' As for your injuries, it was all 'accidental'." Officer Johnson said with a disappointed look on his face. He stood up and began heading for the door. "We know what really happened, though. We can help. Thank you for your cooperation, Rose. I need to go tell my bosses. We'll make sure he can't hurt you or anyone anymore."

The nurse lowered Rose's bed back down as she laid in shock. Her mother would not choose Derrick over her. No way. They were off. Or maybe this was all a dream. She was feeling nauseous and dizzy like she may pass out at any moment. Her vision blurred and the beeps above her began to increase in cadence.

“Relax, Rose. Your blood pressure is rising. You need to get some rest. The I.V. bag is hooked up and we’ll drip some morphine in. You’ll feel….” The nurse’s voice trailed off as Rose lost consciousness again. Derrick’s drunken face was seared into her brain. Rage filled her at the thought of her mother hugging and kissing him, tossing her aside.

CHAPTER 18

Rose was sitting up in bed reading a book the petite nurse—whose name she found out was also Rose, Rose Blanchard, a twenty-two-year-old from Virginia who had just relocated to the area—had brought her from her own apartment library. They had the same taste in fiction: mysteries with a helping of romance, and Nurse Blanchard was happy to bring half a dozen books for her patient to devour during recovery. It turned out patient Rose had already read two of the six books Nurse Blanchard brought her, but she was too polite to say anything and decided to start with the four she had not yet read.

After running several tests and scans over her first couple of days in the hospital, doctors had determined Rose to be severely malnourished leading to underdeveloped bones and a failing kidney. Of course, the reason for her "visit" was a bullet wound in her thigh—a bullet that missed her femoral artery by less than an inch—rendering Rose lucky to be alive given her rural home's distance from the hospital. Another thirty minutes, the doctor had stated, and she could have died. Due to the brittleness of her bones, about a baker's dozen of them broke from her fall from the roof, most of which required surgery to place various pins and screws. Her kidney even needed a toned-down version of dialysis before transplant was needed, but thankfully it was not that far along. And the bullet itself required surgery to remove and re-attach various ripped body parts in her skinny, mangled thigh. Rose was recovering well and would be able to leave the hospital in due course, but as she was about to learn, where to go next would be the real issue.

Halfway through her first book from Nurse Blanchard (about a female detective who fell in love with a killer she was investigating), Rose's mother strolled over in her wheelchair, looking around the wing, wide-eyed. Nurse Blanchard had tried to run interference during her shifts, keeping an eye out anytime the mother tried to talk about Derrick with her daughter, but could only do so much when she was not working; the other nurses merely clocked in, did the bare minimum and clocked out. None of them liked Nurse Blanchard much because of her "over-compassion."

"Get your check and leave, girl," they would say behind her back.

Jenny had noticed the nurse's annoying habit of interrupting and began to despise Nurse Blanchard, calling her every name in the book to anyone who would listen, including Blanchard herself. Young Rose was oblivious to it all, either lost in the trance of a chapter or asleep in recovery from her various surgeries. Now, with Nurse Blanchard relieved of duty after an unsanctioned triple shift, Jenny saw her opportunity.

"How're you doing, sweetie?" Jenny asked, with an agenda unbeknownst to Rose.

"I'm feeling a bit better. Sore everywhere but I'd say the pain is subsiding. Since most of the incisions were in my lower body, my upper body was just soreness and bone bruises. So those are starting to heal." Rose had the vocabulary of an English professor, despite her uneducated upbringing. She quickly pivoted, turning the conversation to the night of the shooting. She had avoided talking about Derrick in front of any of the nurses or doctors, but now was her chance with most tending to others in the room. "What happened the other night, Mom?"

"Do you not remember anything?" Jenny asked, trying to mask her glee at the question from her seemingly oblivious daughter. She was clearly probing.

"No, it's all a blur. I remember being at the library and then waking up here," Rose lied, baiting her mother. She was in a chess match against Jenny at this point.

"Oh no, honey. They did say you had a nasty concussion. Well." Jenny took a deep breath, pausing and pretending to get emotional thinking about what she was about to say. Whether the emotion was genuine or not was not clear, but it was likely misplaced for the purpose of deception. She was probably using the dramatic pause to conjure up a believable lie, Rose thought. Or maybe she had been brewing one the entire time she laid in her hospital bed. "You and I had dinner together and watched a movie. After you went to bed, Derrick came home and wasn't feeling well. He was dizzy and lightheaded, so I went to make him some food. On our way to the kitchen, he slipped and fell, shattering glass everywhere. I told him it was alright; I'd clean up and he'd better just go get into some dry clothes and climb into bed. I think he needed to sleep it off, ya know? He's been working so much lately."

Rose already knew her mother was fabricating everything beyond dinner. To add insult to injury, Rose had heard Derrick and her mother arguing earlier in the week, something about how he was *missing too much work* to go hunting. Jenny only knew because she opened his mail and noticed a plethora of sick days taken in the last month. Rose played along with the lie and appeared to listen intently. She was curious to see how her mother would gloss over bullet wounds in her own daughter.

"Later that night after we'd both gone to sleep, I noticed Derrick was sweating and talking in his sleep. I felt him and he was burnin' up. Musta had a fever of well over a hundred. I went to the kitchen to fetch him some Tylenol or something. And a glass of water. When I turned around, he was running around the house full on hallucinating. He was talking about Robert E. Lee, Stonewall Jackson and Abe Lincoln so I knew he was completely out of it. I mean he was talking like they were alive, well and in the room. I tried to calm him down and noticed he was holding his pistol. This made me nervous because he never takes that pistol out the case. Ya know, the one with the fingerprint lock and all?"

Rose nodded at the fabrication. She had seen the gun a dozen times, usually when Derrick was drinking and showing it off. He even shot a squirrel in front of her with it once, laughing at the horrified look on her face the whole time. She also knew he did not own a case for it, let alone a biometric one.

"At one point, he looks at me with this dead stare, where he's looking at me and through me all at the same time. Like the movies or somethin'. Sweat dripping down and clearly hallucinating, he yells something about Gettysburg and aims the gun at me. I try to wrestle it from him and I manage to get it. Thank God I did and that's how I really know he wasn't feeling well. Ya know, since he's three times my size and I managed to out-wrestle him? Anyhow, once I've got it, I go to take the bullets out. Mind you, it's been decades since your granddaddy taught me how to handle firearms, so I accidentally shoot myself in the stomach. I go down and nearly lose consciousness but thank the Lord I don't cause this part is hardly believable. I swear on your brothers' it happened, though. We see someone outside trying to break in. Derrick, like a daddy bear, snaps out of his hallucinations, bandages me up, gets the gun and goes to get the prowler. He finds the prowler—some black fella from the area, probably a druggie lookin' for a fix—and shoots at him. He misses and ends up hitting you in the leg. You were on the roof trynna get the prowler too."

Jenny paused there as if to perceive if her daughter bought it all. Rose's acting must have been spot on because Jenny, who appeared pleased, kept on. Unbeknownst to Jenny, Rose was disgusted with how idiotic of a lie her mother had conjured. "Then the cops showed up, tried to concoct a whole story about there never being no prowler and 'domestic violence', whatever that means, all because they had no clues or leads about the black man trying to rob our house and were all embarrassed about it. Trynna frame Derrick. Can you believe that, honey?" She pauses once more for a moment. "I'm just glad you and me are okay. Derrick is worried sick about you, but the police won't let him within a thousand yards of the hospital because they made up that crock of *bullcrap* and want to convince you of it."

Rose looked away, unable to control her emotions. How quickly her own mother was able to abandon her daughter this way, she thought. How everything had devolved to this was beyond Rose. Her mother was not always this cold. It all happened so fast and to think about it brought tears to her eyes. She knew what she had to do.

"You're lying," Rose mumbled, unable to turn and face her mother.

"What?" her mother asked as she took her hand.

"You're lying," Rose mumbled a bit louder, pulling her hand away from her mother.

"Rose, sweetie… Look at me when you're talking," her mother said in a tone that turned marginally more serious. Rose snapped her teary-eyed gaze back to her mother, thinking the cold woman next to her felt like anything but a *mother* to her. Rose let Jenny see the tears as she sat in silence, knowing the woman heard her allegations both times. Rose felt abandoned and there was no turning back. She knew she could not even try to convince her mother.

"I don't know what you mean," Jenny stated coolly. "I just told you what happened like you've been bugging me non-stop to do and now you call me a liar."

Rose just laid in her bed and allowed the tears drop down her face. She was too deadened to wipe them away.

"Are you really gonna believe what the police say over your own mother? Are you kidding me? How foolish could you be to believe the lies they're feeding you."

"I'm making sure Derrick goes to jail," Rose said without skipping a beat. "I'm cooperating with the cops and I am making sure he goes to jail. I don't care if I have to testify against you, but one of us has to be the mature one here, *Mom.*

"He's been beating you for years. I pretend not to hear it for some reason, thinking you could take care of yourself and afraid I'd get beaten too," Rose continued on after taking a moment to compose herself and speak with a force to her mother. The anger and sadness inside her acted as a numbing agent, warding off the physical pain. The emotional trumps the physical in this moment, allowing her to focus on a speech she had thought about a dozen times, sitting alone in her room, frightened near to death as her mother was knocked senseless in the rooms below. "But I can't… I can't let it go on anymore and you shouldn't either. That abuser belongs in jail where he can't hurt you anymore. And I'm going to help Officer Johnson make sure it gets done. You should too."

Rage and confusion covered Jenny's face as she listened to her disobedient daughter. She rose slowly from her wheelchair, lifting with her arms until she's leaned over her daughter's face. Through a half-wired jaw, she sneered, "You ungrateful little shit. If you don't stick to the story I just fuckin' told you, don't bother coming back to the house. You're not welcome."

She collapsed back into her wheelchair; a measure of physical exhaustion and pain washed over her anger. The confusion had vanished and the certainty in her words was not meant to be questioned. She added, "You're turning out just like your shit brothers, you know that?"

"I'm sticking with the truth, *Mom,*" Rose trembled. She hoped the emphasis on the last word would jolt sense into the woman before her. Rose could tell it would not. Something had broken in her mother. She had never seen her like this, and she had certainly never been talked to by her like this.

Without another word, Jenny wheeled herself back to the end of the long room, leaving her daughter to cry into a pillow until she fell into a painful asleep.

CHAPTER 19

Caroline's new SUV was already taking its first road trip, one that would certainly test the "sport utility" of the vehicle in doing so. The trip was impromptu, in the middle of the night, through the backroads of rural South Carolina, to the outskirts of Florence. Bobby was behind the wheel after confirming through a handheld breathalyzer (administered by another member of the local law enforcement community in attendance at the retirement party) that he was well under the legal limit, having had only a handful of light beers hours earlier. He did, however, wreak of cigar smoke which, at any other time, would have incensed Caroline to the point of banishing him from her new ride. The smell her son was omitting brought on a rush of memories of her childhood, making the drive seem longer than it already was; her father was a heavy cigar and pipe smoker.

It had been an hour since Robert made the phone call to Detective Covington. The Detective was clearly inebriated, struggling to pronounce the simplest words and slurring through much of the call from the parking lot of a low-end strip club. Despite his state, he convincingly assured Robert that his news regarding the mother potentially abandoning the child was accurate and that Diamond was heard threatening the girl in a local bar after posting bail. Covington went so far as to offer to go to Florence with him to prove it. Certain the story was well within the realm of possibilities and Detective Covington had not steered him wrong in the past, Robert insisted he enjoy the remainder of his night-turned-early-morning; he needed to do this with his family. He hung up the phone, looked around the room and pondered how he would break the news to Caroline. Tears welled up in his eyes as he started for the back patio of Henry's, where they had shared so many happy memories. A sad one was about to intrude and overtake the happy, though. Little did Robert know that the night would only get worse along the drive.

For the first half of the journey, the Escalade was guided by a police cruiser and flanked by two more, all with lights blaring. Robert was sure Covington had arranged it, half to show his loyalty to the Remington's and half to cover his own ass in case the driver was significantly over the drinking limit from a party *he* had attended. As the SUV pulled onto I-95, the escort peeled off with short bursts of sirens as if to say "you're on your own now", just passed the town of Holly Hill. Robert had made that very turn north onto I-95 dozens of times, possibly over a hundred times throughout his life, and every time he would think about the same thing: Holly Hill and what it had accomplished. The little town of less than fifteen hundred had sent a literal man to the moon, a few men to the Major Leagues and a few more to the NFL. Robert still remembers watching Willie Randolph make his Major League debut for the Pittsburgh Pirates when he was in high school. Despite it being the deep South and Willie being black, Randolph was Robert's favorite Major Leaguer back when Robert himself still played ball. He could've been orange, yellow or purple with red stripes, batted .015 with three hundred strikeouts a year and Robert still would have idolized the man just because he came a small town not far from him in S.C. He was what Robert thought about when people said you could be anything you set your mind to. The man won five World Series rings. Fast forward over three decades and Brett Gardner lifted the World Series trophy for the same team as Randolph, the New York Yankees. Gardner was another Holly Hill native (and a College of Charleston alum) that made it in the Big Apple.

But Robert did not linger on happy thoughts much during this drive. He was mentally and physically exhausted, sitting in the back seat with his wife, consoling her as if she was the reason her sister was abandoning her child, letting her husband threaten her. He let his fingers roll over the brass knife in his pocket. The brass sweat in the humid air, moist in his pocket. He ran his thumb over the "Remington" name inscribed on the handle, thinking of the generations that held it before him. As Bobby stopped off at a 24/7 convenience store for some coffee to keep him focused on the road, Robert let his mind wander to the power of the blade. He had used it before, but he preferred using other, less identifiable weapons. Or, best of all, other people to insulate himself. However, he knew he may end up using it by the end of the long day ahead of him. He had come to grips with the fact that one retirement may be short lived. As his adrenaline pumped, mixing with the alcohol in his system, he became ambivalent. He thought about the things he saw in the Persian Gulf. How easily it had become to kill a man in cold blood and watch the life seep from his eyes. How he wanted to leave the practice of law behind and stay in the Army forever, hunting the scum of the planet. The ultimate power of taking another man's life had fueled Robert's own for quite a bit in Desert Storm, as if he absorbed the lives he took, but he had suppressed it for decades. Despite the time that had passed, the memories refused to fade, and Robert was sure he would be able to take a life today if he saw the opportunity. He would do anything for justice.

Or was it that he would do anything to feel that rush again?

"Here you go, Dad," Bobby said, opening the front door with three, steaming hot coffees. Robert snapped out of his daze and grabbed two of the cups. He sipped his black coffee and stared out at the darkness as the SUV lurched north toward a new chapter in the Remington story.

CHAPTER 20

Thank God it was pay day. Without it, Coral would not have been able to front the cash for a trip to Spartanburg as it would be about six hours round trip. She would need to fill up her Civic at least once and with no company credit card—and only minimal reimbursement after the fact—she would be on the hook until she filed an expense report and her stingy boss approved it. What she would need to leave out of the report was that she was traveling *outside* of the Low Country for a story *without* pre-approval. A big no-no in the world of the *Low Country Ledger.*

Coral had seen the piece about the Clark men the previous evening and she knew she needed to speed up state—as soon as she sobered up. It was just after ten in the morning, and she hadn't had a drink yet. Only black coffee and a bagel from an always-busy little bagel place in a strip mall near her apartment. Her head pounded like a thousand tiny hammers inside her skull, but she was determined to make headway on her Remington piece. It had been a long time coming.

It all began when she was perusing the court dockets in the Low Country and kept seeing Remington's name pop up. Nothing suspicious, he was just the attorney of record on a number of big criminal trials over the years. This fact alone made him interesting, especially given there were limited trials of such magnitude in the area. He had represented murder suspect followed by murder suspect followed by murder suspect with a few drug-dealer-type defendants mixed in. It seemed to Coral that Remington never lost the cases she paid attention to. To check the pattern and see if the man or his cases were worth covering in detail, she decided to start attending all of his trials.

Coral learned off the bat that Remington was a magician with words in a courtroom. His bed-side manner with the jury was like a therapist, reassuring them he would help them see through to the truth. His truth, which also happened to be *the* truth, he would tell the jury in trial after trial. And it worked. Acquittal after acquittal. He was the redneck Johnny Cochran.

Coral became infatuated with Remington's craft. She downloaded and printed piles of his case materials. She would show up at the Clerk of Court's office so frequently that the Clerk assumed she was a paralegal at one of the local firms. Coral never felt the need to correct the Clerk either—just keep the copies and case material coming, without questions, please.

Most of Remington's cases had neutral facts—some good for his client, some not so good. What Coral noticed, and began reporting, was how deftly Remington was at keeping what seemed like the most important facts in each case out of the trial. Trial after trial, the jury's knowledge of the case was limited to only facts preferential to Remington's defense. It was a masterclass every time.

Over the first few months of her Remington consumption, Coral managed to squeak a few mundane articles out about the defense attorney's artfulness in a courtroom before her editor demanded she move along. Fair enough, she had thought at the time. You could only ride one horse for so long in this business, and she moved on professionally while still keeping an eye on Remington's caseload in her free time, hoping something interesting would pop up.

Then, her mundane man started looking less mundane. His work—and the ramifications and aftermath of it—demanded attention. A pattern formed.

Remington had represented a man named Jose Fernandez on a murder charge paired with aggravated assault with a deadly weapon, arson and possession of a stolen firearm. Before jury selection even began, Remington managed to get the assault, arson and stolen firearm charges all tossed on technicalities that Coral did not understand. Something about the chain of evidence seemed to come into play, but in a convoluted way that went over her constantly half-drunk head. Despite the narrowed scope, the solicitor for the state would make snarky remarks about evidence being suppressed and charges dropped, threatening appeal, when the jury was not present. Unsurprisingly, these remarks did not seem to endear the solicitor to the judge.

From what Coral managed to glean from some police contacts and her own digging, Fernandez was a low-level criminal who bounced around the country, living off petty crime. Apparently, Fernandez received a bad tip that a wealthy family—the Ratliffe family, living in a pre-Civil War mansion South of Broad Street—would be out of town. Given this treasure trove of information and luck, Fernandez decided to strike.

One night, in the middle of an especially blistering summer, Fernandez rode his bike from the North Charleston motel where he was staying under the name of Jesus Torres to the mansion on Church Street, a block from the Battery. He arrived just before two on a Tuesday morning. Ironically, the attempted burglar locked his bike to a stop sign two blocks over on Water Street, apparently weary of petty criminals stealing in the area.

He walked casually to the front gate of the mansion, wearing a backwards, Riverdogs hat, dark jeans, a matching jean jacket and construction boots. On his back was a tattered black backpack that contained a carton of cigarettes, a book of matches, a half-eaten bag of Doritos and a gun with extra 9mm rounds cast about the bottom. The bullets jangled with each step, but the professional burglar did not seem to notice. Perhaps it had something to do with his .22 BAC. Or maybe the trace amounts of crack cocaine in his system. Just maybe.

The gun was a Glock 19 he had had for years. It had scratches across the barrel and looked like it had been to war, though it had not to his knowledge. Fernandez bought the Glock off a gun enthusiast outside of El Paso, Texas and it remained his trusty sidepiece since. He was pretty sure it was a ghost gun, but did not ask questions during the transaction, which went down in the back of a smokey, biker bar. Made no difference to him.

Unbeknownst to Fernandez, the clinking of the 9mm rounds sounded exactly like the collar of a neighbors' black lab that Bones, the beloved pet Doberman of the Ratliffes, loved to play with. As Fernandez slipped through a part in the antique brick fence and once-attached wrought iron gate, Bones perked up from his snooze. The guard dog was just under a year old and spewing with puppy energy, so when he was ready to play with his black lab buddy, no one was stopping him. To add to the pent-up excitement, Bones could recognize the crinkling of a Doritos bag a mile away, even if it was tucked deep inside the backpack of a burglar trying to remain soundless. He *loved* any kind of chips.

Fernandez heard that the family was wealthy from Louisiana oil money, despite residing in this Charleston home for generations. Their net worth was estimated to be around one hundred million (Fernandez had googled it about ten times the week of the attempted burglary, according to court records which the jury was not allowed to hear for some reason) and Fernandez, who received the tip from a repairman who was fixing a leaky sink and overheard the family discussing their plan, was told that a minute safe with jewelry, gold coins, cash and other valuables resided in a small floor vault under the kitchen. The safe was rumored to be covered only by a carpet;

Fernandez did not know the code, but was told it was small enough to pick up and carry out if needed. He hoped the safe was as rickety and antique as the home and he could just shoot it open. That's why he brought the gun, which he had never used on a person. It was only for show and the occasional opossum.

Once inside the fence, Fernandez, drenched in sweat, tried to scale the side porch and enter through a second-floor window. That was the plan at least. After losing his footing and grip three times, the burglar gave up and peered through a window on the porch next to the front door. Seeing no sign of life, he took a moment to light a cigarette and take a deep drag. He was out of breath from the failed-climb attempt. Surely the tobacco and nicotine would help his lungs.

The repairman clocked no alarm system or cameras in his detailed review. He said the old homes downtown had to go through rigorous review and approval before anything could be changed so no security system for a rich person's home in this area was not too good to be true, it was common. Instead, the pompous S.O.B.s would rely on old fashion security: they would shoot anyone who dared step foot in their home without an invite. Especially if you had dark skin, the repairman warned. Just like Fernandez.

Chuckling at the thought of a rich, geriatric redneck pulling a 12 gauge on his brown ass, Fernandez flicked away some ash onto the porch and jiggled the door handle. Locked. Fair enough. Looks like it would not be *that* easy. He stepped back and admired the small stained-glass paneling wedged on either side of the front door. To even an untrained eye, the glass looked to date back to at least the 1800s. To Fernandez, his three-year-old son could've painted them. He saw nothing special and proceeded to rear back and kick one of the windows in with his dirty boot. After clearing shards of glass with his jacket, drunkenly avoiding cuts, he reached inside and unlocked the door.

Crop-dusting more ashes just outside the door onto the porch—he had *some* respect—Fernandez continued through the narrow entryway toward what must have been the kitchen, per his rough blueprint, cigarette hanging from his lips. There was a closed baby gate affixed to the kitchen's entryway. This meant nothing to the burglar at the time, but would in retrospect. He lifted up the latch and stepped in. Before his boot touched the kitchen's historic tile floor, a burst of light overwhelmed his eyes and a pain shot through his arm.

"Holy shit!" He yelped as he fell hard backwards to the ground.

What looked like a black missile had jumped and latched onto his right arm, piercing the jean jacket's rough exterior. As Fernandez's eyes adjusted to the light, he saw a Doberman pull back from his arm and attach itself to his backpack. The man held on for dear life as the Doberman yanked and pulled and humped in reverse to pry the backpack free. The straps began ripping as did the zipper. Fernandez managed to pull the gun out just before the beast scrambled backwards with the contents of his backpack. Fernandez watch as the dog rifled through his Doritos bag in the corner of the kitchen. Above the sharp-fanged killer was a portly black woman in a robe. She had thrown the lights on and was stunned with fear at the sight of the man. Without thinking, Fernandez fired the Glock three times in quick succession, instantly dropping the woman. He clicked to keep firing, but there were no more bullets; they were scattered about the floor of the kitchen. Without stopping to find the treasure and entire purpose of his entry, Fernandez sprinted back out the front door. Barreling toward his chained bike, he encountered a worried and nosy neighbor on the sidewalk. Without giving the robed man a chance to do or say anything Fernandez whacked him with the butt of the Glock and carried on, deciding to leave his bike.

The genius burglar—and now alleged murderer—was picked up by Charleston PD within ten minutes as he carried up East Bay Street. They informed the perp that the woman he shot was dead, the Doberman had run away and his cigarette butts had burned the porches clear off the historical home. He was going to jail.

These facts—all confirmed by each source she spoke to—and Remington still got Fernandez to trial with just the singular murder charge. But Coral's interest in the case sparked up a few weeks *after* the man's acquittal.

CHAPTER 21

Coral occasionally scanned the obituaries in and around Charleston for any newsworthy deaths. She was looking for local celebrities, local politicians, or even noteworthy criminals she had come across in her work. Anything out of the ordinary. Or in the ordinary, worth a piece.

Two weeks after Remington managed to help Jose Fernandez walk on all charges—nothing short of a miracle Coral thought—she saw it in the *Low Country Ledger*'s obituaries: "*Jose Fernandez, 38, died from a hit-and-run in Mount Pleasant on Friday night. Fernandez was on a bike when a vehicle was seen driving erratically, striking the now-deceased. Fernandez was announced dead at the scene. The driver is still at large, but said to be driving a Jeep or small pick-up truck.*"

A short blurb with no further commentary. No plea for tips. Coral also found it interesting that no mention was made of Fernandez's arrest or trial in any of the local obituaries that ran the hit-and-run. Usually there would be at least a note or reference. Upon further digging, she was able to find out that the local police had made a "request" to the higher ups at her paper, advising them to avoid mentioning Fernandez's "run ins with the law", given he was found "innocent by a jury of his peers". They went on to note that the authorities were merely looking out for the paper, trying to help them avoid libel and slander allegations, for which her editor was apparently very pleased. This did not sound right to Coral. Why would the police care?

She dug further.

Apparently, her contacts at other local news outlets and publications were told the same thing and all blindly listened. There was no use in disobeying the police who were merely trying to help the publications. Right?

Coral dug even further.

The officer that made the request to each of the publications and outlets she spoke to was Detective Joseph Covington. He was a burly African American cop for Charleston County. The political type, from what Coral heard, and she recognized him from her work around the courthouses. The self-serving detective ensured he was pictured, quoted and all over arrests that could make positive headlines. She had also heard that Covington had been known to let a politician or two slide anytime he pulled them over. People owed him. Important people. He owed people. Also important people. He was a *quid pro quo* cop, which was not unusual in the grand scheme of things; he wanted to do his time, earn his pension, get out with the right contacts and land a cushy job afterward.

Oh, and Coral happened to find out that Detective Covington was coincidentally good pals and golfing buddies with one Robert Remington.

While excavating all she could on the Fernandez hit-and-run, Coral hit dead end after dead end. Despite her suspicions and Detective Covington's unnatural involvement, Coral moved on and did not write a story about the connection—at the behest of her editor. The grouchy old editor insisted the story was a nonstarter and would only irritate any contacts she had with the police. Fair enough, Coral thought at the time.

A few months went by and it happened again. Not a mysterious death (yet), but an unwinnable case being won. In this case, Remington managed to convince a jury in Summerville to dismiss all charges, including a charge of murder related to a hate crime for his twenty-two-year-old, white supremacist client. From what Coral saw of the trial and reporting, this should have been a slam dunk for the state, but, instead, Remington prevailed. Then so did *real* justice, so it seemed, just two months later. Another coincidence? Coral was not convinced.

This time, Coral was prepared. She watched for headlines or obituaries involving the man. She followed him to and from his job at a dive bar on Folly Beach on occasion. Nothing happened for weeks. Then weeks turned to months and Coral gave up. She was coming to the conclusion that the Fernandez hit-and-run and Covington's outreach was all her writer's brain trying to produce a story out of nothing. She moved on to other trials, other stories and tailing other titillating leads.

Then, a week after she moved on, she read it. "*Local bartender shot dead on Folly Beach. John Stephenson was gunned down walking out of the Devil's Punchbowl, a Folly Beach bar known for cheap booze and an eclectic crowd. Stephenson, 22, was known to be affiliated with a South Carolina sect of the Ku Klux Klan. The execution style murder is thought to be associated with such affiliations, with authorities saying the leading suspects are members of a predominately black biker gang called the Vipers.*"

No mention of the trial and at least two contacts noted being phoned by Covington to keep a lid on the story. "Just another gangbanger death. Nothing to write," was what Covington told each. This was all the fuel Coral needed. She was going to put all her eggs into the Remington basket. There was something fishy about him.

Remington's next two clients, however, were easy cases, especially for Remington. There were little to no facts to assist the prosecution outside of hearsay and circumstantial evidence and even Coral was convinced before the trials that each were clearly innocent. A jury quickly found the same and, against the hopes of the journalist, both were alive and well six months after their respective trials.

This did not stop Coral though. She looked back at Remington's previous clients. Three others had died within two years of their trials: two overdoses and one random stabbing. She dug into those trials and found that Remington got them off, but from what Coral could scrape together, all seemed guilty as Judas. She studied the clients that survived, even tried to interview some but generally found them unpleasant to be around and wildly uncooperative. Each, though, seemed innocent. There was a pattern forming: clients who appeared guilty died and client that's appeared innocent lived. All got off because of Remington, though. This pattern was enough for Coral to decide to run a full court press on Remington. She pulled all of his cases since he passed the Bar Exam decades earlier, scoured over thousands of pages of court records, interviewed the uncooperative (yet, importantly, living) clients, witnesses, solicitors and the like. She had them all sign NDAs. She was nervous. She did not know what the man was capable of, but she would get him. She would file the biggest story of her career on Remington; a full exposé of the myriad of coincidences he was involved in. It would only be facts; the reader could do the rest. This would change her career—and life—trajectory. She would end up in a big city working for a big paper.

Coral daydreamed about it all as she traveled toward Spartanburg, swigging from a bottle of Jack Daniels she picked up outside Columbia.

CHAPTER 22

Rose laid in her hospital bed and stared at the ceiling without emotion. It had been about five hours since her mother berated her and she felt as though she had no tears left to cry. Everything had seemed to hit her all at once: her numerous pain medications were wearing off, she felt overtired despite having done nothing but sleep and rest, and now, she experienced a new sensation she had never felt before: abandonment. To make matters worse, her pillow was cold and wet from all the tears that pooled and refused to dry beneath her.

She thought back to the various instances in her childhood when her mother would disappear for days at a time only to reappear with needle marks on her arms, bruises on her face and a hollow, defeated look in her eyes. At the time she had no idea; just a simple, innocent girl, but as she grew up, Rose came to comprehend that her mother was disappearing to use drugs and sleep around, the drug use visible, while the sleeping around was learned during shouting matches between Derrick and Jenny. But even back then, mind clouded by drugs and promiscuity, she would always return and Rose never truly felt *alone* alone. Derrick or some other boyfriend or girlfriend at the time would look after her, doing the bare minimum—like leaving only slightly expired cereal and milk in the house. Her mother would eventually return full of remorse and sorrow for leaving her baby, attempting to convince herself and her little girl it would never happen again.

Rose's current situation felt unlike her mother's previous missteps, though Rose could not rationalize why or how. It was if she knew it was the end of a chapter. Or more like the end of her favorite book, a book in a series that would have no more sequels.

As she rested, stared and pondered, Rose knew it was the drugs that made her mother do the things she did back then. Now, her mother had no such excuse. She was sober and was not taking anything stronger than ibuprofen at the hospital, yet with a clear-headed, confident look in her eyes was able to curse at her baby girl, threaten her and cast her away like an old newspaper.

Was Rose actually in the wrong? She did not think so. But maybe? She thought back to dilemmas in the hundreds of books she read over the years. She had no other sounding board to play with, no one else to talk to, so books were and always had been her guide. Fictional characters in the young adult genre. Only her own contemplations and her books. Most of the time, she had read it was advantageous to be on the side of the police. They held the power and were right and just. But sometimes, the police were corrupt and had an underlying agenda. Could that be the case here? Of course not. *Stop thinking that way*—Derrick mercilessly beat my mother and shot us both, she thought. Maybe she just needed to talk to her mother again. She decided to try later that evening after the nurses brought them dinner.

"Hey there, Rose. How're those books treating you? What'd ya start with?"

Rose snapped out of her meditative trance, startled to hear someone talking to her. The nearest occupied bed was about ten feet to her right and the other, the same distance in the other direction, had become empty earlier that day. Sitting on the empty bed to her left, atop clean sheets was Nurse Blanchard. She had swapped her scrubs for white-washed jeans and a Virginia Tech Hokies t-shirt. Her hair was curled, she had light makeup on and she looked like she was headed out for a casual date. Her presence injected a bit of joy in Rose. Maybe she was not *completely* alone.

"Hey, Nurse. It's good. I started with the detective series one. I'm about halfway through and don't know where it's going. Love those types—the unpredictability keeps you wanting more," Rose said eagerly, happy to have someone to talk to. "Why're you here? I thought you were off until tomorrow?"

"That's good! I like those kind too. From our talks, I figured you'd like the detective ones," Nurse Blanchard offered, talking as if the girls were two friends in a high school cafeteria before switching gears. "I am off! But figured I'd stop in to see how my favorite patient was managing. I was passing by anyway. How are you feeling?"

"I'm just physically and emotionally exhausted," Rose sighed. She considered going into detail concerning the talk with her mother, then thought better of it. Her mother would come around; no use in bothering Nurse Blanchard with her unnecessary, petty issues. "Hey, seeing as how there's a bed open here now, can you move my mom there? I'd like to be close to her."

A subtle, but visible change in Blanchard's expression waved across her face. Though veiled, Rose had a feeling bad news was bubbling under the surface. The nurse must have had an ulterior motive for her arrival.

"If you can't that's fine, too! Just figured if you could. Or if you could have someone on the clock or whatever do it instead. No pressure. I don't want to screw up protocol or whatever," Rose blurted out hastily, face reddened. She did not want to burden her newfound friend; the nurse was all she had at the moment. To kill the tension, Rose craned her neck in search of her mother on the far side of the room.

Nurse Blanchard took a deep breath and stood up from her spot on the bed next to Rose's. She slowly approached Rose and sat on the edge of Rose's bed, facing her patient. She found Rose's hand and held it in her own. Rose noticed hers was soft, as if she had just used a creamy lotion or moisturizer. She also noticed the nurse's smell, which was a subtle yet hauntingly fruity perfume; it reminded Rose of an apple orchard she had visited with her mother as a child.

"I have something to tell you," Nurse Blanchard said through troubled eyes, begging forgiveness for what she was about to say.

Rose's heart sank with the next sentence. "Your mother checked out about two hours ago against her doctor's wishes. Said she needed to get back to Derrick. I'm sorry, Rose."

Rose had no words. She felt discarded after their last conversation, but assumed her mother would come around. Her mother surely could not have meant it when she said she was not welcome home. Rose's mind raced through a thousand possibilities before she broke down in tears once more, leaving Nurse Blanchard with nothing to do but attempt to console the young girl. Rose did not bother asking any other questions. She knew the price she was paying for cooperating with the police. If her mother would not help herself, Rose would at least try on her behalf. Her mind was made up.

***

Nurse Blanchard had spent another half hour or so sitting on the end of Rose's bed, half consoling her and half trying to get the girl's mind off the subject of her mother entirely. They discussed books, writing, different authors, movies, aspirations and dreams. Rose was thankful for the nurse's company despite the fact her mind was elsewhere. Without her mother, she had no family at all. Rose never knew her father and had the feeling Jenny did not really either. She knew Jenny had at least one sister, but did not remember meeting her or her family; she was fairly certain they had cut Jenny off due to drug use based on a shouting match with Derrick she had overheard a year back. Maybe Rose could reach out to Jenny's family, but that was unlikely. She would have to figure out a way to survive on her own when she got out, she resolved. Maybe she could live with Blanchard for a bit. Get a job. Go back to school. Grow up entirely too quickly.

After Nurse Blanchard left, admitting she did have a date with a resident at the hospital, Rose returned to her book. Nurse Blanchard and the young resident were seeing a movie as their first date, which Nurse Blanchard was not thrilled about since there was no opportunity to talk. She was excited and nervous nonetheless. Though Nurse Blanchard did not want to appear as though she was bragging about her "normal" life, it took Rose's mind off her own situation for a bit, so the nurse obliged, gossiping and chatting like a schoolgirl. Rose hoped she could one day find a doctor to take her to the movies. She spent the next chapter of her book daydreaming about that possibility.

As the sun went down, so did the light in their wing of the hospital. Each bed had a reading light above it, but it hurt too much for Rose to reach up and turn it on. She could only read so much when her mind was elsewhere, anyway. When the sun settled below the horizon and the only illumination in the wing came from various machines monitoring her fellow patients, Rose dog-eared her spot and set the book down on her night table. She lowered her bed almost flat and tried to count sheep, hoping the sandman would come and take her. Perhaps for good, she thought. Shaking off the intrusive feelings, she struggled to remain positive.

A nurse ventured in shortly after she reached thirty-seven on her mental sheep counter, handing her a pile of pills and a cup of water. Rose could not keep up with her daily pill regiment and had not realized she needed more pain meds, though was appreciative for the numbing agents. Slugging them down, she was grateful, too, for the drowsiness they caused. By the time she had drowned the second handful with a gulp of water and got back to sheep number twelve, Rose was out.

***

Around midnight, Rose felt a sharp pain in her thigh that jolted her awake. Her bed was covered in sweat, or possibly urine. She was breathing heavily through her nose, yet suffered as if she was drowning. She strained and struggled to yell for a nurse, but nothing came out. She recognized her eyes were open and took a moment before she realized she had been blindfolded. Her own hospital gown was stuffed in her mouth, exposing her bare, sweaty breasts to the cold hospital air. The pain in her thigh grew more intense as something pressed harder against it. Possibly a hand or a shoe, Rose could not be sure.

"You keep your mouth fucking shut, you dumb little *cunt*," a voice snarled about three inches from her ear, the hot breath seeping through her gown. "Or else I'll fucking *kill* you."

Rose thought she recognized the voice, but was too focused on the pain in her leg to place it. The driving force into her wounded thigh only intensified until she understood that at least some of the liquid in her bed was her own blood. She heard the monitors above her increase in cadence as the odor of alcohol stung her nostrils. The throbbing only intensified further until she succumbed to the agony and lost consciousness.

CHAPTER 23

The Escalade slowed to a crawl down a one lane, gravel road. Small drainage creeks lined each uneven side of the street as Bobby peered into the night ahead. Only the headlights, which had been set to high beam for the last half hour of backroads, and a faint moonlight lit the path. A light misting of rain had started to fall, leaving Bobby extra cautious in the new terrain. A female's British accent broke an hour-long silence by saying "You've arrived", but there was no structure to be seen.

Robert had been to the house a few times—without Caroline or Jenny's knowledge—and feigned ignorance in the backseat. He lightly shook his wife's hand to alert her of the need for direction; he needed to play the part of lost. Caroline had laid on Robert's shoulder for much of the trip, eyes wide and staring blankly out at the gloomy abyss. She was lost in thoughts and feelings ranging from anger to guilt and back.

"Stay on this road and it'll be the first mailbox on the left. About a hundred yards further," Caroline stated without moving from Robert's shoulder, eyes glazed and puffy.

Flashing lights became visible through the trees ahead and the rain picked up, pelting the car. Bobby eased into the short, mud-packed driveway next to two police cruisers and an ambulance. All three had their lights on, but mercifully left the sirens muted. The house in front of them looked as if it could have been a handsome home fifty-plus years ago. It had the bones of a large porch, a few handcrafted shutters hanging by windows and a peaked roof with missing shingles. The structure had clearly fallen into disrepair due to years of owner neglect. Robert thought this an ironic metaphor for Caroline's once comely sister, who had turned sour-looking, in his humble opinion, as if the beautiful Shelby genes had been drugged out of her.

A police officer in an oversized "F.P.D." poncho greeted the Remington's as Bobby shifted into park. Before allowing the passengers to disembark, the officer held up a dripping wet hand and approached the driver's window.

"I assume you're the family?" the officer, a female in her mid-thirties asked through Bobby's half-opened window. The officer, noticing the rain sneaking through the window, opened up an umbrella she held by her side. Bobby nodded as he opened the window fully. The officer started, "I gots to warn y'all, I don't think none of y'all wanna go in der."

The officer peered into the backseat to take inventory of her audience. At the sight of Caroline, the officer whispered to Bobby in her thick southern drawl, "I'd keep her in da car, son."

As if triggered by the murmur, Caroline climbed out of the driver's side, rear door into the pouring rain. Robert stumbled after her, barely shimmying from one bucket seat to the other. He stepped out of the car directly into a puddle up to his shin, soaking his pant leg and favorite pair of suede loafers. Caroline, who had managed to avoid the puddle, was halfway up the porch steps by the time a lean male officer with a skinny waist and gangly arms held one up as a barrier.

"Ma'am, this is an active crime sce— ", he began. He did not have time to finish his protest before Caroline shoved him aside and stormed through the open front door. She took two steps in before freezing in horror. Robert hurried after his wife, shooting the officer an apologetic look.

"Without crime scene tape, I'm afraid she's within her rights, sir," Robert lied. What he said was not entirely true, but if his wife felt strongly enough to assault an officer for something, he was going to support her any way her could.

"Ahhh, yes. The defense attorney brother-in-law," the male officer glared at Robert, noticing his soaked foot. It was a look of familiarity.

"I'll stay out here, don't worry," Robert stated, acknowledging his foot and taking the words out of the officer's mouth, ignoring the gaze. He whirled around to make sure Bobby was on his way to console his mother. Like a respectable son, he buzzed past Robert and threw an arm around his mother in the living room. Caroline did not make a sound and instead stood in a state of shock. At the sight of her brutalized sister, Robert could not blame her. He had received the text from Covington on their drive. The news had gotten worse and their destination changed from the hospital to the crime scene. He had broken the inevitable to his wife softly, but knew the scene would ruin her. He tried to convince her to go and check in to a hotel, but she refused.

The blood began just inside the doorframe and tracked to the limp, mangled body of Jenny Shelby-Diamond. Her face was barely recognizable, having been caved in above the left ear. Blood poured from her mouth onto the dirty carpet below into a puddle the size of a balloon. A larger puddle sat beneath her midsection, where it appeared she had been shot numerous times. It was a grizzly scene even for someone like Robert, who had seen tableaus like this too many times to count.

"We believe da cause of deth was loss o' blood." The female officer had snuck up beside Robert and followed his eye to the cadaver just inside. She removed her hat in a sign of respect for the fallen woman.

The skinny male officer joined them and continued where the female left off. Robert thought this pelican-beaked officer looked familiar too. "It looks like she walked up the steps and into the house, which, from her medical file was a small miracle seeing as how she was shot just a few days ago and was still stitched up pretty good from that. Upon entry, there was some kind of argument and he took this," the officer held up a large, plastic bag containing the sawed-off barrel of a Rawlings baseball bat, soaked in blood, "and knocked her to the ground. In her state, she wouldn't have been able to put up much of a fight. Yet, somehow, she did. I'll let the E.M.T. explain."

"The splatters on the couch and coffee table," an obese E.M.T. with a nametag that merely read "Tommy" walked onto the porch from inside, pointing with a gloved finger, "they weren't her blood. It looks like she grabbed a beer bottle off the coffee table and cut the man's leg with it. He stumbled back over the coffee table before lunging and hitting her several more times with the bat. Then he pulled out his pistol and shot her."

"Fo'teen times. Sonuva bitch," the female officer scowled.

The name of the perpetrator went without saying. Robert knew at least one or two of the first responders had to have known Derrick, probably helped bail him out of jail and showed up out of guilt tonight. Two police cruisers were not necessary for a rural D.O.A. like this. Just as that thought crossed his mind, he turned to see the second police cruiser peel out of the muddy driveway. Undoubtedly Derrick's inside cops, hiding and hightailing it away once the family arrived. They were complicit, as far as Robert was concerned. Might as well have shot the poor woman themselves. *Cowards.* He made a mental note to get their names for later.

Robert turned back to look with pity at his wife. She had fallen to her knees next to her dead sister, still unable to shed a tear. A piece of her always knew this day would come; she had spoken to Robert about it numerous times. A call telling Caroline her little sister was dead. She had always assumed it would be an overdose or drunk driving death. But she forever knew what laid before her now was a possibility as well. Caroline had done all she could to help her sister. She had brought her to rehab facilities all over the South, spoken to shrinks, the police, her friends. In the end, nothing worked and Jenny only caused her heartbreak. Caroline had all but let go of any hope she had left for Jenny when her preacher gave a sermon on forgiveness. A devout Southern Baptist, Caroline took the message to heart. Jesus had forgiven, so why couldn't she? Caroline decided to give her sister one last shot and had begun sending her money again and calling her regularly, all without asking Robert. Robert knew, though, and Caroline figured he would find out. He did not say a word, though, because he was a good husband, a family man who would turn the other cheek if need be. He had gone through a similar scenario with his own father, but Robert never stooped so low as to mention it. All he could think about now, as he fingered the knife in his pocket, was revenge.

And he did not want it to occur in a courtroom.

CHAPTER 24

"Do you have any idea where he went?" Robert whispered to the officers. He turned away from them and looked at the driveway for the old truck he knew Derrick drove. It was not anywhere in sight. "Did he shoot and run immediately? Pack a bag? Is there an A.P.B. out on him, his vehicle?"

The lanky officer, who Robert noticed was "Deputy David Larkin" from his badge, shook his head. "Sir, we're not yet sure. Our working assumption is this was the husband, a Mr. Derrick Diamond. The E.M.T.s here place the time of death sometime yesterday afternoon or early evening, but it's hard to pinpoint it. We came up here on our regular patrol route after some folks at the hospital said a domestic violence victim checked herself out—against medical advice—and said she was headed home. When we pulled in, we noticed the front door was slightly ajar. This is an open investigation, so we can't definitively state that it was Mr. Dia—"

"Let's get one thing straight, Officer," Robert cut the man off, his tone getting harsher as his whisper turned into a growl. "We know for a *fact* it was that mutt. He's been knocking her around for years and your pals have done *nothing* but cover for his ass. I've read the reports and talked my friends in law enforcement. The reports were nothing more than a toned-down version of the *facts*. And I don't recognize you, but I sure as hell would've recognized your pals based on how quickly they high-tailed it out of here. So, if you could do me and this poor woman lying dead in there a fucking *courtesy* and call out an All-Points Bulletin for whatever dumpster-fire, shitbag on wheels he drives, that would be great. I've done enough of these cases to know that police incompetence, ignorance and—dare I say—corruption in the first hours after a murder lead to a mutt like him free on the streets. As it is, we're already hours behind based on time of death. We're just lucky we were on the way up here already when we got the news. Not from you or local PD, might I add."

As Robert spoke, he inched closer to the officer. The officer had about two inches in height on Robert, but Robert's commanding presence dominated the adversary, who was at least fifty pounds lighter than the newly minted retiree.

"Listen, *sir*," the officer chirped back, standing his ground. "I don't like your accusatory tone regarding officers in *my* county. I'm not sure how things are done where you're from, but 'round here our boys demand *respect*. And we get *respect* because we abide by the laws."

Robert felt as if he was back in a courtroom, mere days after retirement. His blood began to boil. He knew how to end the argument then and there.

"You just let me know if I need to get SLED and Chief Mosby involved in this, boy. He's a dear friend of mine and I'll be damned if I sit and let Derrick's pals like you fuck this one up," Robert calmly smirked as he poked the red-faced deputy in the chest. Robert's temper was getting the better of him, but unlike his younger days, he was now capable of being both political and calculated in his responses.

Before another word could be uttered, the petite female officer who sounded like she was from *Swamp People* stepped in between the enraged men. "Listen, I knows dis her' is an 'motional sitiation, but let's just shake our dicks 'n move on her'. 'Sides, we got da girl to worry 'bout."

Robert had forgotten all about his niece. If Derrick did this to his wife, who knows what he would do to the poor girl.

"How far is the hospital?" Robert asked as he took a step back from the officer.

"About half an hour," Deputy Larkin spat out. The rain drops on the tin roof of the patio grew in volume as the Robert peered in at his wife, wondering what he should do.

"Did you send officers there? Or is there some sort of security guard at least?" Robert tried not to panic, asking in a hushed tone so his wife would not hear. "That's the initial reason we came here, you know. Threats against her. Then we heard about all of this."

"Sir, Margie and I here are the only ones on patrol this time of night. Not sure why those other two officers showed up, 'cause they were off duty…." Deputy Larkin paused, as if putting the pieces together in his head, now understanding what Robert was huffing and puffing about. "Anyhow, the hospital got twenty-four-seven, round the clock security. That little girl's fine."

"And how qualified is that security? And how many in number?" Robert retorted. He knew hospital security jobs were coveted by retirees. Usually, out of shape seventy-year-olds looking to watch television, read about World War II, get away from the wife. and collect a paycheck in retirement.

"Well, Bert's usually by hisself. He's prolly mid-sisties?" Officer Margie cautiously posited, confirming Robert's suspicions. He just envisioned an overweight, wrinkly and slovenly man slumped over in a chair, asleep at a monitor in an ill-fitting uniform. He glanced at his watch. Nearly 5 A.M. He glanced back at his wife who had not moved. Bobby noticed his father and shot an inquisitive look.

Rose. The daughter. We've got to get to the hospital, Robert mouthed to his eldest boy, pointing to the car. Bobby nodded in understanding and turned back to his mother. Before he could say anything, Deputy Larkin's radio went sprung to life.

"All units to MUSC. All units please report," a static-laced voice gargled across the radio. Robert shot the officers a worrisome look which they returned. Deputy Larkin slowly picked up the radio, lowering the volume by the turn of a rusted knob.

"10-4. Marg and Larkin on the way. Over," Deputy Larkin shot into the ancient-looking radio. He turned to Tommy and the other E.M.T.s, who had stopped what they were doing to allow Caroline to mourn. What could they do at this point? Jenny had been dead hours by the time they got there. "Tommy, you and your guys got this? We've gotta get out of here. Make sure you got the pictures and remove carefully."

Tommy nodded without a word.

Robert was not sure if Caroline or Bobby heard the radio. Even if they did, he doubted the words would register for either of them. Robert realized he needed to treat his wife like a delicate victim, a key witness in a big trial right now. She needed to be coddled in her current state of mourning. It was clear the woman was overridden by shock.

"Sweetie," Robert said gently through the doorframe. "There's nothing we can do right now so we better go check in on Rose. Does that sound good?"

Caroline staggered to her feet with the help of Bobby, guiding his mother from the elbow. She had gotten blood on her knees, which Bobby quickly tried to wipe off with his sleeve.

"Leave it, Bobby. It's fine, honey," Caroline said, pushing his arm away. "Is Rose there?" She asked, turning her blank gaze to her husband. He nodded. "Well, we better hurry on over there. No sense in letting two Shelby's die tonight. That girl needs family."

Robert nodded and hurried his wife through the door, down the front porch and into the car. Bobby followed and started up the engine.

"Follow us," Deputy Larkin told Bobby before hopping into the cruiser and blasting the sirens.

As Bobby followed the wining cop car, Caroline continued staring vacantly at the front door where her baby sister laid dead.

CHAPTER 25

Ten minutes into the rain-soaked drive from Derrick's property to the hospital, Caroline broke. A flood of emotions washed over her and she buried her exhausted expression into Robert's wet jacket as the gravity of what she just witnessed seemed to have smacked her across the face. Robert had grabbed a Gamecocks blanket stowed in the third row and wrapped his wife tight in it to keep her warm from the chilling rain. Now, he was letting her wail away into his chest in it. Robert rubbed her shoulders and held her firm, knowing that nothing would right the wrong she had just encountered. Robert had seen shrieks of emotional pain like this occasionally in the courtroom, though what the wails of his wife truly brought him back to was his time in the Army. The first time men and women lost their brother-in-arms, the same reaction would wash over him or her eventually. Or when a suicide bomber took out a mother's child. Same shrieks, similar tears. Pain was a universal language known to all. It knows no race, creed, religion. It'll catch each and every one of us eventually.

Right now, that victim—the second victim—in all of this was Caroline. That was her baby sister lying dead on her own living room floor. Caroline loved her despite all of her flaws. She had avoided talking about her little sister due to all the pain she caused her over the years and the result was that Bobby, Liam and Ben hardly knew the woman existed, save for some childhood pictures planted around Sully's and plenty more hung at the Shelby Charleston home. But when she did talk about Jenny to Robert, it was happy memories. Memories of her and her sister as children, playing in the waves of Folly Beach or sharing a snow cone in Disney World. There was nothing Robert could do other than to be there for his wife. And let her mourn.

For his own appeasement, Robert needed revenge. He fingered the knife in his pocket again, contemplating.

Bobby pulled the car under an overhang that read "Emergency Department" at a quarter to six in the morning. Bobby shifted into park and turned to face his sobbing mother and steadfast father. Robert had been awake for over twenty-four hours and had not started to feel it thanks to the adrenaline that coursed through his veins.

"Bobby, why don't you park the car and stay with your mother. Maybe go grab some food or coffee if she wants it. I'll head inside with the officers," Robert said before turning to his wife. "That sound okay, honey?"

Caroline nodded; eyes closed tight.

After giving his wife a kiss on the head, Robert hopped out of the car and followed the officers through the automatic doors to an over-caffeinated, elderly receptionist who pointed them down the hall.

"Not often we have gunshots here, ya know," Deputy Larkin shot over his shoulder to no one in particular. "Every now and then a hunting accident, but nothing like how those two Shelby women got shot. Domestic disturbances? Sure. But not with guns. Ain't right."

Robert tried to ignore the Deputy as he let his eyes dart from room to room for a name. *Rose Shelby. Rose Shelby. Rose Shelby*, Robert thought on a loop, hoping he would not forget the poor girl's name. He also silently prayed that the girl had not had the Diamond name thrust upon her and was merely "Rose Shelby". She was never spoken of in their household and Lord knows Jenny did not send out Christmas cards, so Robert did not know the girl at all, barely her name. They had only met a handful of times over the years, each of which when the girl was young. He was sure she would not recognize him. From what Robert remembered, he was pretty sure Jenny's other kids turned out fine and even cut ties from the waffling drug fiend. Robert would soon find out for himself whether Rose had turned out like so many screwed up children of addicts he had seen in courtrooms around the state, or if she was a miracle. Then, some decisions would need to be made. He had already done a great service for Rose once in her unknowing life, he may need to do a second.

"There she is," Robert pointed at a sign at the end of the hall. He was silently proud he remembered the girl's name correctly. He was even prouder there was no "Diamond" to be found in it.

Robert turned the metal handle slowly to a dimly lit, single occupancy room. Monitors *beeped*, *buzzed* and provided most of the light in the room. The remaining light came from a single bulb in the far corner, next to a heavy-set man in a rickety rocking chair. The man, who Robert presumed was the security guard from his wrinkled short-sleeved button down, various pins and utility belt, was swaying slowly and reading a well-worn paperback folded in half between sausage fingers. Upon seeing the three new arrivals, the security guard placed a crisp dollar bill into the book and stood up with a resolute, guilty smile.

"Larkin, Margie," he nodded, shaking each officer's hand with both of his own. He turned to Robert and extended his hand, repeating the process, as if Robert and the guard were old drinking buddies. "Officer Bert. Head of night security here. I'm sorry for what happened to your little girl, sir."

Robert had half a mind to scold the man, though he knew it would do no good after the fact. The second Jenny and Rose were brought to the hospital, extra security should have been placed on them in order to ensure the domestic abuser did not try to finish the act, he would say. This attack was predictable, Robert would admonish. He knew to stay calm, composed and out of lawyer-mode, so he bit his tongue.

"Not my daughter. My niece," Robert said after shaking the man's chubby hand. Robert looked the incompetent retiree in the eyes as he shook firmly, letting his gaze do the talking. Bert got the picture, shrinking.

"Err—well," Bert stumbled, clearly frazzled from the heat Robert was giving him. "Firm handshake, sir. You a military man?"

"Yes, I was in a past life. Long ago. In the Gulf," Robert stated. Bert turned into a fidgeting, nervous mess from the handshake. The question's intention was surely to flatter Robert and change the subject from the girl lying close to death, Robert surmised. "Can you tell us what happened to my niece?"

"Well… from what… from what we gathered," Bert was turning into a stuttering wreck under simple questions he must have known were coming.

"Calm down, officer," Robert went into "good cop" mode. "I know you're understaffed here. This isn't your fault and I didn't mean to insinuate as such. My heart is just grieving with the condition of my niece. No one's fault but Derrick Diamond's."

Some head of security, Robert thought.

"O' course. O' course." Bert composed himself before attempting to find common ground with Robert. "I was in Korea myself, you know? Anyway, well, I was doing my rounds early this morning and noticed some broken glass and a tray table knocked over outside the big patient wing." Bert pointed down the hall to a bank of sliding glass doors where Robert and the officers had just come from. "I carefully avoided the glass which I later discovered was a bottle of whiskey and checked on the patients in the room. I heard the usual cadence of beeps, except one patient had a windfall of alarms going off.

I raced down to one of the last beds in the wing where two nurses were working on your niece."

Bert paused, took a sip from his water bottle and glanced at Rose. He dabbed his brow with a handkerchief before continuing.

"I rushed over and asked the girls what happened. One of them said they saw a man stumbling out of the room when they got an alert in the nursing lounge that the patient's vitals were going ballistic. They didn't have time to call me because they left their radios in the lounge, but it appeared that the man had applied pressure to the wounds, blindfolded and gagged the girl. She was losing a lot of blood. A doctor on call ran in and they ended up putting her in a medically-induced coma. Her body had lost too much blood, was going into shock and needed to be stabilized. That was all a couple hours ago. Then they moved her to this room and I've been watching her since. Still in the coma and all. Don't know what'll happen next or when they'll take her out of it."

Bert offered Robert the seat he had just left upon finishing the explanation. Robert waved him off and approached the girl. Robert was not all that familiar with medicine beyond the baseline level needed for many of his cases; anything beyond that, he hired an expert that was usually a retired (expensive) doctor of some kind. From what he saw, Rose's heartrate and blood pressure were stable and somewhat normal, though she had sweat and bled through her nightgown onto the sheets. Robert pointed this out to Bert, who hurried to fetch a nurse to clean her up. As he pieced together the timeline, he mutely grasped that Bert had waited to call the officers.

"Sounds like it was the stepfather," Deputy Larkin broke the silence.

Well, no shit, Robert thought. "Seems like it. I'd like to talk to the nurse or her doctor on the situation. I'd like to get her out of here."

"What do you mean, sir? I doubt she's in any condition to be moved. 'Sides, she's still a minor. She'd need to become a ward of the state. Or check the momma's last will and testy-ment." Larkin rebuffed.

"I'd like to talk to the doctors and nurses regardless," Robert said, trying to ignore the Deputy. Even though it was not his area of law, Robert had drafted an ironclad will for Caroline's sister over a decade ago that gave any of her underage children "then in [her] custody" to Caroline. He remembered this clause was specifically drafted in case she had lost custody due to a run in with the law. Robert had mentally prepared himself for this since the document popped into his mind, halfway between Charleston and Florence.

"Mr. Remington?" A nurse asked as she entered the room with Bert. A second followed and silently changed the sheets and Rose's gown. Before changing her, the second nurse failed to give any kind of warning to the men in the room who each awkwardly looked away from the girl's limp, half-naked body.

"Yes?"

"My name is Rose Blanchard. I'm one of your niece's nurses," the young nurse said the tongue-twister over a slight tremble in her voice. "I'd say I started to grow close to your niece. She was—is an intelligent, sweet girl."

"Thank you, Nurse Blanchard," Robert said before turning to the two officers and security guard in the room. "Do you mind if I speak with Nurse Blanchard in private?"

"We'all be right out der," Margie mumbled, pointing to the hallway. Despite being accustomed to thick southern accents, the officer was becoming more difficult to understand the more sleep-deprived Robert became.

"Truth be told, Nurse," Robert began once they were alone. "I didn't really know Rose or have a relationship with her or her mother. As you can probably guess from the state she is in, she didn't have a good home life. My wife—her mother's sister—tried her best to keep Rose's mother on the right path, but her husband was a real lowlife… as we can see."

"So I've noticed. I actually wasn't supposed to be working this shift. I got a call about what happened and rushed down here. I kind of see her as a little sister. I don't have any siblings, you see, so some patients I grow close to. I've watched some pass from natural causes or of some infliction they suffered before coming in, but never from an attack in a hospital. And I hope this won't be the first," she added the last part after a short pause.

"That's very nice of you, Nurse. Can you tell me what you know about what happened?"

"Of course. It was her stepdaddy. No doubt in my mind. He was a drunk from what I read in the files and we found a broken whiskey bottle in the hallway. Even had to peel some of the shards of glass from her wound. And that other nurse that was just in here said she recognized him when he ran—more like wobbled—out. From pictures on the news."

"That's what I figured. Don't think it takes a detective, or those bumbling idiots in the hall, to figure that out. The drunken stepfather, Derrick," Robert scowled. "What about her condition? I mean, can she hear us now?" Robert asked, realizing he had been talking at a normal decibel despite the patient just feet from him.

"She may be able to hear a bit, but she won't remember it. They had to give her a blood transfusion and restitch her leg up, but other than that she seems stable. No new internal organ damage according to the doctor and seems like she'll recover fine, this will just add some time to the recovery. Doc thinks we can ease her out of the coma after a day or two. Just need to monitor quite a bit."

Robert was relieved at what he was hearing. She looked worse than she was: she was gaunt, frail and could pass for twelve even though she was seventeen. He reached out and squeezed her hand and his mind flashed back to seeing her as a baby. Fury overcame him for a moment before he snapped back to the present. She should have a real father here by her side.

"Thank you, Nurse Blanchard. That's all very good news. If you'll excuse me, I'm going to call my family and let them know. Seems we'll need to stick around for a bit while she recovers."

CHAPTER 26

"The ironic thing is, I might actually need a lawyer," Carolina said blandly to Country as he sported a thousand-yard stare at the wall not five feet away.

The men were sitting on opposite sides of an oversized, lopsided table in mismatched wooden chairs. No one else was present. Only a single lightbulb hanging by a chain from the plywood ceiling offered any vision for the soldiers. It was just after four in the morning in Saudi Arabia and Country was up for his morning run. He did not like being so far outside the U.S. time zone and did not sleep much. His colleague had not slept all night. For very different reasons.

The men had been deployed to Saudi Arabia for just over a month. They were part of what would become known as "Operation Desert Shield". The United States had decided early on that Iraq's threats and build-up of forces under Saddam Hussein (yes, *that* Saddam Hussein) in the summer of 1990 would be problematic, yet failed to act against the country they had recently removed from the list of State Sponsors of Terrorism (in spite of all indications suggesting otherwise). By July 23, 1990, U.S. intelligence (specifically, the CIA) reported back to the Situation Room at 1600 Pennsylvania Avenue that Iraq gathered almost 35,000 of its armed young men at the border of Kuwait. All of the friction stemmed from war debts held by Kuwait and the United Arab Emeritus that Iraq took out to fund its war with Iran in the 1980s. Iraq took umbrage at having to pay back its debt, oil being pillaged from its region, the west's interference generally, the decline of its ally, the Soviet Union and the very existence of any non-Arab nations in its general vicinity. By August of 1990, Iraq had invaded and fully occupied its neighbor Kuwait and the U.S., along with a handful of other international powerhouses, decided to do something about their aggression.

The result? Country, Carolina and thousands of other American troops were deployed to protect the oil in Saudi Arabia. That's how Country and Carolina found themselves staring in the dark at one another over cups of bean water that did not deserve the title of coffee.

"Walk me through it again, brother," Country said, sipping his hot bean water. He was back in the courtroom in his mind, latching onto favorable facts for his brother in arms and mentally defending the unfavorable, of which there were many.

"I was on standard foot patrol at the border by myself. My mind was wandering to a conversation I had with the guys earlier. I was lost really. Don't even remember what it was but I was daydreaming from the heat. I don't even know what it was. Bullshit I guess…just bullshitting and shooting the shit since nothing usually happens this side of the border, you know? I'm literally shooting the shit in my own mind. And then…then I heard bullets start to fly. *Clack…clack-clack-clack…clack*," Carolina mimicked the shells dropping to the ground, his voice rife with hesitation and sleep deprivation. He's babbling. "I held up my weapon and approached the sound with caution. I'm sweating because—well, it's hotter than two rats fucking in a wool sock—but also you know…*sweating*. I've read the reports and I've seen the stories of solo Iraqis or a few military aged men crossing over here to wreak havoc. I've never prepared to fire my weapon like that, you know? To actually shoot to kill. Hunt another man, not a deer from a tree stand or a duck from a blind.

"I hear the gun discharge a few more times with some laughter echoing across the walls of the village up the road. I hear some shrieks, but can't tell what they are. I slowly turn by the corner house on Private Drive leading with my gun in one quick motion."

Carolina abruptly stands up, hands running through his hair, yanking. He grits his teeth and turns his back to Country, pacing the length of the room slowly. Country notices tears in his eyes.

"I don't know, man. It all happened so fast."

"Deep breaths. Keep your voice down."

"I shot them. I just shot the kids. I thought they had guns. I thought they were grown men. I don't know. They were brown and wearing their little scarves or whatever the fuck. I couldn't tell. They were tall. But I unloaded a clip on them. Three of them." Carolina is not crying anymore. His face is zombie-like. Emotionless.

"Again, Carolina. Where are the bodies? Are you sure they're all dead? They could be sitting out there. They could be coming to attack us because of it." Country had heard the story twice already. His mind could not conceive what he was hearing. Surely Carolina was hallucinating or suffering some sort of panic attack or traumatic break from reality. He still had not been told the conclusion of the story. Country needed more information to have any chance of helping his friend.

Carolina just shook his head. He was in denial.

"Brother! You have to tell me! Like, bro, are there three dead bodies out in the middle of the street right now?"

Carolina just continued shaking his head, avoiding eye contact.

"Fuck this," Country said. He snatched a light hoodie off the back of his chair and headed out the door. "I'll find out for myself."

Carolina sat at the table. No response, just shaking his head.

Ten minutes into a brisk run that was well ahead of his standard pace, Country found himself rounding the corner Carolina had just described. He was almost two miles from their station. It was still dark and there was a dry, coolness to the air. He smelled death. Or maybe not. It might've been in his mind. He did not know what death smelled like and talked himself out of the silly conclusion. He slowed to a walk rounding Private Drive and stopped dead in his tracked. Shell casings littered the sandy road right where Carolina described firing shots from. Country knelt down to inspect them further. He had litigated *about* plenty of crime scenes, but never showed up to one with evidence still ripe for the taking.

He had a decision to make.

CHAPTER 27

Robert steered into the hospital parking lot, his wife in the passenger seat, Bobby, Liam, Ben, Portia and Addie piled in the rear. He thought it odd and slightly inappropriate that Addie would accompany Bobby, apparently a new fling that was sticking, to a funeral for an aunt he did not know, but he kept quiet. The funeral probably could use a few more heads to make Jenny appear more popular and liked during her life than she actually was. As it was, Robert could only round up a handful of Jenny's loose connections for the unexpected occasion and the last thing Robert wanted was for his wife to be upset over the low turnout for her sister. Life had not been kind to Jenny so they surely hoped the next one would treat her better.

Robert sported a black suit and tie with matching black wingtips coated on the sole in a bright red. His cuff links were real, black studded diamonds and his tie bar matched, though he kept the latter in his pocket. His white button down was silk and had his initials on both cuffs. He was embarrassed at his extravagance in the informal, country town, but was nevertheless grateful Ben and Portia stopped by the house and grabbed some things for him and Caroline. Or else he would be wearing bright, beachy colors to a non-bright event. Beggars can't be choosers, Robert thought as he bit his tongue getting ready that morning.

Caroline was in a sleek black dress with a slit halfway up the leg that Robert could not stop staring at. Though his wife was in no mood and likely would not be in their shanty motel for some time, she knew Robert loved that dress. Was the dress tragic-funeral appropriate? Much like Robert's own outfit, not really. Ben and Portia really outdid themselves in the clothing retrieval process.

Oversized, black Prada sunglasses shielded Caroline's eyes as Bobby helped her from the front seat onto the hospital asphalt in her low heels. The mourning older sister resembled Jackie-O in the quaint town. In her hand was an ornate urn that depicted a Charleston sunset with an angel welcoming the sun. In it was Caroline's baby sister.

"Why'd we let her be cremated if it was a murder?" Ben asked Robert quietly. Caroline was walking with Bobby and Addie a few feet ahead, out of hearing range.

"I called in some favors and had the autopsy expedited. It was clear cut and they had all they needed. I made sure of it," Robert assured his youngest.

"Cause of death?"

Robert reached an arm out, stopped walking and held Ben back. He did not want Caroline to have to relive it. She had already heard the results.

"Loss of blood. She was beaten badly, but still alive. Likely brain dead from the bat to the head. Laid on the ground, alive, until she bled out. The autopsy revealed ravaged organs from years of drug and alcohol abuse, too. Let that be a lesson to you all." Robert motioned for them to continue walking. He turned to Liam, who had stopped along with Portia and said, "Don't pretend you're interested in autopsies and police reports, Mr. White Shoe Lawyer."

Liam shook his head and chuckled. "Un-de-cid-ed. Told ya once, told you a hundred times, old man."

The overdressed bunch followed Jenny's urn to her daughter's room. It had been three days since the murder and Robert had been informed no sightings of Derrick—at the service or in general—had been reported. Rose remained in the hospital in a medically-induced coma, slowly but surely improving. With the doctor unsure when Rose would be healthy enough to pull her out of it, despite earlier optimism, Caroline decided to go ahead with the funeral. It was a short, quiet and sparsely attended service. Robert called in some of his law enforcement contacts to deter looky-loos from trying to attend, knowing such a murder would be the talk of the small town. Once at the service, Robert met a handful of formerly-close acquaintances of Jenny who all said the same thing with a snarl: "We lost touch shortly after she married Derrick."

"Only two at a time, please," a nurse that Robert found to be off-putting barked at the group. "And only family."

"Take the stick out of your ass, Charlene," Nurse Blanchard hissed, rounding the corner by the nursing station. "Do whatever y'all want. She's just pissy because her doctor boyfriend—*who is married*—is moving to Charlotte."

Charlene glared at Nurse Blanchard before snatching a clipboard and storming off. Portia, Addie and Bobby chuckled.

"How is she today?" Caroline asked without removing her sunglasses. Even with them covering half of it, one could tell her face was red and puffy from crying.

"She's a strong girl, doc says. Vitals are strong and we think we can ease her out of the coma today. We've already started lowering her dosages. Could come to as soon as tonight."

Caroline nodded without expression as she and Robert continued into Rose's room. Nothing in the cramped single, room had changed since three days prior, except the décor. Robert had filled it with stuffed animals, gift baskets and balloons in case the girl woke up alone. That was unlikely since Security Guard Bert remained steadfast in his corner chair, reading the same book in his porky fingers. The guilt of letting the attack occur under his nose clearly steered his presence.

"I'll get out of your hair. Let you spend some time with her. I'll come back later," Bert stated as he slipped out of the room. Robert gave him a friendly pat on the shoulder as he passed; he was warming up to the quirky, nervous old man who usually could not take the hint when it was time for him to leave.

Caroline approached the bandaged girl and planted a kiss on her forehead. She felt odd and a sense of awkwardness holding the ashes of her mother in front of Rose's comatose body and set it down on a night table. Caroline kissed her own hand and placed it on the urn before leaving the room with Robert.

***

Robert picked up his phone and scrolled through the contact list. Once he found the name he wanted, he tapped the screen and waited for a voice on the other end. As it rang, he took in the room around him. With no window to the outside, it was impossible to tell, but it was early evening. He was emotionally exhausted from the funeral that morning and the days leading up to it. He sat alone in Bert's chair and observed the unconscious girl in the bed across the room from him. Ben, Portia and Liam returned to the Low Country while Bobby and Addie had gotten their own room at the budget motel closest to the hospital and taken Caroline back to rest. Robert had volunteered to stay behind and wait for Rose to come to. They would take shifts.

"Counselor," the baritone voice on the other end of the line said.

"Detective Covington. Give me the good word."

"I wish I could, Boss. We've got nothing on his whereabouts. I sent word through my contacts in the state, North Carolina and Georgia to locate him only and let me know. Put a bounty on it, per usual. Nothing."

"Well. Where does that leave us?" Robert sighed audibly through the phone.

"I did get a *bit* of intel that could be helpful. Your boy Diamond spends a lot of time at a small bar called Po Dunks. It's about half an hour from the hospital the girl is in. He's friendly with the owner and some of the staff."

"Names. Give me names."

"I'm not sure that's a good idea, Boss. I give you names, you go cause a scene and this comes back on my ass. I got people to protect and a family to feed, ya know. And don't need you doing any dirty work. Those days are behind you. We've got people for that, Boss."

"Are you kidding me? You know the kind of favors of *you* owe *me*? The shit *I* have done for *you*?" Robert lowered his voice to a sharp whisper. "The amount of money I've put in your greedy little pocket? Besides, I'm retired. I may want to let the justice system see this one through. I'm undecided."

"Alright, alright, Boss. Just wanted to give the warning. Whatever. You're right." Covington paused for a moment and Robert could hear papers shuffling on the other end of the line. "I've got the owner as a 'Big Earl' Atkinson and his two drinking buddies down there as Shawn Kurtz and David Larkin. All four usually drink there half the nights of the week."

Robert felt the blood rise to his face as he asked the next question. "You mean David Larkin as in Deputy David Larkin?"

"Yes, sir. He's a Deputy up there and Shawn Kurtz is Sheriff Shawn Kurtz. Not a big department, only about a dozen officers, if that."

"You've gotta be fucking kidding me," Robert muttered. "I'm going to fucking kill him."

"Something wrong, Boss? You know this guy?"

Robert had stood up from Bert's chair halfway through the phone call and began pacing the small room. Out of the corner of his eye, he saw movement in the bed. Rose's eyes were open as she slowly sat up and took in her surroundings. She stared perplexed at the well-dressed man standing in her room. Then, she turned her sights on the urn next to her bed. She picked it up and held it, inspecting it closely.

"Who are you? What is this thing?" the girl asked Robert.

"I've gotta go," Robert hung up the phone and approached the girl's bedside. He was at a loss of where to start. "Let me go fetch Nurse Blanchard."

CHAPTER 28

Nurse Blanchard stormed into the room followed closely by the man Rose had pegged as a modern James Bond, given his sleek attire. She thought he seemed familiar from somewhere though she could not place him. A movie or a book? Maybe he was an author. Or an actor? Why was he here?

"Rose! Glad to have you back with us. How're you feeling? Sore I bet." Nurse Blanchard adjusted some dials by her bedside and wrote on a clipboard clutched against her body, eyes darting from notepad, to patient to monitors and screens. "Take it easy. No sudden movements. Stay lying flat as your body adjusts."

A searing pain shot through Rose's midsection as Nurse Blanchard spoke. It started in her sternum, darted through her abs and ended in her upper thigh, radiating agony the entire way. It was an achiness combined with sharp pains, emanating. Throbbing. She eased back to her original position and grimaced in the bed, squeezing her eyes tight and clenching her fists. She bit her lip to divert the discomfort, noting her cotton mouth and dry tongue as tears welled in her eyes. She opened her eyes, looking for something to drink. Nurse

Blanchard had a glass of water ready and handed it to her after placing a bent straw in it.

"Thank you so much," Rose said, taking the glass and finishing half of it. She put the pain to the back of her consciousness and eyed the strange man. "Sir, I'm not sure I know you."

Robert stepped forward and offered the smile of a politician hoping for Rose's vote. "Hi, Rose. I figured you wouldn't remember me. It's been quite some time. But I'm your uncle. Robert Remington. I married your mom's sister. Aunt Caroline."

Rose scoured her brain for a memory of Robert and Caroline. She had nothing. She did not even recall that her mother had a sister, though she did not recall much at the present moment, given the pain taking her focus. Robert noticed the girl's blank stare and jumped in. "That's okay. It's been years since I saw you. You were quite little then."

"And the drugs you're on numb everything. Don't forget you suffered a concussion just a few days ago. Your brain is still healing. Some memories may flood back in the coming days," Nurse Blanchard jumped in. Both of the guests in the room seemed on edge, as they watched Rose with caution. Rose did not understand why Nurse Blanchard was on edge; she considered her a friend at this point. A comforting presence during these uncomfortable times. *Usually*.

"Why am I in a separate room now?" the patient inquired, looking around anxiously. She had no recollection of the previous days. "Is everything okay, Nurse?"

"What's the last thing you remember, Rose?" Nurse Blanchard asked after glancing at Robert.

"I remember sitting in the long wing with my mom. I was in my bed; she was in a wheelchair. We had gotten in a fight over something, but I can't remember what. She wheeled back to her own bed at the other side of the room and I cried. I was real upset." The girl paused and thought for a moment while the two adults watched on intently. "Yeah, that's all I can remember. What happened? What day is it?"

Robert and Nurse Blanchard shared a concerned look with one another before Robert gestured for the nurse to explain.

"Well…" the nurse-turned-friend looked into the girl's wondering eyes and began to tear up. She contemplated how much to tell the girl and how much to hold back. "You've been in a coma for almost four whole days I think it is. Well, let me take a step back. You know why you were in the hospital to begin with, right?"

"Of course. That scumbag Derrick shot me after beating my mom. Right?"

"Correct. Okay. So, a few nights ago, someone busted into the hospital in the middle of the night. By the time us nurses saw the person, he…" the nurse closed her eyes and tilted her head as if unable to go on. After a pause and a nod of restlessness from Rose, she continued. "The man had you blindfolded with a rag and stuffed another rag in your mouth. Your night gown was pulled up over your head and he had shoved his fingers into your wounds. Reopening them. He was talking to you. Taunting you, it seemed. We saw him after who knows how long and scared him off. He was drunk. That's when we started working on you and put you in the coma to help the healing process. We rushed to help you and didn't have enough hands to try to stop the man."

"So, we can safely assume it was Derrick that did this to me? Again?"

"We think so. We're quite positive, actually," Nurse Blanchard said. "But don't worry. We have a security guard named Bert who usually sits in that chair over there when family isn't here and of course you have me, Robert here, Caroline and your family. He can't hurt you anymore."

"Where's my mother?"

A pause. An echoing silence.

The nurse slowly welled up with tears and shook her head. She motioned for Robert to help and she hid her face from the girl. Robert had to deliver news like this before and never relished the opportunity to do so. He had selfishly hoped the nurse would tell Rose though saw he needed to step up for his newfound niece. He approached the opposite side of the bed as the nurse. Rose darted her head back and forth between her uncle and the nurse. She began to cry and whisper "no" as if she knew the answer.

"Rose, your mother was killed by Derrick. She checked herself out of the hospital, went home and he killed her. We held the funeral service and she was cremated. She's in that urn next to you. I can't begin to tell you how sorry I am for your loss." Robert stated coolly. He had learned, albeit the hard way, to never beat around the bush with these things. Quick, fairly detailed, but never too much, and to the point. Like a Band-Aid, he had to rip it off. Don't hold too much back or you'll be doing this dance again before you know it.

"No. No-no-no-no. She wouldn't have checked herself out. He attacked her the other night. He attacked her daughter. We were shot! We were in the hospital because of it!" The girl fought back tears, inhaling and exhaling heavily as she delivered the words in a whispered shriek. A look in her eyes indicated she was scouring her concussed mind, memories flooding back. "That was the fight. That's why I was upset the other night. She tried to get me to deny what Derrick did. She got *mad* at *me* for what *he* did."

All Robert could do was rub the girl's shoulder as tears crept into his eyes. He felt terribly helpless for the child. She was so weak, small and frail. Without any family beyond himself and his wife, who she did not even know. He was watching her come to the reality that her biggest hero was in fact a fraud. A dead fraud. He had learned this the hard way years prior. Welcome to reality, kid. You just never assume it's your own mother.

"Why'd she go back to him? I didn't know she was going to leave. I could have stopped her. Why didn't I?"

"Shhh. Sh. Sh. Hush that kind of talk. None of this is your fault, honey," Nurse Blanchard said as she held the girl gently in her arms. "It's alright. We're here for you. Momma's in a better place, Rose, honey. No more pain."

Rose pulled back from the nurse and pulled herself upright in the bed, fighting through severe pain, obvious in her face. She grabbed the urn, having mentally grasped its contents. She held it close to her bosom and cried. A cerebral, deep-rooted cry Robert heard earlier that week from his own wife.

The poor child, almost beaten to death by the same man twice, was in severe mourning.

CHAPTER 29

Caroline, Bobby and Addie arrived at the hospital an hour after Rose broke out of her coma. Introductions were made and Caroline and Rose mourned together as the two closest loved ones on earth to the now-deceased Jenny. Having called in the reinforcements, Robert saw his opportunity and made his break.

"I'm going to head to the motel and get some sleep if you don't mind," Robert said to his wife an appropriate amount of time after her arrival.

"Okay. Are you going to set an alarm clock? We only have the Escalade here." Caroline questioned.

"I actually had a rental dropped off here. Waiting outside for me. Figured it'd be easier to have more than one car if we're going to take shifts. I don't want to leave the girl alone at all until we head back to the Low Country. Between you and me, I don't know if Bert is the most menacing guard." This last line brought a smirk to Caroline's face, the first Robert had seen from his wife in days.

"Good idea, babe. You go get some rest."

And with that, Robert headed for the parking lot.

Once outside, he pulled a key fob from his pocket and clicked the unlock button. Hearing a faint "honk", he continued pressing the remote and followed the reverberating sound as it became louder. Finally, at the very end of the much-too-large parking lot for the miniscule hospital was a black Mercedes Benz Class G550. Otherwise known as the G-Wagon. In his practice—and with his *other* sources of income—Robert thought it ostentatious to be seen in such things as luxurious cars or gaudy designer brand clothes. Now that he was retired, he answered to no one, had to drum up zero business and was looking to indulge his flashier side. Although it was just a rental, Robert was thinking about buying a new car for himself after seeing how nice his wife's Escalade was. He had even become a tad envious.

Robert climbed into the driver's seat and pressed the push-to-start button on the dash. The entire digital dashboard popped to life, complemented by the roar of the AMG engine. He gripped the carbon fiber steering wheel with both hands and marveled at the feel of the German car in his grip.

"Oh, you've outdone yourself," Robert said aloud at the luxurious finishes in the interior and the purring of the engine. He pulled out his phone, connected it to the Bluetooth Bose speakers and clicked play. *Kickstart My Heart* by Motley Crue began to play and Robert turned the volume up. He punched in the address of his destination on the GPS, shifted into reverse and focused on the song. He remembered blasting this same song in his Humvee when deployed and let it take him there. Motley Crue had recently released the pulse-pounding jam at the time and him and his fellow troops played it on a loop through their boomboxes and the Humvee cassette player. It fired them up before a mission or just lifting around the yard all the same. When it played, he felt like a savage. And they really were savages back then. Some, unfortunately, a different kind than others.

Robert forced unwanted memories of savageries out of his mind, sang along, bobbed his head to the rock and followed the GPS. It would lead him to his next act in a long line of *justified* savageries.

He still was a savage. The right kind.

***

It was nearing 10 in the evening by the time the G Wagon pulled off the unlit, two-lane road into a gravel lot. Two patrols cars sat in the only two handicap spaces next to the main entrance while half a dozen other cars lined the small porch's wooden fence in front. As the two-hundred-thousand-dollar SUV shifted into park, two men and a woman smoking cigarettes and drinking longneck Budweisers stood up from their barstools. Both men were rail thin and wore untucked short sleeve button downs with grease stains spattered across the front. Their tattered jeans and steel toed boots combined with their relative frailty made them look lost. By the time Robert turned down the AC/DC, shut off the engine and placed a wingtip on the gravel, the spindly men and their overweight female acquaintance were practically fondling the front of the SUV.

"Jeeeee-suz. You mussa be lost, missa," the woman practically shouted after spitting on the gravel. She was wearing unflattering daisy dukes and an undersized t-shirt with the logo of a band Robert had never heard of. She was a portly woman about ten or fifteen years younger than the men she was with. She could have been a sugar baby if she lost a hundred pounds. And if either of the men had any money, which Robert doubted.

"Yea! This here is Florence, *South Carolina.* Not Florence, Italy, double-o-seven. Ha!" one of the men exclaimed with glee. He removed his ragged Clemson Tigers hat and slapped his buddy with it as they doubled over in laughter, each revealing several missing teeth. Robert felt like saying they were not in Florence at all, but he suspected they were not familiar with geography and would take offense to his comment. He did not have the time nor the patience for a sideshow. By the look of the crew, they probably went into

Florence for big occasions and never much else; probably never left the state. Florence was their Paris, New York, L.A. Robert always thought Florence to be a nice, albeit older, town with sophisticated folks. He did not like the southern, uneducated, bumpkin stereotype of the Palmetto State in general, having been stereotyped that way himself anytime he fought a case against a big city attorney. But this bunch fit every stereotype he had ever been objectified as.

"No, I reckon I'm in the right place," Robert said calmly. "You like the ride? It's my boss's. Lettin' me use it while my Cutlass is in the shop."

"Oh really?" the other man said with the smirk. He pulled off his Dale Earnhardt "3" cap and peered in the window, smudging it. "We don't have no Cutlass at Fred's. That's where we work, ya see?"

"Sorry 'bout that. My brother-in-law's a bit of a mechanic on the side. He's helping me out. Other side of Florence," Robert said in a folksy twang without hesitation. He was winging it.

"Anyhow, I best be getting inside. I have an *appointment* with some folks." Before any more questions could be asked, Robert locked the car and waltzed inside.

The bar was quaint yet surprisingly modern-looking for its location. A few whiskey-barrel high tops with matching stools covered the dark, concrete floor, most of which were taken by burly-looking men and a few hardy women munching on burgers, sloppy-looking sandwiches and onion rings. Straight ahead was a bar with five flatscreen televisions, each of which showed a different basketball game, save the screens on each end, which both showed Clemson and South Carolina baseball games. The bar held a dozen barstools, only two occupied. Behind the bar top was one server tilting a glass and catching foam from one of the six tap handles. Robert noticed that the counter had a slab of ice running its length, a feature he had only seen on trips to New York. The only two men seated cooled their glasses on the slab and chatted, canvassing the games. Robert took mental inventory of it all, glancing at his watch.

Robert pulled out a twenty from his black suit jacket and approached the bar alongside the two men. Their backs were to him as they were discussing—more like debating rather raucously—the physical attributes of a woman they apparently both spotted around town that day. One stated she had to wear a DD bra, while the other scoffed and insisted C cups at most. They were slurring in their spirited debate as Robert got closer, though he remained unnoticed by the modern-day Socrates and Plato pairing.

"I'll take a Miller," Robert said to the bartender as he laid the twenty on the far side of the ice. The tall, tattooed barback nodded as he snatched a glass and began pouring. After planting the glass in the ice, Robert nodded, raised a cheers to no one in particular and downed the beer in three big gulps.

"Make it a bottle of Budweiser you've got back there this time. I need to *feel* something," Robert said sarcastically with a grin. The barback chortled and handed him the bottle. He reached for a bottle opener, but Robert waved him off, raised the bottle cap to his canine tooth and peeled off the cap in one fluid motion, spitting the cap into his open hand before placing it on the bar. The barback nodded in approval.

"So, what's a guy gotta do tuh get a ride like dat one out there, cuz?" The porch crew had followed Robert inside, obviously eager to bother the well-dressed interloper some more. Robert slugged half his bottle and turned to the man in the Clemson hat.

"What do you say I buy you and your little posse here a round and, as I told you before, I attend to my appointment here, sir," Robert said with a friendly smile before taking another sip, losing the folksy schtick that obviously did not work.

"Why don't you answer muh fuckin' question first, dickhead," the man asserted as his friends gathered closer behind him as backup.

After a long look at the man, Robert stood up and stretched an arm over the bar. In doing so, he revealed the cuffs of his white button down from under his jacket. He pulled each diamond cufflink out and placed them in his pocket with a smile to the small crew next to him. The men were about twenty years his junior and a third of his weight; Robert did not see an issue other than the guns in each man's waistband, haphazardly hidden. After pulling off his matching diamond tie clip, Robert pulled another twenty from his jacket and ordered four more Budweisers.

"One for me, and three for my new friends here."

"We ain't your fuckin' amigos, pal. Answer muh fuckin' question before I fuckin' do *whup* yo ass." The man took a drink from his new Budweiser before pouring the rest on the ground, watching Robert the whole time.

"Well. Now why would you do that? I try politely to let you know I don't want to engage with you and I even buy you and your pals a drink, but now you've gotta go and make me angry by being rude. Why on earth would you do that?" Robert asked peacefully.

The man in the Clemson let out an audacious laugh close to Robert's face before raising his greasy shirt to reveal a pistol in his belt. Before he could reach for it with his free hand, Robert swept his wingtip through the man's ankles. By the time the man's face smacked onto the cement floor, Robert took his bottle and smashed it over his friend's head before he could finish opening the switchblade in his jean pocket.

As both men lie in agony on the floor beside him, he eyed the woman. Her eyes were darting between her friends and Robert, contemplating her next move.

"Sweetheart, I really do not want to hurt a woman. I actually make it policy to avoid it at all costs, but if you make one move toward me, I will drop you like a sack of fat potatoes. Please, do us both a favor, especially my conscience, and get you and your boys out of here before someone gets hurt."

The woman complied and practically dragged her buddies out of the door, leaving only a tooth and some blood spatter to show for their efforts.

A few of the men at the whiskey-barrel high tops had stood up, pondering what to do. The two Robert had just made quick work of were almost certainly regulars that the rest of the crowd would feel obligated to defend. Robert was afraid of this.

"Everything's cool, gentlemen," Robert said serenely as he sipped his Budweiser and returned to his seat. He held up a steadying hand and motioned for the men to sit. All submitted.

"Sir, who the actual fuck do you think you are?" one of the men at the bar said. Robert turned and met the officer's stern stare with a cold smile of his own. As soon as the officer recognized Robert, the color drained from his face.

"Detective Larkin. Nice to see you again. Sheriff Kurtz—glad I could finally meet you as well."

CHAPTER 30

Coral was late to the party. The bodies were gone, which she had expected, but so were the gaggle of reporters and all save two local cops. The caution tape tied between Roman columns blew in the wind as she stepped up the front porch. One of the two cops had been eyeing her since she parked on the street and walked confidently up the stone driveway. It was not obvious she was a reporter and she made sure of it that morning. She wore a black pantsuit, only slightly wrinkled, with reserved black flats and aviator-style sunglasses. She could pass for a high-level cop or even some sort of Fed.

"Morning, officer," she said, stopping just before the caution tape. The officer—standing on the other side of the tape by the front door—was a county boy. And a *boy* he was. He looked fresh out of high school, if that, with a scrawny, short build and an innocent grimace. He was trying to act tough though Coral saw right through it. She was not certain that the boy *would not* wet his pants once she, a woman, started talking to him.

"Morning, ma'am," was all the officer managed to stutter out.

"What's the status here? How're you local boys on leads?" She asked as she glanced at her phone, scrolling and trying to look uninterested. The severe interest a journalist gave was always a dead giveaway.

"Ma'am, do you—" the boy began before she cut him off.

"Leibowitz was certain a standard suicide-homicide. But everyone knows Leibowitz is a has-been. Now a wannabe. Washed up and dumb as a sack of nickels. I said our county boys would know better. Would prod. Get to the bottom. They'd be able to tell for sure."

The boy was unsure how to proceed. Coral had convinced him she may be in law enforcement and he did not want to insult the woman by not knowing. But he had been under strict orders not to let *anyone* behind the tape and not to talk to anyone about the investigation. This, however, was a grey area. He thought he would press a little.

"Leibowitz, ma'am? I'm not sure—" he started, reddening in his cheeks. He was flustered. Some high standards these boys in blue had for entry to their ranks.

"Don't tell me you're not sure, officer. Leibowitz is never sure and look where that's got him. Back running a footpost hauling doubles on the night, out in the boonies with the *hoodrats*." She cut the boy off and injected some of her favorite cop-show gibberish to confuse the wits out of him. "I know you county boys have more sense in you than someone who's plummeted from grace like an angel whose wings were shot to shit and fell into hell. What's the status on these DOAs. We know they're not John Does. They're John Someone and John Someone's son and they were tied up in that Remington case. What's the angle?"

She was losing steam on her jargon, but making headway with the village idiot in front of her.

"Well....ma'am it's a standard murder-suicide. I think it's open and shut from what my boss is telling me. Looks like they were both going to be indicted for the murder of that boy. Could've come back from a grand jury as early as day after next.

Guilty as all hell it looks it. And this here all but confirms it. Couldn't live with theyselves."

Coral shook her head while removing her glasses. She stepped under the caution tape and looked the boy in his eyes. She glanced down at his badge before returning a sharp stare.

"Officer Petty. You must be a goddamn disciple of Leibowitz. You sound like Jefferies and that fucking Cassidy too. Have you got your head so far up your boss's ass that you don't see there's more to this? The easy answer isn't the right one here. Don't take the easy way out, Petty. That's not how fucking careers are made. That's not what you county boys need. You joined the force to take your head out of your ass. To help your fellow boys take their heads out of each other's asses and do real cop shit. You don't want to go back to your tiny desk in the bullpen and write up a shit report that uses all the standard phrases by the book to make your boss happy. To blindly agree and be a goddamn sheep." She pushed by him in jilted frustration and stepped inside. "You smell the fish and don't call it a fish fry? You wanna pretend it's a steakhouse grilling wagyu? You're better than that, Petty. It's all right in front of you."

She slammed the door shut and left the poor boy in mental shambles. She was not even sure what she said herself and was sure he would spend the next week trying to figure it all out.

Coral returned her glasses to her eyes for cover. She counted two cop cars in the driveway so she knew there was at least one cop more inside. By the look of her encounter with the boy, it was probably his boss who, she guessed, was not as naive as him—not that that was any high standard to meet. But she was already inside and that was half the battle.

She heard the rapid *clicks* of a camera going off upstairs and decided to avoid it for now. She snooped through an impressive foyer with vaulted ceilings. A crystal chandelier dangled between twin, stone staircases that followed dual portrait-covered walls to a balcony overlooking her. She shuffled under the balcony, past a wet bar and into a large den.

This was where the double homicide had taken place. The couches were cream colored and the flooring was white marble, both creating a perfect canvas for the spatters of blood still visible throughout the room. The room itself was magnificent, but to think of the brutal executions that took place in it so recently sent chills down Coral's spine. Or maybe it was not the murders themselves and instead the knowledge that she has been so close to the orchestrator of the murder so many times. Or maybe that she knew the culprit and law enforcement seemed to be turning a blind eye. An ignorant eye? Or a stupid eye?

Coral did not know what she was looking for. The bodies were gone, blood was blood and she was no Dexter; spatter would mean nothing to her. How could she link this definitively to Remington? Was it like a RICO case where it was not one misdeed in particular that would take him down, but the circumstances of the multitude of deaths related to him? No. She needed evidence. She needed someone close to him to talk. Or to catch him herself. Both of these seemed far-fetched and improbable.

She stepped carefully around the blood on the floor and maneuvered to where the bodies had clearly laid a short time ago. One set of sprayed blood surrounded a blank spot that she noted as the perfect spot for a corpse, if such a thing existed. It was behind the couch, before a set of bronze, high-backed barstools lined at a high-top counter that opened into the kitchen. She turned and looked back toward the front door. Clear line of sight. The shooter could have walked in and immediately shot the target. The killer did not even need to walk in for the first kill since the front door was half glass. She could see the back of the boy's uniform from her spot in the den.

Coral walked around the couch to the center of the den. A considerable wool rug covered the floor. It was patterned with red, white and pink flowers. On further inspection some of the red flowers were more speckles of blood spatter. An oak coffee table was shattered and splintered by the fireplace. It, too, showed red and brown stains all over it. She looked around and noted she could still see the boy through the windowed front door from this spot, too. So, the killer could have sniped both men without even opening the front door? No, the door is still intact. No sign of shattered glass. Could the cops have replaced it? No, that would've been too much trouble. The killer had to have stormed into the house and made it clean, especially to mimic the suicide. She had not seen pictures of the bodies and the police had not given details on the location of the bullet holes or caliber of the bullets. She looked around the den for holes, fragments or any signs of stray shots. Nothing. This was a professional job. A man killing his son then killing himself would have sprayed and prayed. No, he would have used a hunting gun around this part of the country.

"Hey! Who are you?" A voice shouted from the kitchen.

An adrenaline spike rushed up her spine and blood dashed to her cheeks, reddening her face.

"Excuse me?" She asked, in an offended tone. She whipped around to see a middle-aged officer storm from the front foyer toward her. He was ready for a confrontation.

"You heard me," he said as he approached her, stopping three feet short of steamrolling her. "I asked you a question."

"I don't like your tone right now, officer…" she looked over her sunglasses for a nametag, but found none.

"That's right. *Officer*. Ergo, I can be here. You, however, *cannot* be in my crime scene, ma'am. What's your name?"

Coral slowly crept away from the cop, thinking of a way to buy time. "I'm offended by your accusatory tone, officer. Your officer at the door—Officer Petty—said I could go ahead in. So don't get mad at me. I haven't even touched a thing." She felt bad throwing the village idiot under the bus, but every man for himself here.

"Fucking Petty," the officer grumbled to himself. He took a step, closing the gap that Coral had managed to create, and scrunched his face. He sniffed twice and snarled. "Is that alcohol I smell on your breath, Miss…?"

Coral bolted by the cop before he could realize she was on the move. She thought he shot a "hey!" at her, but she could not be sure. She was out the door, passing Petty in all his glorious stupor and back to her car before anyone could nab her. She was not sure if she was chased, but did not want to take a chance. She fired up the engine and was a mile down the road before she pulled off the highway into a gas station. Coral backed into a spot toward the rear of the convenience store and had full view of the highway going in all directions. It was reminiscent of her Remington lookout spot off Rifle Range Road. After twenty minutes, she was confident no one was following her and whipped out her cell phone.

"Hey, Rick," she said. "I got your message. Let's meet at the Old Timer Diner whenever you can get there. I'm heading there now. I can wait a bit. I want to talk the Clark case. There's more to it and I know it and I know the cops know it and I know you know it. See you soon."

She clicked end, took a long swig of her drink and turned back onto the interstate.

CHAPTER 31

"You know, it's funny, Sheriff. I'm usually pretty good with feeling people out. I can, generally speaking, tell if someone's lying pretty quickly or get a feel for what type of vibes a person puts off within a few minutes of being around them." Robert sipped his beer. "It's kind of a sixth sense you begin to develop after a law career in defense like I've had. But I've gotta hand it to your boy here. Deputy Larkin is some mighty fine actor. I think he missed his calling. Truly."

"Now I can't say I really know what it is you're talking about, but you—" Sheriff Kurtz began to get up from his seat before Robert cut him off.

"I think it'd be better for all parties if you sit the fuck down, Sheriff," Robert offered. "We've got some chit chatting to get to. Now, I'd offer you the same deal I offered your fine constituents that just left, however from the slurring in your words I'd say you've had enough. I'd like you sober for this conversation so I'll actually grab you a water. What's the bartender's name?"

"Uhh—Johnny."

"Hey, Johnny? If you wouldn't mind grabbing my friends here some tall, ice cold glasses of water? I don't want them driving drunk this evening." Robert chuckled as his gaze shot from one officer to the other. "And I'm sorry about the glass and that Budweiser. If it's any consolation, looks like I have glass lodged in my Louboutins. That's unfortunate."

Johnny rushed over a pair of waters for the officers and shook his head. "No worries, sir," he said as he rushed off to avoid any ensuing confrontation.

"Now lookie here, Mr. Remington. I don't know what you think I did, but I didn't do nothing and you know it. Let's all keep our heads here. I know this is an emotional situation. I don't want to have to take you outside or even downtown," Deputy Larkin's tone began conciliarity and morphed into confrontational as he took a sip of his whiskey neat, pushing aside his water. He was still slurring.

"Sheriff Kurtz, that's where I'm going to have to politely disagree with your drunken colleague. He arrived at the scene—or should I instead say he arrived at the house of his buddy-*slash*-murder scene with some other officers. Now from what I know as God given fact, is that the victim, Jenny, had called you fellows over there on multiple occasions. It was generally well known that your friend liked to slap my sister-in-law around. I will concede that my sister-in-law had her own issues and, God-love her, they frustrated my wife and me. Nevertheless, you all turned a blind eye and allowed Derrick to continue beating his wife."

Robert slammed the rest of the beer and grabbed a water for himself. Wagging a finger in no one's particular direction, Robert continued. "You gentleman may not know, but there was a time when we had laws on the books in this country protecting things like 'marital violence' and even 'marital rape' in the home, but, you see, we sit today in the twenty-first century and our laws—though not completely caught up in every aspect—have been amended to give wives some rights. And funny enough, one right is to not get the *shit* beaten out of them by their husbands!"

"Mr. Remington. Wait just a minute. I don't like the accusations or the tone you're throwing at two officers right now. We did no such—" the Sheriff began before being cut off by an irritated Robert.

"No, I will not wait, Sheriff. You fucking cocksucker. I don't think you really know who I am. I mean *really* know. I think before you say anything you're going to regret you give some of your law enforcement buddies from around the state a call. Maybe at SLED. Hell, maybe ask the Fibbies while you're at it. They've got a good idea.

"As far as I'm concerned and as far as has been confirmed to me by numerous of your colleagues, this was an avoidable murder. If you had done your job as officers and taken *some* form of legal action against that scumbag. Or even if you did your job as a half-decent person and friend, and stopped some of the shit your friend was pulling."

The officers glared silently at the man lambasting them at their own watering hole. This was their turf yet Robert had ambushed them. And they did not know how to take it. Sheriff Kurtz sipped the water Robert ordered for him and leaned back in his barstool, exchanging an annoyed glance with Larkin.

"I digress. Nothing you pieces of shit can do about it now." Robert grinned, taking an onion ring from Larkin's basket. "What I need from each of you now is to tell me where Derrick is. Because let me tell you something: you had better come up with him before I do. Because if I do…. Well, if I do, let's just say I hold grudges. And I have a bit of temper. Don't let my dapper dressing fool you, these hands can get dirty, gentlemen."

Robert placed a half-eaten onion ring back in Larkin's basket and finished off his glass of water. He dabbed his mouth with a napkin, tossed the soiled ball into the officer's basket and stood up from his barstool. He pitched a few twenties on the bar and pointed to Johnny as he began to walk toward the door. After a few steps, he turned to the officers.

"Oh, did you gentleman still want to tango in the parking lot?" No response. "Didn't think so. Let me know where Derrick is. Deputy Larkin, you have my contact info."

CHAPTER 32

"This may be it. This may be the big break. I can feel it," said the man in a creased black suit and red tie. He was carrying a dangerously lopsided cardboard tray of numerous coffees, steam steeping from the small opening on each. Under his arm, he squeezed the top of two white paper bags as he held open the door with a shined black oxford.

"Calm the fuck down, Sandler," a petite woman in a black pantsuit and flats said as she shuffled over, snatching a coffee and one of the brown bags from the man. "You've said that no less than three times about this case and so far none of them were accurate. So actually, shut the fuck up."

The woman took her place back at a noisy, grey metal desk in the middle of the small room. There were three desks to match the woman's, two of which were occupied by hulking men in furrowed, over-starched white button downs, slightly yellowed at the collar for years of sweat. Sandler took his seat at the last remaining desk, abutting the woman's.

"Nah. This is different," he said, stone-faced as he reached into one of the bags and housed an old-fashioned donut in two bites. "The others were all clear contract killings.

He was careful, calculated and had to use outside assistance. This one will be a murder of passion. Malicious. Pre-meditated. Violent." Sandler let each word linger, savoring them.

"Kid, I agree with McGovern: do us a favor and shut the fuck up," one of the other men said with a creased brow. The red-faced man leaned back in his chair and rubbed his face with both hands. Sipping his coffee, he turned to the woman.

"For a junky, his target keeps a pretty low-profile, Darlene. We've tracked and lost him three separate times in two weeks. He hardly uses plastic, seems to have ditched his cell phone and has been through a few states in that time."

"Well yeah, maybe if we got the funding to put an actual physical tail on him it'd help," the fourth desk piped up. He was a black man with a sweaty bald head.

"We're the unit that cried wolf one too many times, Chase. SAC won't give us shit until we show something." Darlene lied, peeling the egg off her sausage, egg and cheese. "You know this is off the books." Before she could toss the egg into the waste can below her feet, Sandler snatched it from her hand.

"You know the rules. I don't let eggs go to waste. Not in this economy. Not protein."

"Well, it seems that he's turned his phone back on and he's back at least in the Carolinas," Darlene said, ignoring Sandler. "We can use this as justification to tail. Chase, take the kid with you and go out to this mutt. Don't be seen, but try not to let him die of his own volition. He's a nitwit, so that might be difficult, but live bait is the only bait that'll work here. And remember, we don't need evidence on this case that badly. Just leverage. We want the big fish."

Chase let out a sigh, clearly irritated. Sandler fired a gleeful glance at Chase who appeared at least twenty years older than the scrawny, twenty-five-year-old. "Let's head out. I've got his coordinates, Chase," Sandler squeaked, jumping to his feet. He dropped a couple manilla folders into a Duke Blue Devils backpack and slung it over his shoulders. Eagerly, he picked up a banker's box from the corner of the small, windowless room and kicked the only door open with his foot. "You wanna drive, or me?"

The fourth agent in the room grinned ear to ear at Chase, who threw a pencil at him in retaliation. "Fuck you," he mumbled as he got to his feet. Grabbing his suit jacket from the back of his swivel chair, he threw it over his shoulder and picked up a worn, black leather attaché case.

"Do us both a favor and you drive. If I do, I might wrap us around a tree on purpose."

CHAPTER 33

Coral had only been at the quaint diner half an hour when Rick had arrived. Just long enough to down two cups of coffee, a muffin and read up on the Clarks. Both Clark men had their social media unblocked and available to the public. The elder's was clearly run by someone other than himself, showing off pictures on the set of *Who Got the Mail?* and at various galas, fundraisers and other local and semi-national events of importance to one politician's check book or another's. Lots of tuxedos and phony smiles. His social media would get her nowhere. She made a note to check to see if she could find his social media manager—either a personal assistant of sorts or someone from his show. They could give a good interview on working for Clark the elder, but were probably under strict confidentiality agreements. Then she struck the note she just made. It would be a waste of time.

The younger Clark's social media, on the other hand, was a treasure trove of his deviance and definitely should have been private to the world—or deleted altogether—though it did take her some time to find it. He posted like a bachelor playboy—with no sign of the kid in sight. Once Coral was on his page, she quickly recalled Remington referencing it in the trial of Clark's baby-momma. She, too, was nowhere to be found. Instead, it was bikini-clad women in places such as Tulum, Miami, Vegas, Dubai, Jamaica, St. Barts, Ibiza and numerous more party spots. Clark had pictures of guns, knives, booze, pills and more. Coral was flabbergasted at how the younger Clark garnered any support in the community, yet he did. Likely through the pockets of his father, though, she thought.

Rick strolled up to Coral's table in a hoodie in jeans. He never was the dresser. She got up to greet him with a peck on the cheek and quick one-armed hug. She had known Rick a few years now and they always shared tips, leads, secrets, general gossip and, more than once, men. Coral met him through a friend of a friend at the Rooster's Playhouse in Columbia, a rundown bar that somehow became a hotspot for law students, paralegals, lawyers, judges, cops and any other trade touching on the law. Coral and Rick were the only two non-attorneys in the bar that night, it seemed, and they quickly hit it off. Though he worked for a newspaper that technically competed with her own here in the upstate, they helped each other out on occasion. I rub your back you rub mine.

"And another Remington lead brings my babe to the upstate, it seems," Rick said with a smile as he sat and ordered a sweat tea and cinnamon biscuit.

"Pegged me there, Ricky baby," Coral said, turning her phone to show a picture of the rear ends of five strippers surrounding a very inebriated—and very happy—Harold Clark IV. "How could he be so stupid? Who even posts pictures like this? How did this dumbass's social media not stop any trial to begin with? I mean, he has zero pictures of the kid."

Ricky frowned and took Coral's phone while sipping tea with the other. After a few clicks, he seemed satisfied and turned the device back over, proudly displaying a different Harold Clark IV.

"Honey, that's his real social media account that just went public *after* the trial ended. He had a fake, public one up the entire trial. It's all picture of him at church, him with that baby boy and even a few with Remington's old client. Made the man look like he was coming up for sainthood. Very strategic. I guess he couldn't wait to start chasing some tail again and needed his clout account open to the public ASAP. Shimmied this bad boy back up." He took another gulp. "We did a forensic dive yesterday. Most of the followers on the other account were fake. Paid for accounts. To make it all look real. Hired a whole consulting firm to do it. Insane, darling."

Coral was not that surprised. She was more surprised at the prospect of someone with the community respect like Clark having a smut-filled social media the whole time and Remington not really highlighting it. Maybe Remington lost his touch.

"Nope. Nuh-uh. I see that look. Your boy, Handsome Robby, he wasn't allowed to discuss the social media. Judge ruled it irrelevant. Snuck in a comparison of it to his client's OnlyFans once, but beyond that the jury heard nothing. That devil Handsome Remy ain't losing a step at all."

"You know me too well, Rick," Coral smiled. If only she could find a straight man like Ricky. Though that obviously was not possible. "So, spill. You know why I'm here. My passion-project."

Ricky was the only soul on earth who knew anything about Coral's full-blown obsession with Remington. It bubbled to the surface when she was drinking margaritas with him once and she made him swear to not jump the story. Ricky quickly assured her he would never touch the story, mainly because Remington was a good friend of his paper's editor and Ricky would never be allowed to publish it. Besides, Ricky had a crush on Remington and thought he could do no wrong. He was, however, becoming more and more convinced of the man's evil-side by Coral. To the point that Ricky would call in favors and ruffle some feathers—quietly—to get any word on Remington. So far, it was a fairly fruitful relationship only one way, with Coral basically gift-wrapping a few big stories to Ricky so she could tell her boss they had already been run and she was not going to redo them—leaving her to focus on Remington and the case of the murderer-defending, non-murderous murderer.

"Well, the latest tragedy to befall a Remington-adjacent figure is his sister-in-law, in case you didn't hear already." Ricky offered with a pause. He quickly admired the look in Coral's eye that told him she had not yet heard this juicy piece of Remington news. He loved breaking scoops, especially to other *scoopers* in the know. He added in dramatic fashion, "And the niece."

"What?"

Ricky went on to recount what he had heard from his contacts in Florence. The shooting at the Diamond home. The subsequent hospital stays for the Shelby-Diamond girls. The mother's jump to defend the shooter, her husband. The girl in critical condition stemming from a follow-up beating and visit from her step-father. The beating to death of the mother in her own home.

"Jesus Christ. That's horrible," Coral said obligatorily. Then, her wheels started spinning. She had done some research into Remington's extended family. "Was this the druggy sister and her husband?"

Ricky nodded.

"Adds up," she said as she pondered. She was almost certain there was not any other family on Mrs. Remington's side. "What about a biological father? What's happening to the girl once she's discharged?"

"No father in the picture. I don't think the mother ever even knew who the father was for sure. From what I've heard, she was pretty loose when she was on drugs back in the day. Straightened up for the most part, but was still married to the clown. The murdering clown, I guess I should clarify. And no clue. Looks like Remington may be taking her; he's up there right now, from what I hear. He's already gotten into an altercation with some cops. They bowed down to him in the end. The man's got swing all up and down the state. Everybody seems to know it and respect it."

"I'm sure they'll give the guy that killed his sister-in-law the chair with that kind of swing. He got a lawyer yet? Or a public defender?"

"Still on the loose. No one knows where he is. Just ran for it."

Coral put down her coffee at Ricky's response. Her mind was working twice as fast as she thought through what this meant for her. She pulled out a five and a handful of crumpled ones and stuffed them under her plate. She bolted upright, gave Ricky a kiss on the cheek and headed for the door.

"Ricky, have I told you how much I love you? This is it," she shot over her shoulder. Before Ricky could respond, she was gone. As fast as Coral arrived in the upstate, she was gone even faster. Next stop: Florence, South Carolina.

CHAPTER 34

In the two weeks since Jenny's murder, Sheriff Kurtz and Deputy Larkin had been astonishingly forthcoming with information following their run in with Robert, calling him whenever any information crossed their desk, though there was little. The belief for a majority of the two weeks was that Derrick had disappeared to a distant relative's place in the swamps of Louisiana, but nothing had come of work with local law enforcement in the state. As local law enforcement put it to Roberts' contacts: "Swamp people stay off the grid for a reason. It's likely he found kin in similar predicaments. We've got a better chance finding a gator that don't like meat down here than finding that man, but we'll give it our all."

That all changed when Robert got a call from Chief John Mosby at three in the morning.

"What's up, John?" Robert said as he stumbled through the back door of Sully's, sleepy-eyed and lethargic.

"I've got something on the Diamond. Turns out he's been at a buddy's cabin in the Appalachians in North Carolina for the last couple weeks. Killed your sister-in-law, spooked and assaulted the kid at the hospital and immediately took off.

And we can definitively confirm he is the murderer. I was able to get screenshots of text messages he sent to one of the boys in blue up there outside Florence." Mosby began before a brief pause. "I ain't even telling you the name because I'll handle it. It's not either of your boys from the bar, though. And don't ask how I even got the screenshots. He was trying to gauge the law's flexibility on this one. Made it clear there's zero. It's personal."

"Fair enough. You heard about the bar? Covington's got a big mouth, huh?"

"Not Covington. You know I have eyes and ears all over this state. If you so much as have a loose stool, I'll know about it before you have time to wipe your ass, Boss. Hell, I might even know before it hits the bowl. Been awhile since you snooped around on your own, though. I told you that you couldn't stay retired from the game you're in."

Robert chuckled. Mosby was right. "So, what's the plan? Do we have some assets up in the Apps? I can make some calls. I have a few buddies that retired off-grid there themselves."

"I got something even better for you, Boss. In the texts I got my hands on, he tells his buddy he's heading to your neck of the woods. Blames the whole ordeal on the girl. Rose is her name? Never wanted her. Now, apparently, he wants to kill her. Not enough blood on his hands as it is, I guess. Real sick fuck."

A normal human being would be worried by this news, maybe even flee. Not Robert, though. He perked up at the thought of Derrick wandering into the Low Country, ripe for the picking on his terrain.

After lingering to think a moment in the breezy sea-salt air, Robert thought of something. "I've got an idea. Listen closely and leak exactly what I tell you to people you *know* will tell Diamond. I want to greet him with his own surprise party."

Before Robert clicked end, he quickly added, "Hey, by the way. You are right to a degree, but I am out of the game. I've struggled with this, but we need to let justice see it's course on this one. Too many close calls. I need to enjoy a retirement with my family, not behind bars. Find him and bring him in. *After* I've had my shot. He'll be alive and mostly well."

***

Later that morning, the Remington clan assembled around a wrought iron table complemented with a crystal-clear glass top for a brunch of French toast, bacon, eggs and muffins, courtesy of Caroline. The homemaker was back into her motherly rhythm and it showed. She smiled as she passed around American flag-themed service plates and pitchers. The emotion stemming from the loss of her sister had clearly dissipated over the two weeks, culminating in her confession to Robert the evening prior.

"The saddest part about this whole ordeal is I don't think I'm even surprised or upset about Jenny's passing, Robert. Does that make me sick?" It was a rhetorical question she asked as they laid in bed reading. Robert knew better than to interject as his wife pondered. "I think in the beginning I was in shock and just emotional at the brutality of it, but not fully surprised. Poor Jenny was lost for years before this. In the end, it's a bit of relief her pain is over. I used to block her out of my mind because anytime I thought of her, I'd think of her lying in a ditch somewhere from a drug overdose. I only feel bad for poor Rose at this point. To grow up without a mother is a terrible thing."

"But to grow up with Jenny as a mother? Is that much better? Not to mention Derrick as a quote-unquote *father*." Robert added, laying down his iPad and removing his reading glasses.

"That's very true. If Derrick is who Jenny settled on, Lord only knows the type of scumbag Rose's *real* father is." Caroline shook her head. Robert nodded in agreement. "All I know is we need to give that girl every chance at a normal life we can. From what I can tell, she's amazingly stable and somehow has a good head on her shoulders. Don't you agree?"

Robert nodded convincingly and they both returned to reading their respective eBooks, minds wandering to Rose's fate until they went off to sleep.

"Would you pass the *real* syrup, Bobby? And extra ice from the bucket for my drink." Robert asked. It was mid-morning but with sixty percent humidity and a high of ninety degrees anticipated later that day, everyone was already feeling the heat. The summer was creeping in. Their only saving grace was the wind that whistled off the ocean, cooling the family.

"Robert, the sugar free is real syrup. You know you need to watch your sugar intake. Now use that," Caroline scolded.

Ahh, the joys of retirement, he thought.

"Nurse Blanchard, what do you think of this? In your medical opinion, shouldn't I be allowed happiness? My wife acts like I'm ninety years old and four hundred pounds," Robert said, turning to their tenant with a wry smile.

"If you were ninety and obese, I'd have you chugging real maple syrup because I know for a fact you don't want to grow old and useless, my dear," Caroline said with a wink, throwing the real syrup bottle across the table to her husband. "In fact, I'd probably smother you with a pillow at that point."

"My wonderful wife, everyone," he said, raising his glass and giving a reserved golf clap.

Robert sat with his back to the house, monitoring the beach. There were a dozen or so locals strolling the waterline, but Robert remained vigilant. Luckily, the Remington's had grown friendly with and knew most of the others on the island, so any tourists were pretty easy to spot.

"How's the food sitting, honey?" Caroline asked Rose who was seated between Nurse Blanchard and Addie. Rose had moved into Sully's once she was released from the hospital and Nurse Blanchard had followed. They had struck up a sisterly connection and the young nurse wanted to move to the Low Country anyway. Seeing an opportunity for a sense of normalcy and a friendly face in Rose's transition, the nurse moved into Sully's and continued caring for Rose as she healed.

So far, the arrangement was working out well for all involved from Robert and Caroline's point of view.

"Wonderful. Thank you, Mrs. Remington. You and Mr. Remington have been more than accommodating," Rose said, covering her mouth sheepishly as she swallowed a bite of pancakes. Robert could not help but be struck at how similar Rose was to her Aunt Caroline: poised, well-spoken and wise beyond her years.

"Honey, you need to call us aunt and uncle or Caroline and Robert. None of this Mr. and Mrs. nonsense. We're your family." Caroline shot a welcoming smile the girl's way.

"Well, I echo the sentiment. You both have been so hospitable and I genuinely appreciate it. I always wanted to move down here but never thought I'd be able to afford it," Nurse Blanchard said as she held a piece of bacon in her hand. A gleam in her eye exhibited a sincere appreciation for the hosts.

"Of course, Rose number two," Robert's moniker for the nurse. "You're more than earning your keep by caring for our little patient here."

The family carried on eating their brunch, sipping iced coffee, listening to the waves crashing in the distance and Zack Bryan playing on the radio. Robert sat in silence, having nothing to add as the women at the table debated the "dreamiest" qualities in various country musicians. It struck Robert as fateful that he and his wife had always wanted a daughter, and it seemed tragedy had just given them the opportunity to have one. They had discussed adoption years ago, but nothing had come to fruition and at this point in their lives, they wanted grandchildren, not dirty diapers of their own babies. Their plan was to raise the girl, who was almost an adult already, as if she were their own. They had discussed it, though it was not so much of a discussion as it was an immediate agreement. They had more than enough in the bank, in real estate and elsewhere, so why not give the girl the life she deserved after a torturous childhood already endured?

"Did anything ever come of that murder-suicide related to the case you worked on, Robert?" Robert abruptly snapped out of his daydream by the question. Addie, who usually was very quiet, had asked. Nurse Blanchard appeared to shoot her a surprised glance as the table went silent. Talk of death did not exactly rank as the most popular of topics in recent weeks. Noticing the discomfort, she retracted a bit with flushed cheeks. "I'm sorry, Bobby had just told me and I was curious. That's all."

"No, no, it's okay, Addie. Glad to hear you pipe up and feel comfortable here," Robert said with a chuckle, though he did not necessarily mean it whole-heartedly. He had his courtroom acting on display. "No, there was a note apparently. Seemed it was a straight murder-suicide. Couldn't stand the thought of going on having done what they did to that poor baby, I guess. Although, who really knows what goes on in the minds of killers?"

Robert stood up from the table, changing topics. "More coffee anyone?"

Inside, Robert found the pot empty and began brewing a fresh one. He liked to get his own coffee as opposed to letting his wife fetch it, as she would slip half-caf into his cup and think he did not notice. He noticed.

"Mr. Remington, I'm sorry about that back there." Robert turned to see Addie, who had followed him inside with her own cup, holding it up almost as a peace offering.

"Don't worry about it, dear. I think we're all just touchy of such topics around the Roses."

"I had just read somewhere that there wasn't a note and the family was calling in independent investigators to snoop around. Seemed like it could've been a set up."

Robert turned his back to the girl as he pretended to check the coffee. Why was this girl, who he never had a conversation with before, pushing on this in *his* kitchen? He jiggled the pot handle and turned to find the girl had closed the gap between them and was just steps away. He was getting irritated.

"Oh really? I hadn't heard that. That's interesting." Robert said with an ease about him, cool under the pressure of an evident interrogation. "Well, I'm sure if they stooped so low as to murder their own family—a baby at that—they probably made other enemies too."

"Yeah, I guess you're right."

Robert and the girl stood there in awkward silence until the coffee brewed. When finished, Robert filled their cups and quickly returned to the back deck.

***

The ringing phone reverberated throughout the Bronco only twice before Mosby answered.

"What's the good word, Boss?"

"Why is our little thing outside the Low Country still being looked into?" Robert barked.

"I can't just shut it down, Robert. I tried. The media is all over it and smells blood in the water. We ruled it murder-suicide too quick and now they're poking around, thinking it's some kind of conspiracy." Mosby took an audible gulp of something on the other end of the phone. Or was he nervous? "Had a couple folks asking about you up here. Off the record. But still."

"What were they asking?"

"One was talking about how it's suspicious the number of cases you've been involved in where someone has been killed or gone missing after the fact. Another said you drove the girl back to Florence."

"Neither of those are questions, John." Robert said, annoyed. For being head of the most vicious group of men and women on the state payroll—behind the politicians, of course—Robert always thought Mosby was underqualified and had a lower IQ than a man in his role should have. He was beginning to think of him as a weak link.

"Okay, well. Uh, they said it in a question form, you know? 'Hey, John. Don't you think it's suspicious that

Remington is involved in these types of cases?' And: 'Hey, John. Did you hear he drove the defendant back to Florence?'"

"Cut to the chase, John. What'd you say? Did they get anywhere? Like actually suspicious or were they spinning webs? Yapping?"

"Well, I told them I didn't think anything of it. That a man in your profession deals generally with scumbags and scumbags are generally the ones who choose murder or to go on the run."

"And the drive?"

"I said you're a good, Christian man. Felt she'd been dealt a raw deal and you were just bringing her back home. Nothing fishy. Quit fishing."

"Okay, good. I heard no lies," Robert was pleased by his minion's response. Not always a weak link. He turned back to the Clarks. "Well, you had the coroner and M.E. come out. All the forensics were done. Everything by the book and all signs pointed to murder-suicide, Mosby. You answer to justice, not reporters. Not the media. Just keep them at bay and feed them something else. I don't care if you have to go commit crime just to get them to investigate something else. Do it."

Robert clicked end on his cell without waiting for a response. Mosby needed to remember the hierarchy.

CHAPTER 35

Despite the slovenly pace of an off day in the Caribbean with nothing to do, it was a regular Tuesday, not the weekend. And this was no vacation. Guess this is retirement, Robert thought as he and his wife strolled through the market in downtown Charleston. They decided to act like tourists visiting the Holy City that day as they had not strolled through the peninsula with either a plan or schedule in decades. The initial intention was to have a beach day out back of Sully's—read, nap, sip cocktails and talk. The weather did not like the plan and instead it provided an unseasonal nip in the air with a strong breeze and clouds. So here he was, shopping with his wife like the old retiree he was.

Robert's wife admired some sweetgrass baskets as the artisan of Gullah decent eyeballed her with a salesman's smile in the midst of making more. Robert passively admired as well, feeling the texture of a small bowl and checking the price of a nearby basket that would work well in his office. His wife shot him a smirk and the price reminded him of why he did not already have one.

"For the love of God, you have to remember I'm retired now. No more income. Look at this shit all you want, but don't even think about it. I'd like to stay out of the poorhouse, woman," he mumbled teasingly.

"Oh relax. If you piss me off enough in your retirement, I'll spend until you find a new job, bucko."

They continued on through the market, communicating without words as Caroline would pick up an item and glance at her husband who would nod with raised eyebrows to feign interest and acquiescence. *Buy what you want*, the look said.

The slow amble of what could be torture for a husband in the Charleston Market continued. He watched as other husbands, boyfriends and children all did the same slow march ahead of wives, girlfriends and mothers, each looking for new ways to decorate their respective spaces. The sweetgrass baskets were ubiquitous in the market and an obligatory buy. The Remington's already had over a dozen, but it did not stop Caroline from buying another six-inch basket for north of three hundred dollars. Despite living in the Low Country and not actually being tourists, Caroline moseyed between various Charleston-branded items at several vendors, picking up shirts, hats, mugs, coasters, and anything else shiny enough or with a big enough pineapple that it caught her attention. She bought shirts and a hat for both Roses. She thought about some local jewelry before deciding she did not know the girls' respective styles and left without any.

Robert, on the other hand, spent a bit admiring the local artists' giant paintings. Boone Hall, the Angel Oak, bridges, Shem's Creek, fishing boats, Spanish moss, the beaches. He loved them all and had variations of each throughout their properties. He stopped at a hat shop in the middle and admired a Stetson cowboy hat before turning to see his wife laughing at him. Maybe another time.

By the time they reached the end, Robert was roughly a thousand dollars poorer and starving. They strolled down

East Bay Street, the water dipping in and out of view, before finding a new rooftop bar and grill to duck into.

"Okay. You've got to spill. I need to know the progress you've made," Caroline said with a sullen look. She took a sip of her pinot grigio before adding, "Or lack thereof."

"What are you talking about?"

"The latest problem. Your latest *target.* Don't play dumb with me. We've been married long enough for me to know your next move."

Robert wiped his brow with a handkerchief. He was sweating a bit in the sun, despite the chill in the air and the breeze. The woman across from him meant business. She was looking to meddle and ask questions in a way she never did. He looked around to make sure no tables or waiters were close enough before leaning in to respond.

"All these years of marriage, and you want me to now implicate you as an accessory? You've done so well. Don't ask questions." He swigged his whiskey neat. "But if you must ask, I am retired, remember? Aren't you proud? No more of that. Not even once or twice removed. A reporter or two is starting to—" Robert stopped himself mid-sentence. "Don't worry about it. I'm in contact with the powers that be and they'll bring him in for a trial. He's not getting off for what he did to your sister and that little girl."

Caroline shook her head despairingly. She glared out at the church steeples lining the Holy City sky and downed a large gulp of wine. "You don't know the half of it, Robert."

"What's that supposed to mean?"

"Nothing. Look, I have never pried into any of your *business.* Because quite frankly it has never concerned me. But this does. This is one man who should be punished for what he did. One that I want punished."

"He will be, I can assure you. I'll line up the judges, the public defender—the whole nine yards. I—"

"That's not what I mean, Robert," his wife sharply interjected. "I've turned a blind eye to all the bullshit you've done. The bullshit that could have cost us everything. And now this? This is the one you've decided to throw the towel in for? No."

"Honey, you know he'll get the needle. Or the chair. Or firing squad if he chooses. It'll all work itself out." Robert had never discussed this aspect of his business with his wife. She had read the writing on the wall after a bit, but never questioned him. They had spoken in euphemisms about the topic and addressed it head-on once, maybe twice while drunk. She was not stupid. She had become like a mob wife: don't ask, don't tell. No accessories after the fact.

"You know that'll take years. He'll appeal and appeal until he dies of old age in twenty years on death row. Let me be very clear: I don't want you to do anything, but I want you to see that things are handled. Handled *outside* of the unjust and deathly slow justice system, Robert." Caroline glared at her husband. She was upset. He had not seen her this adamant about something in a while. Something was off.

"Look, Caroline. I understand why you're upset—"

"No you don't, Robert. I need you to see to it on this one. I mean it. Not you. But one of the others."

"Caroline? Talk to me. Why are you so stuck in on this? I understand it was your sister, but you want me to risk my life—our futures—for this?"

"Robert. I don't want you involved. Just make some calls. Please."

"What? Why?"

Caroline flagged down the waitress and ordered a double tequila soda. The woman was not much of a liquor drinker, but on certain occasions she was usually stressful situations, which included the happenings of the last two weeks.

"I spoke with Rose last night. Uh—Rose number two. Blanchard. The nurse," Caroline babbled. The waitress handed her the tequila and she downed it, telling the impressed waitress to bring another. "He'll have another whiskey neat, too."

"Slow down." Robert raised a hand to calm her drinking. "And?"

"Robert, the things that monster did are awful. Just awful. He doesn't deserve to breathe the same air as us. The same air as that poor little girl."

Robert downed the remainder of his current whiskey neat as he took his new glass from the waitress. He had heard and seen a lot in his life. At war, in the courtroom, dealing with brutal cases and, of course, at his own hands in the right circumstances. But he was not ready for what was about to come.

"Last night, when you were in your office, the girls and I were watching television. Some girly movie. At one point, a woman in the movie gave birth to a stillborn baby. Rose got up and went to bed shortly after that. I didn't think anything of it, but Blanchard stayed and finished the last twenty or so minutes of the movie with me. It ends, I start tidying up and getting ready for bed and I hear muffled cries from Rose's room. I look back at Blanchard, who was still on the couch. She had been scrolling on her phone and stopped to look at me, clearly hearing the same cries. She had this look in her eyes. Like discomfort at something she knew. Something that she knew and I didn't." Caroline closed her eyes and took a deep breath.

"I walked over to her and whispered to ask what was wrong. With her and with Rose. She tried to get out of telling me. Saying she promised she wouldn't tell. And how it didn't matter anymore. I pried and made her tell me. She made me swear not to tell anyone. And to never bring it up to Rose. Fine, I said.

"The first night Rose was in the hospital, she was in and out of it. They had her medicated pretty heavily for both physical and mental pain. She was having nightmares and talking in her sleep. Or not even sleep because the nurse described it at some state of consciousness where she was awake but totally out of it. She was crying and yelling Derrick's name. They figured it was trauma from what she had seen and heard over the years with her mom. And of the shooting, of course. Thought nothing of it really. Then the next day, Nurse Blanchard ordered some tests just in case. Rose was only seventeen and didn't attend school anymore, but she figured the tests would need to be run eventually. To check everything internally after the shooting." Seeing that her husband did not understand the nature of the tests she was talking about, Caroline cut to the point. "Robert, Derrick raped Rose."

Robert dropped his drink to the table with the loud thud of glass on glass. A few other patrons on the rooftop gave him a quick glance before returning to their own conversations. Caroline had tears rolling passed the bottom rims of her oversized sunglasses and down her cheeks. Her hand was shaking as Robert took it in his own. He was angry. Angry at Derrick. Angry at Jenny for putting her daughter in that situation and not protecting her. Angry at himself for not thinking. The thought never occurred to him that this might have happened despite the fact that it was commonplace in his cases involving lowlifes like Derrick. He was at a loss for words at he stared at his wife in disbelief.

"No. She told me he never touched her. Told Blanchard and I shortly after we got up there."

Caroline shook her head. "Robert. They know this because she was carrying a child when she was shot. First trimester and she lost it, for better or for worse. Blanchard showed me the ultrasound on her phone."

"Well, uh, how do, uh....Do we know it was his?" Robert stuttered.

"Rose confided in Blanchard after the tests were run. Poor girl didn't understand she was pregnant, just thought she was sick. Said it had to be Derrick's. Never had sex with anyone before Derrick started molesting her. Happened a few dozen times, she said. Always when Jenny was gone. The monster would hold her down and...and...." Caroline let out a blubbered wheeze. Robert squeezed her hand tighter. He downed his whiskey with the other hand. His rage was bubbling up, but he fought it to focus on consoling his wife.

He began to ask more questions, but Caroline waved him off to stop. She had more.

"So, she lost the baby in the shooting. Loss of blood to the womb or something. Rose's body was fighting for its life and made the decision to supply blood and oxygen to her over the fetus. Nurse Blanchard said she spoke with Rose about the rapes a few times, had a therapist come in and help her, too. They were gearing up to break the news to Jenny when she left the hospital. The therapist called her a few times after she left to talk it through, but never got her. Then Derrick attacked Rose in the hospital and she shut down. Stopped acknowledging the rapes. Said she didn't know what the therapist, doctors or Blanchard were talking about. Blanchard said the doctors and therapist called it dissociative amnesia. Apparently, Rose genuinely doesn't remember anything to do with the rapes, the baby or talking to anyone about it. Her mind flipped a switch and blocked out the trauma to protect her. Saw it on an episode of SVU once."

Robert's mind was numb as his hand trembled holding his wife's. They sat in silence for a few moments that felt like an indeterminably long period to Robert. Caroline sobbed silently, resolutely behind her glasses. Now Robert understood why his wife had decided to speak up. But he disagreed with his wife. Derrick needed to die before being apprehended by the police, yes, that was for certain. But his would not be at the hands of one of Roberts' cronies. Derrick's brutal murder would be at the hands of one Robert Remington.

CHAPTER 36

Country booked it back to headquarters. Once inside, he found Carolina pacing the kitchen. The sun still had not risen, but most of their fellow soldiers were up and about. Carolina looked to be in his own mental torture chamber, replaying his misdeeds in his head. As Country approached, Carolina perked up.

"What's up brother?" he asked, perking up as if nothing was wrong. Country led him outside to a corner of the fence-lined yard where they were out of earshot.

"I got rid of the shell casings. Threw them along my run into the river. Now listen to me. *Listen to me closely*," Country stared into the killers' eyes. Carolina beamed back. "I am not getting involved in this. You clearly hid the bodies. I don't know what happened. I don't know what you did with the bodies. I know nothing. You hear me? You know nothing. You keep all this shit to yourself and don't tell a soul. You lie low and you keep your mouth shut. With any luck, whoever the fuck you killed had it coming. And whoever the fuck you killed was killed by some sand gnats from across that border. Right? You hear me?"

Carolina smiled like he won the lottery as he gripped Country in a tight hug. Country returned the hug with a strong grip of his own. He was not certain he had done the right thing. He was sure it was an honest mistake on Carolina's part, but he had heard plenty of stories of soldiers snapping, committing an atrocity and then spending the rest of their lives paying for it. They were savages doing savage things to other, more criminal savages. A single fuck up should not cost a soldier his career, his life and his reputation. That could have very easily been Country who fucked up, right? He would want Carolina to have his back the same way. He may have some trouble sleeping for a bit, but no blood was on his hands. He was merely helping his brother in arms out from spending the rest of his life in a foreign prison.

Little did he know at the time, Country would learn to deeply regret his decision. It would change the trajectory of his life.

CHAPTER 37

Rose had not yet admitted it to her newfound family. Or even to her live-in-nurse-turned-best-friend. She did not want anyone worried any more than they needed to be. They had all done so much for her in just a few short weeks. Why add more unnecessary stress to these kind people?

Besides, Rose had told herself every night that the nightmares would fade. That she was safe. She knew she was lying to herself, though. He was still out there. The nightmares would remain until she knew otherwise. Until she saw his corpse. His cold, lifeless face.

No. She yanked back her thoughts about Derrick lying dead in a casket. She would focus on positivity and positive affirmations. That would surely do the trick, she thought, knowing better.

The nightmares began after her mother died, when she was still in the hospital. They had grown increasingly more vivid with each night at Sully's. Despite her posh new surroundings, she could not sleep through the night, feeling as though she was in a constant state of imminent peril. Her therapist had blamed it on cortisol and fight of flight adrenaline. She would nod off after midnight, bone-tired and stressed to the core. By two in the morning she would usually wake in terror, hyperventilating with a puddle of her own sweat surrounding her.

The dream was constant. Always similar with slight variations. She was trapped at the rear of Derrick's dilapidated home, watching through cold, wrought-iron gates as the ceiling caved in slowly above her head. A grandfather clock ticked vociferously against her eardrums as she pressed her cheeks against the metal posts, watching Derrick bludgeon her mother to death. Sometimes, she would be watching herself beat her mother as Derrick applauded. Derrick's laughter would reverberate across the house. And then he would charge Rose. He would beat her until she would awaken from the dreams. She would remain awake through the morning when she heard Nurse Blanchard or her aunt rousing about the kitchen. Knowing she was not alone anymore was some solace, but not enough.

The clock beside her bed that morning seared a bright 2:52 A.M. into her sleep-deprived, dry eyes. She dabbed and massaged her forehead and temples to disperse the beads of sweat that emerged every night in her sleep. Sitting upright against the mahogany headboard, her senses felt heightened in her semi-delusional state. She felt everything harder. Sights singed her eyes. Smells were robust. Sounds were brasher. Thoughts were even shriller in her head. She gazed around the room aimlessly, head drubbing, before deciding to wave the white flag on sleep for the night. The terrors won again, albeit a bit later in the morning than usual. Progress.

Rose swung her legs out from under the damp sheets and let her feet touch the hardwood planks below. They were cool and sent an unwelcome shiver up her spine. She opened the nightstand drawer and removed her latest novel—courtesy of Aunt Caroline's personal library—and a clip-on book light. She did not want the rest of the house to be disturbed or know she was awake by flipping on a lamp. She had gotten the booklight at a school bookfair years earlier and used it every night, even in her now-distant, former life at Derrick's when she had use it so the bright lights did not attract unwanted attention from a drunk Derrick.

After collecting her items, she silently slid across the room to an old rocking chair. Once in the chair, Rose turned to her side, slid open a creaky, wooden window as silently as possible and opened her book.

Less than a chapter into her early morning read, Rose heard creaking floors outside her door. Always curious, she dog-eared her page, stopped rocking and checked the clock. As 3:13 A.M. shot back at her. Between her nightmares, her lack of sleep and the horror-skewed nature of her latest book (about a boy whose neighbor was a serial killer), Rose was on edge. She tried to tell herself she was hearing things, but the screeches culminated in the starting of a car engine close by.

Rose hurried to her bedroom door, peeled it open and ran to a front window to see what was going on. A Ford Bronco was idling in the street across from Sully's. Its lights were off, but the rumble of the engine was audible. Letting her curiosity mixed with insomnia get the best of her, Rose threw on a pair of Caroline's Crocs and slinked down the driveway, stopping for cover behind a palm tree. Rose peered through the fronds to find it was Robert's car, removed from the driveway, with an empty driver's seat. Ignoring all instincts and channeling her adventurous books as her guide, Rose approached the car and peeked in. The front and back were empty and nothing could be heard beyond the engine. After allowing a brief pause of confusion, she walked to the passenger side and inspected the vehicle for signs of entry from anyone. After confirming none to be seen, Rose tried the rear door. It was unlocked.

"What the hell?" Rose whispered as she lifted a foot to climb in. Before she could steady herself, Caroline's oversized Croc caught on the floor mat and Rose face-planted, slamming the door behind her. As she writhed in pain, her incision wounds searing, a man's voice approached. She found a blanket in the rear of the Bronco and hid herself under it.

***

"All I'm saying is keep your patrols away from my Charleston home for a bit, okay?.... Yes....Yes, I understand, but do your best. Or get out there and physically stop them. I don't care. You know what this is about.... Yes, well I received new information.... Don't worry about it.... Yep, morons lost him.... I just got a notification of movement from my security cameras downtown. He's there alright. The info dump worked. Mosby has a rat, but helped us this time. We'll worry about that later.... What am I saying? I'm retired. You'll worry about that later.... Yes....you're right. Semi-retired. Going to my real retirement party as we speak. I'll call you when I need you later. Gotta go. Bye."

Robert ended the phone call and climbed into the driver's seat of the Bronco. He was sure to keep the lights off and park across the street the last few nights in case this moment arrived. He did not want to wake the Roses. Caroline woke up when he got the notification. She knew what was happening and was ecstatic.

Robert received the camera notification exactly three minutes before he was on the road to Charleston. By the look of it, Derrick was playing the prowler, sneaking slowly around the property and checking windows, just as Robert had hoped. Robert would speed downtown and be at his house by the time Derrick realized he had been fed bad intel and the Remington's—more importantly, Rose—was not there.

Zooming through Mount Pleasant, Robert checked his pocket to make sure his trusty knife was with him. He felt the cold steel and smiled. He reached blindly into the backseat for the "go-bag" he had kept in the Bronco for this very event. Once he had the duffle bag in his grasp, he pulled it into the front passenger seat and caressed through it, glancing back and forth between the road and the bag. In it, he felt and mentally inventoried all his tools for the evening. He had envisioned this moment ever since Caroline told him what Derrick had done to Rose. He practically salivated thinking about it. Just days earlier, he thought he would never get to experience the hunt again. Boy how he was wrong. His thirst would be quenched tonight if he had anything to say about it.

CHAPTER 38

"Alright, Sandler. Good job so far. I think tonight's going to be the night," Chase said in the passenger seat of the surveillance van. They had tailed Derrick Diamond for weeks now with nothing to show for it. It had become evident, even to the oblivious rookie, Sandler, that the police responsible for hauling the wife-beating murderer in were either incompetent or had been told to leave Diamond be. They had spotted at least one officer tailing the felon from time to time, though the officer did not seem to notice their FBI surveillance van or ever try to actively contact the man. While Chase found this peculiar, he had a feeling Remington had put the officer up to task and wanted to finish Diamond himself. That's what he hoped. The fly in the ointment was, ironically, that the other tail lost Diamond shortly after he drove through Florence. Diamond ditched one stolen vehicle for another and successfully dropped the officer. Only that tail, though. Chase and Sandler were still with him, booking overtime en route to Charleston. They just hoped Remington would fall into their trap.

"Thanks, Chase. I *was* right. We're gonna nail this guy. I checked his houses in the database and all of them have camera equipment and security. If Diamond's going where we think, which he should be, and Diamond wants to do what we think he is, we've got them nailed." Sandler pumped his fist and flashed a toothy grin at Chase. Chase glared back. He was a grizzly twenty-three-year veteran of the Bureau and could not stand the unwarranted positivity Sandler spewed. The boy was not a pragmatist in Chase's eyes, which meant he was not a real Fibbie. He had not seen or done the things Chase had done. Chase had been on dozens of operations and jobs like this one where all seemed to be falling into place just to implode at the last minute. This was what Sandler lacked: a frame of reference. Still, after two weeks on the road with the kid, Agent Sandler was starting to grow on Chase.

"Alright, cool it, zippy. We're not even close to out of the woods yet. We're tailing a guy who we hope is tailing a guy to get a guy to admit not to a crime we hope is about to commit, but to a crime that we believe he committed decades ago. You see how to any realistic-minded person, that doesn't sound like a slam-dunk?" Chase yawned. He was amused by the positivity and, though he would never admit it, even slightly encouraged by it. A positive outlook was contagious, his wife, an elementary school teacher, constantly told him. Of course, he would not be sharing this with his personal driver at the moment.

Sandler smirked and kept to himself. He could tell Chase was starting to like him. Now if only that bitch Darlene would come around on him. His ass was on the line for taking a rogue, off the books mission like this, the same as the other five members of the crew.

"Look. He's turned into that gas station. Stop off," Chase pointed to Derrick's old beater. They had watched Derrick hot-wire it days earlier around the South Carolina and North Carolina border.

"Got it. I'll loop around so we don't look suspicious," Sandler said, speeding up and passing the pull-off for the station. They were outside the suburb of Summerville, just shy of North Charleston. It was nearly two in the morning and the men had not slept outside of the van in almost a week. Chase was exhausted. Sandler, less so due to age and, mainly, adrenaline.

"What? No! What the fuck are you thinking?" Chase exploded as they passed Derrick pumping gas. He sat up in his seat and shot his glance back and forth between the station and his driver.

"We were too close! I didn't want to spook him," Sandler said with a worried look in his eye, his voice cracking. "The book says that a good tail—"

"'*The book, the book, the book'*. Fuck the book! Look around kid! This ain't a motherfucking book. We're on the road at two in the morning following a murderer. You listen to your goddamned superior, which, in this case, is me. You dumb motherfucker," Chase whacked Sandler over the head. The older agent's neck and face boiled red. He checked the rearview mirror against the road ahead. "Alright. You can't turn around here 'cause if he sees us it'll look suspicious. Just go another quarter mile and pull off by that exit. Then turn all the lights off. We'll wait until he pulls out."

Sandler did as he was told and remained silent. He was easily flustered and, along with his glimmering positivity, it was his biggest flaw.

After five minutes of silence, Chase jumped in. "Look kid. You're doing your best. This shit takes time. Just listen, do as your told, keep your head down and don't say talk too much. You'll be fine. And stay away from Darlene. She hates you."

This last comment produced a smirk on the younger agent's face. He began to talk then thought better of ruining the moment, heeding his partner's advice. He mimicked zipping his lips and sat back. Chase grinned. The kid would be alright.

But after another ten minutes, the men began to worry. This was the longest Sandler had been quiet the entire time they were together. He was itching to say something and break the tension.

"He had to have stopped for a smoke, right? Filled up his car, went inside, and took a leak. That's ten minutes right there. Then he took a look at what he wanted, but there was a line. Finally got his smokes and took a drag outside. That's at least another ten."

"Dipshit, there was no one in the parking lot and the sign said no restrooms. And he wouldn't give a shit about smoking in a stolen car. What is he concerned about leaving a smokey smell for resale value?" Agent Chase rolled down the window, lit and took a drag of his own cigarette. "Jesus Christ, kid. We're this close and we lost him."

"No, no. Wait a minute. We'll head back to the gas station to make sure he's not there and worst-case scenario we know he's either going to the Remington Charleston residence or the one on Sullivan's Island. We can make up time and pick him back up."

"Let's do it. Double time."

The all-white surveillance van was disguised as a normal work truck any construction worker would have. It had rusted spots on it and the paint was chipping. From the outside, no one would ever guess it had state of the art, Hollywood spy-level equipment lining the back. It was most likely a truck seized in one raid or another, turned state's property and revamped for its current purpose. The issue was that despite the overhauled interior, the engine, tires, axles, chasse and entire structural integrity of the vehicle was based upon its original and never touched. It was like an iPhone running on 1G internet. So when Agent Sandler turned into the grassy median to steer the lug back toward where they last saw Derrick, the uneven pothole conjoining the grass and asphalt made quick work of the front driver's side tire and entire front axle. The agents inside bounced up and down like they were on a roller coaster. Chase tried to lunge for the wheel, but it was of no use. The axle snap caused the truck to tilt just enough that it ended up on its side in the median, glass shattering and an airbag exploding on Sandler. Sandler shrieked like a little boy and Chase screamed obscenities, the former in fear and the latter in rage. There was no backup car within a hundred miles for the Fibbies. They would be missing Derrick's last dance that evening.

CHAPTER 39

Coral had been practically living in her Civic since her diner date with Ricky. Her editor begrudgingly approved her expenses to the upstate in exchange for two stories submitted in each of the next two weeks. This meant that while living in the cramped sedan, she also wrote in it. She was starting to remind herself of the Lincoln Lawyer. Except even less money and no driver. And no law degree, but, in her mind, she practically had one from all her reading on Remington cases.

From what Coral had gathered, Remington was emotionally driven. If a case involved an act of murder against a marginalized community, Remington would feel the need to strike. What she had not determined—yet—was how Remington would react when someone close to him was killed. The journalist understood that the Shelby women were not exactly close to Remington and his wife, but they were family nonetheless. On top of that, one was brutally bludgeoned to death by her own husband while the other was just a young girl, shot point blank in her own home by her own step-father. Coral was all but certain that Remington was ready for revenge.

From the diner, she had sped to the hospital the girl was at. She had managed little to no information from doctors, nurses and staff. Good for them upholding confidentiality, but come on. Any crumb of information would have helped. It probably did not benefit her that she had no money to bribe them with. Bigger newspaper outfits had big slush funds for situations like this. Not hers.

In spite of the fact that she was, as usual, in the proximity of her journalistic subject, Coral had never made contact with Remington nor anyone in or around the Remington family. She hoped Remington did not know who she was, though she had a suspicion that he was at least aware of her. Hopefully not her proposed story. Coral had always thought it best to avoid direct contact with subjects, especially if a piece would not be flattering. While some journalists liked to face the music head on, she liked to sit back, write and present Remington an opportunity for comment at the very last moment. She hoped to avoid conflict and agitation of the subject. In her past, she had begun her research by reaching out to subjects and quickly learned this was not the route for her. On multiple occasions, she had to file for a restraining order after subjects of less than flattering pieces began stalking and threatening her. She quickly changed her approach.

After hanging around the hospital officially proved fruitless, Coral swung by the Remington's motel and poked around town. She found that Remington had already threatened the local police who were not on his payroll, yet. She was told Derrick was a heavy drinker and real scumbag, but had friends in law enforcement and frequently got off easy. He even had a girlfriend on the side that everyone seemed to know about, but she was not talking, either. She found that no one knew Rose Shelby's real father given that the mother was a loose one back in her drug days. As for the girl herself, she had dropped out of high school, gotten a job and spent most of her time at the local library reading and keeping to herself. The only thing Coral managed to scrub from a nurse was that, based on a quick "Ew! No!", the there was no history or evidence of Derrick molesting the girl.

Everything was a dead end. She had to have patience and just sit back and observe. And it seemed to be paying off as she followed the brake lights along King Street. The Bronco turned onto Beaufain Street and Coral smiled. She let her subject skate unfollowed to, undoubtedly, the Shelby Charleston home. She stayed straight on King and would loop around to the home on Colonial Lake Park from Broad Street to give Remington the false belief that he was alone.

By the time Coral pulled out front to the house, the Bronco was nestled into the driveway with massive iron gates closed behind it. The lights were off and nothing but the gas lanterns by the front door illuminated the property. Her Civic kept an unsuspicious speed to the end of the block, turned and kept going. Coral parked her car a block and a half away and got out to walk to the property. But after she locked her car and it gave a singular *beep*!, she thought better of her plan and climbed back in. She was not there to stop a crime. If Derrick was indeed at the home and Remington was there to kill him, she would not stop it. Or even call the police. They were both scum of the earth and could battle it out to their hearts' desire. She just wanted proof in her own head—and potentially some photographs to match—that Remington was in fact the murderer she had hypothesized he was for so long.

She started the Civic back up, flipped off the headlights and crept down the block, parking two houses down from the Shelby compound where she had a full view of the gate and all porches, though part of the front door and some windows were blocked by shrubs and the retaining wall. It was the best spot she could get while still feeling safe. She reclined her seat, took a sip of her Vodka-infused coffee and readied her Canon.

CHAPTER 40

It had been at least an hour. Maybe more. Maybe way less? Like ten minutes? Rose's concept of time had disappeared as her adrenaline spiked. She had been frozen under a scratchy blanket in Robert's backseat, not sure where the car she was apparently a stowaway in was headed. She heard the end of a phone call that sounded cryptic; it reminded her of a mystery novel, but provided no clue as to her destination.

She had narrowly avoided being grabbed as Robert blindly searched for a bag that was under her legs. She was in too deep to reveal herself now, despite the pain in her body. How would it look if she popped out and admitted she had snuck into the Bronco and spied on her newfound uncle? After all he and his wife had done for her and her friend? She had to remain hidden. No noises. Pretend Derrick was driving the car.

Finally. The Bronco slowed to a stop and the engine shut off. Robert let out a grunt as he leaned over the center console to grab something from the duffle bag. Rose heard a metal *click*, a recoil and her uncle grumbling something to himself. She was almost positive what she heard was the cocking of a gun and a quick prayer, but could not be sure. She peered through the thin blanket to watch Robert ease out of the driver's seat into a crouched position. Now she was certain she heard a gun, as she saw the metal glisten in the moonlight. She had noticed earlier that evening that it was a full moon. It kept the world slightly illuminated in Rose's otherwise dark reality.

Robert quickly disappeared from view. He looked to have entered through the front door of what must have been a home. After giving it another sixty seconds, she tossed off the blanket and sat up, looking out the windows. They seemed to be in Charleston based on what she remembered of the architecture she saw during a middle school field trip years back. The houses looked old, but eloquent. Gas lanterns illuminated bright colors and lopsided porches. Yes, this must be downtown Charleston. That would make sense; she heard the Remington's talk about their home here. She recalled her mom had talked about it too. It must be where Jenny and Caroline grew up. But why would Robert sneak here in the middle of the night with a gun?

Rose had come this far, no use in quitting now. She stepped out of the Bronco and quietly closed the door behind her. The driveway was made of uneven, smooth river rocks. Her aunt's ill-fitting Crocs were not made for this terrain—even in sport mode—so she made sure to slide her feet slowly up the drive with care. Once on the front porch, she lowered herself down into a squat and waddled to a window. Luckily, the curtains were drawn and she had a clear, albeit dark, view of what appeared to be the living room leading into the kitchen on the far side of the house. After a moment of seeing nothing, she impatiently scampered down off the porch to get a different view. Rose squeezed herself between a couple of large bushes and the side paneling of the home until she was square in the middle of a window, sticks jabbing into her back. This one looked at the foyer of the home, yet still no sign of life inside. A moment later, she returned to the porch, contemplating her next move as she stared at the brass doorknob. She was feeling courageous tonight. Her wounds ached, but she saw no signs of open stitching or blood. She would take her chances.

Once inside, it was hard to ignore the opulence even amongst the obscurity. There was a massive, antique chandelier in the entryway. The flooring into the lower walls were black and white marble that led into intricate wainscoting. The interior was not quite as large as what she had seen in movies, rather, each room was clearly delineated by bright, picture-covered walls and substantial wood doors. No open concept here.

Rose quickly shook her head clear of interior design ideas and jumped back to the matter at hand. She needed to find out what Robert was up to. After clearing the entryway, foyer, living room and kitchen, she decided to venture up the stairs. Her uncle had to be *somewhere* in this dated mansion.

Cautiously creeping, Rose heard thuds and grunts as she ascended. They grew louder with every restrained step. Her mind raced back to one of her novels, making her nervous that she was intruding on an affair Robert may be having. Her movement slowed and she crouched lower to the floor with each step, to the point she was practically knee to hardwood at the top stair. The floor seemed to creak with each breath she took. There were three doors immediately at the top of the stairs. She had to choose an opening and burst in to hide since she was too open at the top of the staircase. Rose chose the entryway closest to her and practically summersaulted in.

Empty. Thank God. It was a small bedroom with an oversized, four-post bed. She allowed herself to catch her breath and stand tall, stretching and listening. The thuds and groans continued. She thought maybe they were getting closer, but she could not be sure. Rose crept back toward the entryway to the bedroom and was ready to peer into the next room when she was knocked back onto her rear with force.

"What the fuck?" The voice standing over her sent a chill down her spine. She kept her eyes closed tight and writhed in pain on the floor. Each wound throbbed with an intensity that made her lightheaded. She grasped at the most intense pain, the bullet wound, and found an opening with warm, sticky blood pouring out. Was she shot again? Despite the physical pain, her mind was in a tailspin at the voice. It was a voice she had hoped she never heard again in her life. The voice she had heard in the hospital, threatening her life.

As she gnawed her teeth together and opened her eyes, she was thrust from the ground with a strong hand, twirled one-hundred-eighty degrees and locked into place. From the quick glimpse she got, Derrick was bloodied and his face was swollen. His shirt was ripped and he wreaked of sweat and cigarettes. One sweaty arm was wrapped over her shoulder, culminating with a hand gripping her opposite hip tightly. His other hand was under her armpit, pointing a gun up at her cheek.

"I missed you, princess," his hot breath spewed into her ear. She could've thrown up as he continued to huff heavily, his beer belly expanding and contracting against her back.

"Let her go, you *piece* of *shit*!" Robert yelled, from the entryway to the bedroom. He held a gun out, pointed at Rose and Derrick. "You shouldn't even be laying a fucking hand on her!"

"Try and stop me! Take one step and I put a bullet between her teeth. That's why I'm here. I don't give a fuck about you. I don't want your money or nothing! So leave me and my bitch of a daughter alone!"

Robert's face was covered in sweat and reddened, though no blood or bruises were visible. In fact, no sign of the altercation that he and Derrick were clearly in showed besides a torn collar on his Tommy Bahama. Robert was winning, apparently. Until Rose just gave Derrick the upper hand.

The tension filled the room. Robert stared. Rose whimpered. Derrick grasped tighter. The barrel of the gun was pressing harder into Rose's cheek with each passing second. She was freezing cold and sweating pure adrenaline. She was terrified. Robert looked on helplessly, keeping the gun steady. He had no clean shot.

In an instant, Rose turned the tables. She mustered all her might and all her courage to let her chin drop to her chest slowly and without any sudden movements, gearing up. Then, with one quick thrust, she snapped her neck back as hard as she could. The back of her already sore skull connected with her hunched captor's jaw and she felt a *crack*. She was not sure if it was her own bones or Derrick's as she felt a dizzying discomfort emanate within her skull. Derrick was caught off guard, falling backward and releasing both her imprisoned and his gun. Rose turned and watched Derrick stumble. He seemed drunk, but she did not smell it on his breath as she usually could. He was disoriented from the head shot combined with Robert's apparent beating. The daughter and stepfather locked eyes for a moment before both their gazes anxiously settled on the gun. The black barrel was practically touching Rose's feet about three feet from Derrick. Robert was saying something, but Rose heard none of it, ears ringing. She and Derrick lunged for the gun at the same time. Rose's body blocked Robert from having a clean shot at Derrick with his own. Rose snatched it just before Derrick could and uncomfortably pointed it with two trembling hands at Derrick.

The corners of Derricks mouth jerked upward into a devilish grin. "Ha! Do it, you little bitch. You don't have the balls. You're just like your slut of a mother." He laughed and took a step closer.

Behind Rose, Robert had lowered his gun. He reached out and put a hand on her shoulder. She shuddered at the touch while keeping her scowl, and the gun, pointed at her former abuser.

"Rose, put the gun down. You don't need to prove anything. I can take care of all of this. He can't hurt you anymore, just get behind me."

A shot rang out and deafened Roses' ears. She stumbled backward and heard it again. And again. *Bang! Bang! Bang! Bang! Click! Click! Click! Click!*

A buzzing in her ears reverberated and she went into a daze. She felt arms around her. They pulled her back after she had stumbled and fallen to the floor. She had unloaded the gun into her mother's killer. She tried to shoot the cold-hearted monster even after the last bullet fired. She tried to will more bullets into the chamber with each pull of the trigger. Blood filled her aunt's Crocs from the body that spat it out in what felt like gallons in front of her. She had pumped lead into Derrick's face and chest, leaving no doubt regarding his chance of survival. She dropped the gun and stared as the blood trickled onto her feet and legs, Robert dragged her back out of the reddish-brown puddle growing in the room.

"Rose! Rose? Are you okay?"

Rose nodded. She began to smile at the view before her. She felt good about what she had done and wanted to soak in the feeling. She had killed him. She had done what her mother should've. She had done what her mother could not.

"Rose. The neighbors would've heard those shots. We've gotta get his body out of here. You have to help me. Fast!"

Rose nodded and got to her feet, her gaze never leaving her artwork.

CHAPTER 41

She heard muffled yells followed by shots that rang out in quick succession. It was exactly what she had hoped to hear and now she had been rendered motionless and unable to move since. She held her breath as if the sound of her exhaling would alert the shooters of her presence. From two houses over. Across the street. In the grey night.

It had been fifteen minutes since she parked the car and began her stakeout when the shots were fired. Another ten minutes had already elapsed, during which Coral was unable to do anything. Her mind was like a hamster on a wheel going nowhere. She was weighing all the pros and cons yet unable to focus on the whole purpose of her surveillance. Was the alcohol clouding her? Was it adrenaline? What's the issue here, dammit!

Finally, she saw the front door swing open. Just as it did, her eyes darted away from it to watch a police cruiser pull onto the street and park in front of the driveway's gate. A tall man in plain clothes stepped out of the driver's seat. He secured something on his belt and looked up and down the street. Coral slouched farther down and snapped a few pictures with her camera held up on the dash. The man was humongous. The object on his belt was a gun, clearly visible in her snaps from the gas lantern reflecting off it. The cop disappeared behind the open front door, into the house. Coral studied the pictures she had just taken and a chill went down her spine. Everything was coming together. It was the cop that was warning all the journalists not to run stories on Remington cases. It was Detective Covington. He was surely here for more Remington cleanup.

Coral took a slug from her alcoholic coffee, an attempt to calm her nerves. After swallowing a massive gulp, she looked down at her hands to see the unsteadiness; she was quivering like a beached fish trying to flop back into the ocean. One more drink, this one straight from the vodka bottle in her glove box, and she latched her camera around her neck and emerged from her car. She hurried across the street, glued herself to a neighbor's fence, stooped down and waddled to Remington's gate, keeping the fence as cover. She took a deep breath, made the sign of the cross and turned to peer through the cold iron. She had been dreaming of this moment for years and now she was face to face with it, nervous as a shelter dog.

Through the fence, she saw no sign of life. Covington's squad car was ten feet to her right and just in front of it was the Bronco she had followed here, yet not a single light illuminated the house.

Wait. She thought she saw something. There it was again jetting across the windows. It was a flashlight. Multiple flashlights. They were in there and they were trying not to be noticed. She pointed and snapped, hoping to get a few pictures to prove that they—Remington and Covington—were sneaking around in Remington's own house at nearly four in the morning. Nothing she had so far on her camera would help, but she learned from her numerous Remington-defended trials that circumstantial evidence in abundance could help sway a jury. She would gather all she could.

She scooted back into a bush to hide herself. She jutted the lens out of the bush just enough to get pictures as the men would leave the house. But she sat and saw nothing for ten minutes. Twenty minutes. Thirty minutes. At forty minutes, she feared they had left without their cars and scattered out back. She checked the road behind her and saw no changes. She would wait it out a bit longer.

She was fighting back yawns as an hour approached. Her skin began to itch from the bush. She wished she brought her booze, but it would be a fool's errand to dart back for the bottle now.

After an hour, she had run through every possible scenario she could imagine and some she had not a clue how she imagined. Remington and Covington were having a secret affair in there. Robert and Covington were torturing Derrick—or a mystery target—in there. Robert and Covington had actually left because they knew she was in the bushes and they were at her apartment torching it.

As she gave up on replaying make believe scenarios in her head, her mind roamed to her warm bed with a bottle of Jack Daniel's. She would start slipping soon as the adrenaline wore off. So would the booze. But then, she finally heard something. The old garage. The big door was opening with loud creaks and scrapes that yearned for a can or two of WD-40. She steadied her camera and snapped. The door rolled up at a dramatically sluggish pace to reveal Covington. He bent beneath the half-opened garage door and lumbered out, carrying a big box of some sort. Or was it a stack of something? She zoomed in to see. It was a big stack of lumber. Thinner than two-by-fours but thicker than plywood. It looked to be pieces of wood flooring with smudges all over. He threw them into the rear of the Bronco and went back inside the garage. A moment passed and he was back with a roll of something. A rug. This, too, went into the Bronco.

A moment later, the garage opened the rest of the way and Covington emerged once more. He was followed closely by Remington. A tarp was between them as they were half-carrying, half-dragging something in it. They opened the police cruiser and struggled to get the package into the rear trunk.

It was a body. It was Derrick. It had to be. It was the right size. It was the right target. And Coral snapped it all on her camera. Two of the biggest investments she made in her life might actually pay off: the money she had invested in the camera and the time she had invested in tailing Remington. She knew he was fishy. She had him. She would publish then let the cops—excluding Covington—do the rest. First, she had to follow them to see where the body went. Then, she would storm home and write like her hair was on fire. Like her life depended on it. Because it might. One neighbor's stray camera spotting her in the street may lead to questions. Questions to Remington or the police, which would lead to Covington. She had to hurry. Her life *would* depend on it.

Coral watched the two men shake hands in front of the cruiser. Covington got in, started the engine, putting it in reverse. Coral bowed back into the bush, snapping pictures from her concealed position. Once the detective disappeared off the block, Coral felt safer. Ironic.

Remington returned to the garage once more and emerged with another person. He closed the garage behind them and put his arm around the other person's shoulder. The mysterious silhouette limped with Remington as they approached the Bronco. From the shadows of the hair and petite figure, it looked to be a female. Coral clicked away then looked at her screen and zoomed in. She could hardly believe it. It was the girl. The Shelby girl; Remington's niece. She was covered in blood and had the look of a soldier with PTSD in her eyes. Remington helped lift her up in to the passenger seat of the Bronco, tossing her a blanket before he started for the driver's seat.

Coral thought about dashing to her Civic to follow the Bronco. She would have to sprint, turn on her engine and dim the lights all before Remington pulled out. She glanced across the street to her trusty steed and back at the Bronco. Remington was already in the driver's seat, buckling his seatbelt. She had no chance at making it in time. Her hesitation cost her. It could prove to be a suicidal move to dash for the Civic now. She would have to wait them out.

The Bronco, all its lights turned off, reversed into the road and sped off into the night. Coral stood from the bushes, unsure of her next move. Unsure of what she had just witnessed. It was exactly what she wanted, yet she was at a loss of what to do next.

CHAPTER 42

Chase was driving now. He was fed up with his partner's incompetence and they rode in silence from the gas station they lost Diamond at. After they quickly determined their surveillance van was useless for the night and likely totaled, they abandoned it and hiked back to the gas station and waited. And waited. And waited.

Finally, the closest unit in the area dropped off a new car. Chase told the unit he did not "give two flying fucks what kind of car" it was, they just needed something there as soon as possible for a drug-related case, he lied. He regretted not specifying it needed to blend in when they ended up in a bright red Mini Cooper.

By the time they were back on the road, the men were hopelessly behind Derrick and they knew it; they just hoped their intel was right and they were right about his ultimate target. From bugging Derrick's phone, McGovern was able to get copies of Derrick's messages, albeit on a delay, and relay them to the team. The delay and relay strategy was due to the fact that the bug was not exactly *legal.* That is, they never got a court order or a judge to sign off on it. They did not have time and did not feel like playing politics, so they went low tech with the bug. That was how this whole case had gone given its secrecy. Despite the delay in messages coming through, they were informed shortly after boarding their new ride that Derrick was, in fact, heading to the Remington Charleston house. Apparently, he was under the impression that the Shelby girl was there.

The blood red Mini Cooper pulled Slightly North of Broad after four in the morning and cut its lights. They were on Remington's block and creeping toward the house. Sandler had broken the silence moments earlier when he spotted Derrick's stolen car a block over. They checked to make sure it was abandoned, as they assumed and carried on. He would be in the house; they were sure of it. He thought he was the hunter, but little did the killer know, he was merely the bait. Kept alive solely to catch the bigger fish.

"Hey! What's that?" Sandler practically yelled. He was pointing at a bush in front of the Remington house. A figure stumbled out of it, crossing the street fifty yards in front of them. They hoped it was Derrick, but it looked to be a woman based on the profile. She had something around her neck. Before she was halfway across the street, she spotted the unlit car and its two occupants. Chase and the woman locked eyes for a split-second before the woman bolted. She took off down the street, taking whatever was around her neck and clutching it in her hand. Chase turned on his high beams and floored it. The woman stood no chance. She was on the chunky side and the small car caught her before she managed to turn onto the adjacent street. Chase slowed and anticipated the woman giving up when she made a sharp turn and scaled a brick wall with the nimble quickness of a squirrel.

"Run for her!" Chase yelled at his colleague who nodded, waiting for the vehicle to slow. The car screeched to a halt and Sandler tumbled out after the woman. He jumped the fence and dove to the other side.

Unfortunately for Sandler, a koi pond was right where he intended on landing. He fell right into the water feature, killing at least two fish and swallowing what felt like a gallon of water. After getting his bearings, he stood up in the two feet of water and trudged out, shaking like a dog in the rain. He spotted the woman who had managed to avoid the water and was rushing out of a gate at the far side of the yard. Before Sandler could catch up, a pain shot through his leg. It took a moment before he realized a German Shepard had latched onto his thigh and was growling and shaking violently, teeth sunk in. Sandler shrieked in pain and threw punches at the dogs' fangs to no avail. Luckily for him, it was not a full-grown German Shepard and he was able to limp to the gate the woman had just exited with the dog still in tow. He slammed the gate on the dog and it finally let go, shriveling back to his yard, barking like hell. Sandler made sure the gate was shut before he was off. A voice shouted after him from the porch of home he had just trespassed. Without looking back, Sandler shouted, "FBI! Stay in your house!"

"Fuck you!" the voice on the porch bellowed.

Sandler found himself a street over from Remington's, across from a park. The girl was in the distance, hobbling and heaving behind a smattering of trees. Sandler kept after her until he began feeling lightheaded. He stopped and bent down to feel his thigh. The dog had sunk three teeth deep into the skin, practically strumming his hamstring. He was bleeding. A lot. His suit pants were torn and covered in blood. Sandler lowered himself down against a tree to catch his breath. Before his ass managed to hit the ground, he passed out.

Meanwhile, Chase was drifting, skirting and skidding through the streets of Charleston like it was *Need for Speed.* He was turning the wheel with such veracity he feared the little British car would give out or roll on him, but it held its own. Once on the next block, he peered out at the night for some sign of life. There she was on the other side of the park still at a light jog. His partner was nowhere to be found. That did not matter to Chase. His priority was this fugitive.

He floored it through the middle of the park until he was ten feet from the woman. He slowed and readied for a surrender, but none came. He knew just what to do and had done it half a dozen times before. He pressed his right foot hard on the gas, kept the wheel steady and stomped quickly on the brakes. The resulting maneuver was intended to whip the car into the fugitive and then quickly slam to a stop before running her over or doing serious damage. And it worked like a charm, leaving the woman writhing in the grass.

Chase put the car in park—in the middle of the park—and locked on the figure before him. He quickly flipped her over onto her back, pointing his gun at her chest.

"Who are you and why are you running from me?"

"I'm…. I'm sorry…. I'm…. just a…. reporter," the woman gasped out, huffing and puffing for oxygen.

"A reporter? Why the hell were you in those bushes?" Chase asked.

"Why'd…. you…. hit me with…. a fucking car?" she yelled out. She covered her face with outturned palms. "Please…. the gun."

Chase saw no threat from this gassed woman. She looked young. She also looked like she had not seen the inside of the gym in about ten years. He reached down and snatched what she had been grasping. An impressive camera was what she was holding for dear life.

"What're you some sort of National Enquirer, tabloid artist looking to peep through windows?" Chase tried turning on the camera, but only managed to snap a picture and momentarily stun himself. Thankfully, his gun had returned to its holster inside his suit jacket.

"No," the woman said, offended and scared. "I'm a real investigative journalist. I—hey. Why am I answering this. Why the fuck did you just chase me down in your Mini Cooper, hit me and hold a gun to my face? I'm gonna press charges, James Bond wannabe."

Chase whipped out his badge while playing with the camera he had appropriated. After giving up on the camera, he handed it back to the woman and studied her. She looked relieved.

"Thank God. I thought you were going to kill me. I thought you were with them."

"With who?"

"What? No one. Why are you in a Mini Cooper?"

"Long story. Now answer my question. Why were you in a bush this time of night? Who were you after?" Chase asked, irritated.

The woman sat up and returned an irritated scowl herself. "I don't have to answer your questions. I know my rights. Do you have a smoke? I think that's the least you can do right now for me. After hitting me with your fucking golf cart of a car here. You never identified yourself as a cop. Come to think of it, I think I felt a snap in my neck. Yeah, I think I did, *Agent.* I'll definitely press charges now. Uncle Sam will settle quick."

Chase rolled his eyes and returned to the Mini Cooper. He rummaged through the center console and produced a pack of Marlboros and a Bic lighter. He tossed them to the woman. "Now help me out here."

She lit a cigarette and took a long drag. She let out a deep exhale, like a surgeon that just finished a twenty-hour conjoined twin separation. She eyed Chase up and down as she took a second drag. "You tell me what you were doing and then I'll tell you."

"Look, lady. You see what time it is? I've had a long, few weeks here and I'm not playing games. I'll haul your ass in right now." Chase was bluffing. The last thing he wanted to add to his plate was an arrestee. He was not sure they could even have any arrested on this op. To top it all off, he thought of having to stuff her in his current ride. No thank you.

"I know my rights, Fibbie. I don't have to tell you shit. And I'm not. It's for my own protection. Probably yours too." She took another prolonged suck of the cigarette. "I think you may be against me on this, too. Enough of you boys in blue are."

Chase was getting pissed now. He had a feeling she was out there for Remington, too, but doubted she was a journalist. "Can I see some credentials on you?"

"What? You think I carry around a card or a fucking badge? I'm not a dweeb like you. It's not how it works with journalists, you idiot. Besides, for all I know, that badge could be fake."

Chase had had enough. He began reading the woman her Miranda Rights. He forced her against the pathetic car and produced a pair of handcuffs. He was not sure he had jurisdiction or any legal footing to stand on, but he did not care. It was nearly sunrise and he had already had a day. He was bringing this little bitch in. Where? He was not quite sure.

"You've got to be kidding me," she grumbled. "Don't you have to go grab your egghead of a partner?"

"Where is he?" Chase asked after securing the cuffs on too tight for comfort. The girl pointed with a nod toward the other end of the park. He turned to see a body slumped against a tree a few hundred yards away. "The fuck you do to him in the thirty seconds he was alone?"

"Not me. I think the Remington neighbor's dog got him." The woman said nonchalantly, not realizing what she had said. Chase perked up. She may actually be a reporter. She may have seen or heard something. The camera! He had to bring her in now. They were there for the same reason. She had something on that camera she was protecting. Something that would help him.

CHAPTER 43

Coral finally caught her breath ten minutes into her ride as a detainee. The older agent had made her dump the cigarette and this irked her. She was being detained for no reason and she was beginning to think she actually had a lawsuit in the works. She slouched deep in her seat and closed her eyes. She was exhausted from the eventful night. The sun would be up soon and she had not slept a wink. The decision on how to answer questions from the agents in the front seat would be made after a short nap. Or a long one. She had no idea where they were going.

After Old Agent had cuffed and put her in the back of the Mini Cooper, she turned and watched as he went to fetch the younger agent. Old Agent appeared furious and embarrassed at his partner and it showed by the slow pace at which he took to help him. While Coral thought it was karma that a dog snagged the man chasing her, she felt slightly bad for the man at the mercy of Old Agent's wrath. It looked as though he had passed out from loss of blood because by the time he was in the front seat of the Mini Cooper, Old Agent had put a makeshift tourniquet on the mangled leg. She changed her tune quickly when Young Agent was slouched in front of her. She doubled over with laughter.

"Did you fall in that little koi pond? My God, that's fun. I spotted it at the top of the fence and managed to avoid it. Figured a skilled Quantico boy like you would be able to spot a pond! Ha! Jesus Christ that's funny. I wish I had turned around to watch it all happen."

"Keep your mouth shut back there," Old Agent had snarled as he climbed into the driver's seat. Young Agent ignored Coral as he slipped into a hoodie that said FBI.

"You see, if you were wearing that hoodie before maybe we could've avoided all this. The water. The dog. The high dollar lawsuit." Coral laughed to herself. Old Agent put the car in drive and shot Young Agent a dirty look. Young Agent ignored it by staring out the window, disgruntled. They had all clearly had a long night.

"Wake up," a voice demanded after what felt like just a moment after she dozed off. Coral's body ached and the light irritated her eyes as she squinted them open. She could see the sun barely peaking over a building out of her Mini Cooper window. Young Agent was gently shaking her, standing at the open car door. "Come on. I took your handcuffs off. Let's go."

Coral looked down and rubbed her naked wrists. She peered around the car for her camera and phone. She had neither. She was about to ask, then thought better of it. They were not handing either back. She stood up and followed Young Agent into a motel room on the first floor of a dump. Old Agent had led the way with Coral's camera around his neck as Young Agent led her to a bed and told her to lay down. The room was cramped, old and smelled of stale cigarettes. There were two queen beds, a lopsided desk and some other mismatched and stained furniture strewn haphazardly about the room. It was a real eyesore. Coral began to get nervous.

"Can I see your badges? Why are we in some shitty motel room? I feel like I'm on some cheap gotcha television show."

Young Agent hiked a hand up his sweatshirt and retrieved a small leather folio. He handed it to Coral then proceeded to undress his upper body. For some strange reason, he had put the sweatshirt over his wet suit jacket. Coral ignored the badge for a second and watched Young Agent's bare body before her. He was a bag of bones. No wonder a dog made him pass out.

"We're agents, I can assure you, ma'am. We never got a name from you. What is your name?" Old Agent tossed his badge to her. She studied both the badges. Old Agent's was badly weathered and tarnished. Young Agent's was pristine, but wet. She was terrible with names and did not bother clocking either's. She memorized the numbers instead, her specialty. From the look of them, they were real. But what did she know. She was a bit relieved knowing that both men seemed like every other Fibbie she encountered. And at least they were in suits.

"Coral Sands."

"Come on, lady. If you're going to give us a fake name, at least think of a good one," Old Agent scoffed.

"Look me up. *Low Country Ledger*." She eased into the mattress, fluffing a pillow with her head.

Young Agent emerged from the bathroom with FBI sweatpants that matched the sweatshirt he had shed. He was drying himself with a towel as he nodded, looking at his phone. He handed it to his partner without a word. Old Agent nodded smugly.

"Put on some clothes, Sandler. There's a lady present. Come on." He turned to Coral. "Alright, Coral. I have a feeling our priorities and goals are aligned here. Did you snap any useful pictures tonight?"

Old Agent held up Coral's camera as Young Agent put his full sweatsuit on. It was a comical scene when she took a step back to take it all in: an old Fibbie in a suit and tie, a young Fibbie in an oversized FBI sweatsuit, sopping wet, and a struggling journalist all in a dingey motel somewhere in or near Charleston County. She felt like this was how Watergate broke.

"Come on, Coral. Just talk to us. We don't want to make this harder than it has to be."

Was this a threat? Coral was not sure how to approach the question. Despite Remington clearly having cops like Covington on his payroll, these two did not strike her as Remington fans. Still, how could she know if she could trust them? Remington was clearly well connected. Anything she said could lead right back to him and send her to an early grave.

"Well, why don't we start then?" Old Agent offered as he took a seat in the desk chair at the foot of her bed. "You mentioned Remington earlier without realizing it—Freudian slip there—so that's who I think you're writing a story about. Seeing as how you were in a bush outside his second home with a camera at four in the morning, it's safe to say this story isn't going to be a flattering one. Am I on the right track?"

Coral remained stone-faced as Old Agent smirked. She had let him spill his secrets first.

CHAPTER 44

Robert gripped the steering wheel tight with such intense pressure he thought it was going to bend in his fingers. The night was not supposed to unfold this way. He was not supposed to cause more pain for his niece. This was supposed to ease her pain, put her mind at rest. Now, she was a zombie in the passenger seat of his Bronco. Her eyes were wide open but no one was home. He kept glancing from the road to her, thinking her expression might change but it never did. He hoped for any change. A few words. Some tears. Anything. She remained expressionless.

The girl had killed Derrick herself after smuggling herself in Robert's Bronco. She did it by accident. The smuggling, not the killing. That was all he managed to get out of her. She could not sleep, heard noises, got in the car and Robert pulled off, none the wiser regarding his stowaway. She was curious. Why would her uncle be driving so late at night? Where could he be going? Perfectly logical questions.

Robert ran through the scene a hundred time in his head already. It was an endless loop in his mind. What could he have done differently? He could have checked his car for one thing. Or maybe not played with his prey.

Replaying it all in his mind, one big blur and also like a four-dimensional movie, simultaneously. All the same. He had walked in, surprised Derrick and the brawl begun. Robert was trying to get Derrick's hands tied to begin the abuser's slow death. It had become more difficult with age and his age was on full display that night against the massive foe. Robert wanted Derrick to suffer, but did not have the strength of his youth to aid him against the massive man. In his estimation, Robert knew Derrick had to die, but the man did not deserve a pain-free passing.

Before Robert could manage to get the oversized hands of the abuser knotted, Derrick broke free and darted from the room that was staged for the killing. Tarps were down, a table set up and all. That's when Rose arrived. She did not see the room before Derrick grabbed her, but she broke free, God bless her. Then she shot him. Over and over. And over. Robert had not fired a single bullet that evening. Had not plunged a single blade into flesh. He had landed a few punches before Rose arrived and that was it. After Rose committed the homicide, Robert snapped into clean up mode. He was a fixer and he had done it before. In fact, he had done it a dozen times, just never with an unwitting third party like his niece.

He had to calm her down first. He called Covington and made him drive over. Robert tried to console the girl but she just sat in silence after he had pried the gun from her hands. A few guttural moans rang from somewhere deep inside her after a few minutes. Then more silence. The girl was in shock.

At least Caroline knew what had happened, Robert thought. Or at least the intent of what was to occur that evening. He did not have to hide anything in the house. Only from the nurse. Nurse Blanchard. They would have to ease Rose back into normalcy. Blame any shock on the death of her mother. Convince her not to talk. Derrick deserved to die, they would say. It was an accident. An accident for the betterment of the world, they would say. It's exactly what Jenny would have wanted, they would lie.

Robert pulled into the driveway and prepared to carry the girl to her bed. He took the keys from the ignition and before he could get out the girl escaped. She got to her knees on the front lawn and threw up. It was all hitting her. He knelt down and held her hair. Then he led her inside, made her a cup of tea and put her in her bed. The sun would be up soon and he hoped the girl would sleep the day away and process everything another night.

After closing her door in silence, he sat at the island countertop and pondered the night. He was scared. He was sure the girl was twice as scared. Nothing to be done now. They would talk in the morning.

CHAPTER 45

The desert heat had turned Country into a killing machine. All he thought about was killing more Iraqis. The lines in the sand were drawn and the sides were clear: Iraq wanted Western blood and that was it. The Americans and the rest of the West, Country had decided, were just trying to keep the peace for the world. It had not even been fifty years since the end of World War II, the Cold War had just ended and it seemed that Saddam Hussein was the next coming of Hitler and Stalin—maybe combined, Country thought. What would become known as the Gulf War involved the largest military alliance of countries since World War II. The U.S., U.K., and France were all fighting side by side. Country and his fellow countrymen would be on the right side of history, though Country would never be the same man after returning home. The Gulf War had changed his DNA.

He had been in Saudi Arabia and Iraq for seven months. Just across the border from Country's position, Hussein had installed his own cousin as the "leader" of Iraq's nineteenth province: Kuwait. America's initial intention was a wholly defensive campaign to help protect Saudi Arabia. That all ended quickly and the U.S. begun bombing Iraq from the air. Country's fellow soldiers soon breached the Iraqi border and began a ground assault after softening the defenses from the air. Country was one of the men on the ground—not in tanks—storming through the country and killing all in his sight. The Iraqis were putting up a fight, but stood no chance against America's might. Country estimated he had killed fifty Iraqis himself, most with his gun, some with his knife and some with his bare hands. He relished every moment. It made him feel exhilarated in a way he never felt before.

Country sipped his beer and cleaned his gun while the radio blasted Metallica. They had set up a makeshift camp and were hunkered down for the night. He took a draw from his cigar, puffed smoke and filched in his surroundings. Half a dozen of his fellow Army men were doing the same before bedding down for the night. Or before continuing the drinking and card playing a bit longer. He smiled to himself thinking that this beat the hell out any courtroom he had been in. He missed his wife, but other than that, this was the happiest he had been in a long time.

"How many you nab today, Country?" Carter, a soldier from the backwoods of Mississippi, asked with glee.

"I reckon I counted at least five more today. Watched the bullets lodge right into the windpipe of one poor sucker," he beamed with pride.

"Damn. And you love it don't you?"

"Something feels right about killing. Like I was born to do it, under the right circumstances. I mean, I read that story about these Iraqis raping that village a while back and that was all the reason I needed to turn savage. Don't you feel the same way?"

"I mean, they're still people. Still got they families, gods, and what not. I feel a little bad. We all gonna be judged by the good Lord one day. I just hope we're in the right, ya know?"

"Myself? I can't stand the killing." Carolina was playing cards and drinking from a bottle of Jack Daniel's.

"Oh, really? Then why're you here?" Country asked with hidden rage. He had grown apart from his former friend. Carolina had begun drinking more every night, was aggressive with everyone in the unit and was frequenting brothels behind enemy lines whenever he could sneak off. Country had heard a rumor that the man never paid at the brothels, just threatened the girls with a knife each time. He detested what Carolina had become.

"Don't know." Was all Carolina managed to mumble. He turned up the bottle of Jack in his hand and drained the equivalent of three shots in one big gulp. His expression never changed. "You know, I remember seeing something on the Saudi news about some bodies they found of Saudi kids months back. It was about the time we arrived over here. They were full of bullets. American bullets. If you love killing so much, maybe you know what happened there, Big ole Country"

Country slammed his gun to his cot, stood up and growled. "If you're going to make accusations like that, why don't you come say it to my fucking face, you coward."

Carolina did not move from his spot or turn his head to meet Country's gaze just a few feet away at the foot of his own cot. He simply downed another three shots and kept playing with the cards on his bed.

"Why's it bother you so much, if you didn't do it, son?"

"I don't touch women or children, you scumbag. I have a code, okay?" Country said, stomping toward Carolina. Carter and the other men in the bunkhouse stood ready for an altercation.

"Calm down boys. Carolina, ease up on the sauce for once, would you? You've been a real pisser lately," one man stated coolly.

"Yeah. Whatever," Carolina snarled. Country returned to his bed and gun. He had had enough of Carolina. Country helped him out of a jam and now Carolina was trying to frame him for it.

Carolina would go AWOL that night and Country would not see or hear from him for years. Country could not have known it at the time, but the next time they met, one of the men would be killed by the other.

CHAPTER 46

"You must be quite the poker player, Coral," Old Agent smiled. He was friendly and menacing at the same time. Coral could not tell if it was an act, if he was naturally condescending or if he just lacked true people skills. "I'll continue. Stop me at any point if you'd like to share—or add—anything.

"Robert Remington has been quite the fleeting figure for our boss. Special Agent in Charge of our field office, Darlene McGovern, has had quite the hardon for Mr. Remington for a number of years. You see, years back, a sitting South Carolina Senator, Senator Arthur McDonough, was shot and killed. Execution style. It occurred in the Senator's *own home* just outside the city limits of Columbia, South Carolina. The facts were scarce but, it being the first sitting United States Senator to be assassinated since Bobby Kennedy in sixty-eight, the Feds were called in and took over. The local boys couldn't handle the media circus on this let alone that circus *and* the investigation. Well, it turned out even the Feds couldn't handle it. Dead end after dead end. The only physical clues—if you could even call them clues—they had to go off were the fact that the assassin must've known the Senator since there was no forced entry and that around the time of the bullet entering Senator McDonough's forehead, a small knife stabbed his abdomen."

"What about the Secret Service? Or family members in the home?" Coral interjected. She vaguely remembered Senator McDonough's assassination, but it was just a blip on her radar then. What did this have to do with Remington?

"You're asking the right questions, Miss Sands. Arthur McDonough was a military veteran and gun enthusiast. He refused Secret Service access to his private property, stating on numerous public occasions that he could kill any intruder on his own. Obviously, this turned out to not be the case at all. As for family, the Senator was known as quite the skirt chaser. He was rumored to have affairs with various political friends and enemies alike, but never married. As far as authorities could surmise, he was alone that evening. It was a Tuesday night, mid-Summer and Congress was out of session. No contentious bills were coming before the Senate and the Senator hadn't done or said anything out of the ordinary prior to his assassination. He had no aspirations for higher office from what we could gather and re-election was still a few years off. The Senate majority was firmly in his party's favor and him being ousted wouldn't make a difference. From all accounts, this was from out of the blue."

"Maybe someone found out about the affairs? A jealous husband. A jealous lover." Coral was intrigued, but still at a loss. Did they think Remington killed the Senator?

"Good hypothesis, but all avenues there were exhausted. Everyone had *airtight* alibis. There were really three couples the Feds locked in on. Another Senator and her husband, a staffer and his wife and a Low Country attorney and his wife. We're pretty sure they were the most intense, secret affairs the Senator was involved in. But nothing."

Coral nodded, finally seeing the connection. At least she thought.

"No, no. Different attorney. Not Remington. I'll get to that. Now, there were some other loose theories about a sex trafficking ring, spurned business partners and some nephew who would inherit the Senator's fortune—though it would mostly go to various banks thanks to his lavish spending habits.

"The case was dropped. Never formally, but behind the scenes: dropped. We had nothing. I remember working on it as a young Fibbie, thinking I'd crack it. After a while, I was convinced it was a CIA job. Why? I don't know. Felt JFK-esque. A *sexy* theory, you know?

"Years of nothing go by. No substantive tips. I move on to other cases and my life keeps going. Agent McGovern, on the other hand, never let it go. She was a few years ahead of me at Quantico and was obsessed with it from the day it happened. It would be like solving the JFK assassination for her. You see, she's born and raised in South Carolina. She had a rough go as a kid here, but for some reason loves South Carolina to its core. Thought the assassination was an affront to her and the whole state. Now, on paper, we're not working it at all, you see? For reasons you'll understand shortly. Darlene, though, keeps us on it with any spare time we have. Me, Sandler here and our buddy, Agent Quincy and two other agents. We've got to log our time and expenses to other cases, but we stay on this one."

"Where the hell does Remington come into play?"

"Okay, okay. So, with all other angles exhausted, Darlene pulls some strings and gets the Senator's military records. They were redacted and expunged for some reason. I still don't know why. None of us do because the records are normal. One tour, then comes back, hops into law and politics and then he climbs the ladder to Senator McDonough. Okay, so where to go now? Only one tour is a bit unusual, but he played it off as an injury keeping him form serving more. With just one tour, we're able to quickly look at all those he served with. A few fellow soldiers look like good fits, but all come up as empty leads. Including Remington, who served that sole tour with him. Months go by and we're losing hope and interest. The murder had been years earlier and we had nothing. But then we keep seeing Remington's name in the court dockets, followed by obituaries of defendants or affiliated parties of those lawsuits—"

"Winding up dead," Coral finished his sentence.

CHAPTER 47

Old Agent flashed a toothy grin and pointed. "I told you we were onto the same scent!"

"So, why do you think he killed the Senator? From what I can gather, the only people who have wound up dead are the people who clearly committed some crime. Usually a heinous crime. Like they killed someone or child abuse or something. I don't see the correlation beyond they served in war together." Coral stopped herself and thought for a moment before continuing. "You think the Senator did something overseas when they served together?"

"That's one theory yes. Darlene doesn't buy that one. From Remington's pattern, he would have just killed the man overseas. He wouldn't have waited years, until he was a Senator and then done it on American soil."

"Then what's the other theory?"

"This is the reason why we have to work the case quietly. Remington is a wealthy man. Wealthier than his bank accounts lead you to believe. Wealthier than any Low Country defense attorney should be. He's even wealthier than what the managing partner at a white shoe firm in New York would be."

"Murder for hire," Coral blurted out. "You think he killed the Senator for cash. You think he doesn't just kill for a righteous cause or karma; he kills for cash."

"Bingo."

"Then why do you need to keep it quiet?"

"The Director of the FBI. Before he was Director, he was a member of the House of Representatives. Representative Ralph Marconi. He represented District 1. Charleston. His biggest donor? A super PAC tied to none other than Robert Remington. We believe that Representative Marconi paid Remington—who we know for a fact are friends and were classmates in college—to kill Senator McDonough so he could run for that seat. Let me rephrase that: he would be *selected* by the Governor to replace McDonough for the remainder of the term, then he would be the incumbent and difficult to defeat."

Coral sat in silence and let it sink in. It was too far-fetched for her. It was all speculation and loose ends. If she pitched this to her editor, he would laugh her out of the building. She could see why they had made no moves to arrest the man.

"Why wasn't he tapped at Senator?" The obvious question.

"Another hole in our theory. We think Marconi may have thought too highly of himself and overestimated his value to the then-Governor. The murder-for-hire ended up being for naught. But Remington got paid nonetheless because Marconi has family money."

"I don't know. That's a lot. Haven't you been able to get anything on phone calls, wire taps, any of your surveillance shit we plebeians know nothing about?"

"We don't get any of that on the books. We'll set a wiretap here or there on the downlow, but we can't use anything we get as evidence. A judge never signs off because we don't want Marconi wise to us." Old Agent shook his head, stood up and stretched. "Besides, Remington is too smart to say anything on the phone."

"Well, now you can take him in. I know for a fact he killed Derrick Diamond tonight," Coral stated proudly.

"And that leads us to why we took you here. Do you have pictures of him doing it?"

Coral got up from her bed and snatched the camera from the desk behind Old Agent. She flipped it on and scrolled through the pictures. Both agents peered over her shoulder as she spun through, narrating as she went. She recounted her night, Covington's arrival, the flooring being removed, the body and the girl.

"The girl was with him?" Young Agent spoke up for the first time in a while.

"Yes. Here she is in these few pictures. I only saw her exit the garage with Remington. But she had to have known about the murder that just took place." She gazed at each agent, waiting for them to weigh in on the legality and whether they had a case.

"I mean, yes. However, we need more. That's a good angle though. We get the girl to spill to us," Old Agent said to himself, scratching his head like a caricature.

"I don't understand. Why don't you just take him in. Remington. Question him. You get him on this murder and make him spill about the other murder." She felt like a better Fed than both agents in the room.

"We've tried before," Old Agent shook his head.

"What do you mean you've tried? We have evidence here! Circumstantial, but still."

"We've had more evidence than this and he lawyers his way out. We know of at least seven deaths that can be traced to Robert Remington. We've brought him in on three. All three were ironclad cases. He quietly got them quashed. Never spent a second in prison. Was never arrested. Never talked. Never admitted a thing."

Coral was flabbergasted. The Federal Bureau of Investigation first said they could not investigate the murder of a sitting United States Senator openly because the *Director* of the FBI was tied to it. Now they were telling her they could link a man to seven deaths and had not made any progress in arresting him.

"What the fuck?" Coral screeched. "Okay. Well, I'll get my story in print with some pictures and it should shake the leaves on this. It'll get the facts out there and no—"

"No!" Old Agent yelled. "You cannot publish anything on this. It will ruin our investigation."

"What investigation? You're not investigating anything! You've gotten nowhere!"

"You don't understand. We're using the smaller fish to nail the bigger fish," Old Agent could tell he was not getting through to Coral. "What I mean to say is we don't give a shit about murders of some low-life scumbags. From all accounts every death linked to Remington was deserved, *except* Senator McDonough. If he were linked to deaths of innocent people, maybe we'd have already acted. But, take Diamond for instance. You think the world is better off with him in it, or six feet under? Exactly. This is what I mean."

Coral was still processing. Her mind was blazing through the facts she had just been given. So many holes. She did not even believe the Senator link, let alone think she should hold off publishing her work. These men were crazy.

"Look. I'm going to publish my article and my pictures. However, you proceed from there, so be it. But you can't stop me."

Young Agent looked at Old Agent with worry.

"You can't impede my First Amendment right, gentlemen. You know that. Now if you could please let me go, that would be ideal."

CHAPTER 48

"Oh my God, Robert. How could you possibly let this happen?" Caroline scolded. "Do you understand what you just did to that girl? All she's been through already and now she has to live with this on her conscience? She's not like you! She shouldn't have to go through the rest of her life knowing she's a killer! She's just a girl, Robert."

"I know, Caroline. I know. You think I drew it up this way? Because I sure as hell didn't in case you were wondering." Robert was fuming at the mere, ironic fact that his wife was fuming. "You know, I wasn't the one who even wanted to go through with this. This was your call."

"Oh, so now you're going to blame it all on me? Come on, Robert. You've killed so many people and I turned a blind eye and now I open my mouth once and I'm the problem. Don't take me for a fool!" Tensions were escalating. They were arguing about Rose yet had no resolution for how to handle it with the girl. If Rose were anyone else stowing away in his Bronco then witnessing Robert try to kill someone, Robert would have simply killed him. But he had a standard—he refused to kill women or children. So obviously a female child in his own family was not going to be a casualty of his bloody habits.

"Okay. Okay. We need to take a step back, take deep breaths and calm down. We need a solution, not bickering. This won't help." Robert played the peacemaker. He was lawyering. "Now, the issue is Rose: she's seen and actually *done* too much. We need to make sure she stays quiet about all of this and also that she doesn't spiral."

"Yes. Agreed on all counts."

"Alright. I think you need to turn a blind eye. Pretend you haven't a clue about this all."

"Why?"

"Well, then you have plausible deniability in any worst-case scenario. I need to deal with it as if it is only her and I in this. You can keep playing the dead mother card and coddling her and being therapeutic that way. Just in no way hint that you know about Derrick."

Caroline pondered for a moment before nodding. "You're right."

***

It was the morning after Rose pulled that trigger. The girl had barely slept, though that was nothing new in recent weeks. The cause of her insomnia, however, was the real new part. She had showered and was getting ready for a trip down to the beach with Nurse Blanchard. They had planned to sit and eat breakfast with Caroline and Robert before leaving, but the girl had no appetite so she lingered in her room a bit longer. She had a feeling she would not be hungry for quite some time.

After she pulled on a pair of jean shorts and a linen button down over her bathing suit, there was a soft knock at the door.

"Come in."

Robert entered with an empathetic smile. "You mind if we have a talk?"

Rose nodded. She figured it was coming and was relieved. She wanted to talk to someone about it and Robert was the only one she could talk to. She just feared how he was planning to handle it. If he could kill so easily, would he kill her? "Yes, please. I need to talk."

"I don't want you to blame yourself at all for last night," Robert said, taking a seat in the old wooden rocking chair by the window. He waved an arm for her to sit on the bed across from him and she did.

"Why were you there?" Rose asked pointedly, though she at least thought she knew. She's asking the tough questions; this may be a good sign, Robert thought to himself. Better than silence.

"Well, you're a smart girl so I won't lie to you. I think you deserve the truth. I knew Derrick was heading down to the Shelby house. I was expecting him sometime last night and the cameras at the property alerted my phone."

"You invited him there?"

"In a sense," Robert hesitated. He was wading into dangerous waters.

"What does that mean?"

'Well. You see, from all my years as a defense attorney I met a lot of people in law enforcement. I became friendly with quite a few, too."

"Like Mr. Covington."

"Exactly. So when I heard Derrick had escaped, I simply asked some of my friends to keep an eye out him. Well, they were able to figure out he was headed down to the Low Country here and—"

"But why?" Rose interrupted.

"Well, he wanted to get to you, Rose. To hurt you." Robert stated gently. The girl took it all in stride.

"Okay. And you knew this?" She pushed.

"Yes, but I made sure to make him think we were at the empty Charleston house. He didn't know anything about this house. Sully's." Robert paused to see if any questions came. When none did, the girl nodded slowly and he continued. "Well, you see, I tried to kind of bait him. I wanted him to go to that Charleston house looking for you. Then I'd show up and get him."

"So you wanted to kill him?" The tough question. Robert had rehearsed his calculated lie.

"Well. I wanted to hurt him. He hurt your mother and you and I wanted revenge. Then Detective Covington would come and arrest him so he could spend the rest of his miserable life in jail where he couldn't hurt anyone."

"But then I shot him." Rose said was an uneasy calmness about her. She said it as if she was talking about taking an algebra exam or eating a piece of toast.

"Hey. Listen to me. You never, ever have to tell anyone that. Ever. If you ever need to talk about it, it's just you and me. I'm an accessory and just as guilty as you. I have just as much at stake so don't you ever, *ever* think you're alone in this."

"I don't know. Shouldn't we tell the police? Well, the *other* police. Besides Mr. Covington."

"We can't, Rose. They'll arrest us and put us behind bars. We can't tell anyone."

Rose digested the statement for a moment before letting out a sigh. "Okay.... So what now? I mean, someone will say Derrick must be dead. The police will catch us."

"No, no. People like Derrick disappear all the time. He has no real family or real friends. The police will keep looking for him like he's a fugitive—which he is—until they quietly close the case and move on. No one will lose sleep over that scumbag."

Rose nodded. More silence. She was a quiet thinker. Most young people seemed to blurt out whatever came to mind. Not Rose. And Robert liked this. She would not easily talk. It would take time, but they would need to build a trust in each other. A code of trusted silence.

"That all makes sense. Can I tell you something, Mr. Remington?"

"Sure thing. But call me Robert or Uncle Bobby or something."

"I'm glad I killed him. I mean, I feel uneasy about having shot someone. About having killed someone and taken a life. But I'd envisioned killing Derrick dozens of times. I never had the courage to. I'm just sorry I didn't do it sooner."

Robert smiled. He got up and patted the girl on the back. "Me too, Rose. Me too."

CHAPTER 49

"Chase, how's it progressing down there? Did you nail him? Tell me we've got leverage." Agent McGovern was hyper on the other end of the line.

"That's not exactly why I'm calling, Darlene." Chase said. She knew there was an issue when Chase used her first name.

"Okay. Spit it out."

Chase quickly recounted the last twelve or so hours. The tailing of Derrick. The broken-down van. Missing Derrick and Remington's encounter. Coral Sands. The photos she took. How Remington almost certainly killed Derrick. Covington's arrival. The fact that the journalist knew all about Remington—minus the Senator link. He strategically left out the Mini Cooper, though. His boss would not find it comical.

"We have photos then? From this journalist? Where is she?"

"That's the most imminent issue at the moment, Darlene. She has photos from outside. Nothing with Derrick in them. In some, we think that Detective Covington and

Remington are carrying the corpse of Derrick out. Other than that, nothing definitive."

"But…?" She asked.

"But we had to let Coral go. We had no probable cause to detain. And she took her camera and photos with her. Sandler managed to copy the drive so we have them too, but—"

"But she's going to run the photos. Run a story. How much does she know, Chase?"

"Everything. She's been on his tail for years. Knew as much as us. A bit more in some areas. She wouldn't talk at first so we proved to her we already knew. Mentioned the tie in to the Senator. She didn't have that, but was skeptical of our—"

"What! She didn't know about the Senator angle and you spoon fed it to a journalist! Chase, are you fucking insane?" She blared through the phone. Chase raised a hand to his Bluetooth headphone and pulled one out at her shrieks.

"Darlene. I made a tactical decision based on the information I had. I needed to know why she was there. She wasn't spilling. I was afraid she was private contractor. Another alphabet boy. An agency. Or who knows what."

"Alright, Einstein. So now where does this leave us. Since the decision you made was tactical and all."

"Well, she's going to run something. I suggest we go to a judge and get an injunction—"

"Chase. After all this time you know we can't bring a Federal judge into this. Next option." She said curtly.

"Uh. I guess we can let her run it and—"

"Worse than the first idea. Next."

"Darlene, you've gotta play ball with me here. A journalist beat us to the scoop. It's happened before. Remember Rodriguez? The drug thing? Let her run it and maybe she'll shake some cobwebs loose. I can make for damn certain that she doesn't mention us." There was a long pause. "I think this is the route we've gotta take. We deal with the hand we've been dealt. A good journalist did her job and arrived at the same place we're at. Now we've got to finish the job."

"Right and wrong, Chase. You've got to finish the job. And you know exactly what I mean."

Chase was afraid of this. He sighed heavily and paced the length of the motel parking lot. He glanced at Sandler who sat in the passenger seat of the Mini-Cooper a few yards away. He was watching as Chase nodded his head. Sandler grimaced.

"Doesn't that make us just as bad as him then, Darlene? We can't do that. We can control her. Trust me." Chase was pleading.

"Quincy just handed me the file on her." Darlene's voice echoed as she switched to speaker phone. "Nothing heavy. She's an alcy though. Use that to your advantage. I'll come up with something to handle the niece. She saw something and we need to know. She's our next chess piece."

Agent McGovern hung up the phone without waiting for a reply.

CHAPTER 50

Coral had a feeling her time was limited. How limited? She was not sure. She was all but positive she would be pressured to dump the story. Maybe a judge would step in and force her. Maybe the FBI would break down her door and hold her in a jail cell. Maybe the CIA would swing through a window and shoot her. She shook her head. Her hyperbolic nature would get the best of her one day. Realistically, they would probably pressure her boss to force an end to the expose. She needed to finish the story and publish before that could happen.

She had been up over twenty-four hours and it was beginning to show in her writing. She sat hunched over her ancient laptop pecking away at the boisterous keyboard, using the backspace key more than usual. She had written up to deadlines before, just never self-imposed ones. Or FBI-imposed ones. Coral had the framework of a story in her laptop for over a year now. It would end up taking up half of the front page and continue in the centerfold for its entirety. She had left placeholders for photos—which she now had—and needed to fill in some holes in her story with her newfound information from the FBI and the actions of Remington earlier that morning. She waivered back and forth all morning on whether to mention the Senator. Or the FBI. She was leaning toward leaving out the FBI, but including the Senator. What troubled her was she could not figure out how to discuss the Senator angle organically. She did not understand why Remington would kill strictly those who objectively deserved it the most, then a sitting Senator. She had read as much as she could on the Senator and his voting record, but nothing popped out at her. It did not fit the pattern. Or her neat and tidy story. She needed more time and time was the one thing she did not have.

After reading her first "final" draft, Coral made the decision that she would allude to the Senator and the loose connections. She typed up:

> *A source close to the investigation of the execution-style murder of South Carolina Senator Arthur McGovern in his home in 2007 has confirmed that some sects of law enforcement believe there to be a connection between Remington and the murder. The source, who wishes to remain anonymous, lists Remington as the prime person of interest in the cold case. This is an ongoing story. Check back for updates.*

With the advent of online, real-time stories, Coral felt comfortable throwing in this last bit about Remington and the Senator. She wrote it to make it seem as if she would have another story on the Senator soon. This was not true at the moment, but it bought her time, as that was her enemy at the moment and she needed to publish what she could.

A knock on her door startled her. She was not expecting anyone so she snatched a putter she kept behind her bedroom door before jogging lightly to the peephole. Agent Chase was smiling on the other side holding a big bottle of Grey Goose. Coral unlocked the door, pulled the security chain off and peered suspiciously at Chase and Sandler, the latter of which was standing beside the older agent. Before they dropped her off at her car later that morning, she managed to secure their names. She had to in case she wanted to include in them in the story.

"What do you want?" She sneered suspiciously. "Wait. Don't answer that. I know what you want. I've already written the story. I'm on my way to my office now. It'll be out in tomorrow's edition. Maybe even online tonight." She was bluffing. It likely wouldn't be out for another couple of days. During that time, she would be arguing with and eventually persuading her editor all her facts were buttoned up and any libel suit would fall on deaf ears of any judge.

"You know why we're here. We have a duty to at least try to convince you to put country over fame and fortune. That story will blow up this whole investigation and you know it. We brought a small token of our gratitude for you to consider holding back at least one more week." Chase flashed the giant bottle. Coral snatched it from his hand and carried it to the kitchen. She left the door ajar behind her and Chase followed. Sandler remained stationed at his post outside.

"We've all had a long night. Thank you for the gift. I'll consider as I taste it. Do you boys want any?" she said as she opened the bottle and poured some on ice and soda.

"We're both teetotalers, I'm afraid." Chase said, shaking his head and holding up a hand. He was lying. He wanted some of that vodka more than Coral did. Maybe not that much, he was not a raging alcoholic, just an overworked, stressed agent. Either way, he would not drink from the bottle her just gave the woman. Not after what they had spiked it with outside. She had about twenty minutes. "Wasn't even quite sure what to buy. Haven't been in a liquor store in quite some time. Hope you like it."

"Good. More for me." Her drink disappeared in one sip and she poured another. "How'd you know I wasn't a sober yahoo like you both?"

"We're the FBI, ma'am," Chase said with a smile.

"Gentlemen, I know you're stalling for time," she said after downing another couple of drinks and placing the bottle in a barren freezer. The apartment was dark, sad and cramped, even for just one person, Chase thought. After seeing the empty freezer and sorry fridge, he felt even worse. Maybe they were doing the woman a favor. The way she was downing liquor on a weekday morning, he was becoming more and more positive of that fact.

"If you don't mind, I'm going to be on my way and I'd prefer if you both weren't here when I returned. So if we could all file out now." Chase led the way to the door as Coral grabbed her laptop and keys.

"Alright, Miss Sands. Just please give us a call if you change your mind. You'd make a lot of people very happy."

Coral nodded and jogged down the stairs toward her car. She sure hoped Chase was right and she was choosing fame and fortune.

***

Detective Covington could not call out sick. His squad car had been spotted out and about that morning and when a call came in about a robbery in Mount Pleasant, he had to respond. He needed to keep up appearances. The problem was, he had not slept a wink. Oh, and there was a dead body in his trunk.

After leaving Robert and his niece, Detective Covington went back to his side piece's apartment. She was a new side piece and she had brought out all the toys for them to play with earlier that night. They had played a bit before Robert rudely interrupted them, but the price was right and he would not turn down Robert. They had too much on each other. As for leaving the side piece hanging? He was not going to pass up the opportunity with his wife and kids out of town until the next day. He needed to play all he could, so he shrunk back to her apartment as soon as he could.

This meant leaving Derrick's body in his trunk. It was not the first time he had pulled a stunt like this. Once, he left two cold, decaying bodies in his trunk for a week before disposing of them. Time was never really of the essence. He was a cop, he had cover; no one would bother him. Besides, Robert had told him to get rid of Derrick's body as soon as possible, but did not want to know how Covington did it or where. To Covington, that meant it was all at his discretion. And his *indiscretions* were guiding him at the moment. So, when he rolled over and answered his phone off his side piece's nightstand, he was not the least bit worried about going to work with Derrick in tow.

After sharing a passionate kiss as if he was a sailor off to the Pacific in 1943, Covington gargled mouthwash in his driver's seat, swallowed it and was off to the nearest coffee spot. Where that was? His phone would need to tell him because he was unfamiliar with this area of Mount Pleasant. After punching it in and seeing it was two miles away, he was off.

A mile and three quarters later, Covington mumbled some obscenities to himself as he pulled to the side of the road. A BMW was pulled off in the grass with an ambulance and fire truck behind it. No other cop cars were in sight and a medic, hopping out of the back of the ambulance, was waving him down. Covington flashed his lights, popped the siren one time and pulled halfway into the shoulder of the road. He was sticking out into the slow lane of the highway so he left his lights on as he lethargically emerged from the car. The medic met him at his vehicle as Covington yawned.

"Officer, can you help us out here?" The medic had pasty skin and was in his early twenties with broad shoulders and a thick waist. He was a foot shorter than Covington but weighed almost the same. He had the build of a powerlifter and the demeanor of a brain surgeon.

"Look, I'm a detective. And quite frankly, I am exhausted and was on my way to get coffee."

"We think this is a kidnapping case here. There's a little girl in the back. The BMW broke down on the side of the road and some Good Samaritans called it in. Said the driver was just sitting here, ignoring the screaming kid in the back. I think I recognize the kid from the news. I think the dad lost custody and was taking the kid and booking."

Covington nodded. Just what he needed on no sleep with a dead body in tow. He shut his car door and followed the medic. Today would be a long day.

***

Coral could not believe the FBI would give up that quickly. She knew it was too good to be true, that was why she needed to personally deliver the story to her editor. Explain everything face to face and convince the powers that be that it was in *The Low Country Ledger*'s general best interests to publish her story. And to do it as soon as possible.

She took a sip from a label-less plastic bottle as she turned off the bridge into Mount Pleasant. Chase did not see it, but Coral had managed to pour some of the Grey Goose into a water bottle she fished from the trash. She sincerely appreciated the Federal government's contribution to her alcoholism. Any other time, she would be suspicious at the thought of the FBI knowing what she liked to drink. That was a worry for another day, though. Today was all about her story.

After turning north in Mount Pleasant, Coral's vision began to blur. She was used to driving tipsy or even fairly drunk, just usually not with this little sleep. She focused on the car in front of her and gripped her steering wheel tighter. Shaking her head, she tried to snap to. She turned her air conditioning to full blast and rolled down the windows. This usually did the trick. When it refused to do the trick, she gave herself a smack across the face. Nothing. She would pull over at the next intersection she thought.

Focusing with all her might, she pulled into the far-right lane to prepare to pull over. Up ahead, she could see the flashing lights of police, fire and EMS. After her run-in with the FBI, she decided she would wait another few minutes before pulling off. She did not feel like being harassed by local law enforcement too.

Coral sped up to sixty to keep pace with traffic, though the limit was fifty. Still struggling to focus on the road, she turned on the radio. Whiskey Myers blasted through her stereo with "Gasoline". She had tried all her wake-me-up tricks.

Then it all went black.

Coral had lost consciousness behind the wheel. Her foot dropped heavy against the accelerator and her Civic barreled to seventy, eighty, ninety miles per hour before finally coming to an abrupt stop. She side-swiped Detective Covington's police cruiser and continued on to strike both Covington and the medic he had been walking with. The Civic's final resting place was the back bumper of a fire truck that made Coral and the Civic unrecognizable.

Detective Covington was thrown thirty feet down the road. One shoe had flown off while the other hung onto his severed foot. His head skidded like a bowling ball on the hot asphalt before it and his body finally came to rest in a ditch next to the highway. He had died somewhere between impact and the grassy resting place that would soon be covered by flowers and crosses.

CHAPTER 51

Robert sat on the back deck of Sully's taking in the overwhelming aroma of salt in the air. The next few weeks would surely determine whether he would remain a free man, allowed to breathe God's cleanest, most humid air for the rest of his days, or whether he would be huffing fumes in a federal prison somewhere in the middle of nowhere, like Leavenworth, Kansas. It all depended on his newfound seventeen-year-old niece. He felt a twinge in his chest that had been absent for years. It was an anxiety he had not known since his first trial. One he had felt when under enemy fire in the Gulf; a nervousness that caused a pit in his stomach. He tried to shake it away and opened his book, a biography about President Ulysses S. Grant. Surely stories of the alcoholic General Grant would ease his mind.

"Robert," Caroline called from inside the screened door behind him, snapping him back to reality. "John won't stop calling your phone. It's charging on the counter in here and the buzzing is driving me insane. I'm going to pick it up and bring it to you.

"Hey John. I'll have Robert in a minute."

Robert had forgotten about the Clark men, which was probably a good thing. No news was always the best news, he had learned. He prayed Chief Mosby was calling to say all had settled on that front since Robert now had bigger fish to fry in the near term.

"Mosby. How are you? Give me some good news. The case with our friends is all closed, I hope?" Robert said hardily into the phone his wife had handed him. He had made sure to wait until his wife returned indoors before speaking. She had been involved enough recently.

"Not sure on that front, Boss. I have some other news. Covington, Boss."

Robert's anxiety rushed back like a tidal wave at the utterance of Covington's name. Any possible news on Covington at the moment could potentially be the worst news. News he never anticipated.

"Ahh shit. Based on the silence I'm guessing you hadn't heard. He's dead, Boss. Was run over by a drunk driver this morning." Mosby delivered the news as he had certainly done hundreds of times in his career: bluntly and without hesitation.

Robert must have been white as a ghost the way his heart sank at the news. He was not as concerned about his friend's untimely death at that moment as he was about Derrick's body. *Please tell me he got rid of the body*, Robert thought.

"Chief. Listen carefully. Respond slowly and think before you speak. We're on a phone remember. Did Covington have anything or *anyone* with him when he died."

Only the labored breathing of Mosby could be heard on Robert's end of the phone.

"Nah. All I heard was a medic got it with him. Some Bernard Stevens. Ring a bell?" Mosby said after a transitory pause.

"No. You sure nothing else? Covington was working with me recently on that other thing. The *family* issue," Robert emphasized each word and accentuated the word family. It took Mosby a moment, but he understood eventually.

"I see. I have heard nothing on that from the news or my colleagues down that way. Want me to dig around?"

"No! Definitely not. Just call me if you hear anything else," Robert said as he clicked end. He wanted to throw the damned phone into the ocean and punch a hole through the glass table he sat at. Instead, he took a deep breath and ran his hands through his graying hair. What to do now? He had never been in this situation. In the past, he had to make quick decisions to cover someone else's ass before. Never his own. After a lingering few minutes of ponderance, he pulled his phone back out of his pocket and skimmed the news. Early reports with few details were trickling out about a car wreck that killed Covington. There it is! One article from the *Gazette* showed the location of the accident. Robert knew exactly where it was and precisely what he had to do.

Robert hurried through the house, grabbed his keys and was off. He practically took a nosedive on the coffee table trying to slide into his Birkenstocks too fast. He was rushing because he had no one to call to help. He had no Covington now. He was his own Covington; he had to be his own fixer from now on.

Ten minutes later, after going twice the speed limit the entire way, Robert pulled up to a traffic jam. He could see the flashing lights at a distance and envisioned the rubbernecking drivers ogling at the scene up ahead. As the traffic tiptoed forward through a single, bottle-necked lane, Robert saw a familiar face directing traffic. A young highway patrolman named Eddy something or other Robert had met at one of the various law enforcement events he attended every year. His firm sponsored many and one of those useless sponsorships was finally going to pay off. Robert remembered the Eddy fellow as a polite, young black cop who played football at Coastal Carolina University. He was short, but stout and showed promise, seeming to be liked by all his superiors. Robert rolled down his window and held up a hand as he approached Eddy, flashing a turn single at the direction of the accident. Eddy nodded and waved an arm to gesture Robert to pull over on the side. Eddy shouted for another cop to relieve him and one jogged over before he approached Robert's parked Bronco.

"Hey, Mr. Remington. Did you hear?" Eddy asked as he leaned a hand on Robert's car door.

"Afraid so. Poor Covington. He was a great man. Leaving behind a wife and kids all because of what? A drunk driver right?" Robert was toeing the line between rushing through the formalities and being brokenhearted. He needed to act like he was just there for Covington.

"Yes, sir. The woman driving that Honda there drove right through Detective Covington's patrol car and then careened on into both Covington and a medic he was with. They were out of their vehicles and on foot. Struck and probably killed instantly. Covington was just helping out until a patrolman could arrive. At least what I heard."

Robert shook his head as he stared at the wreckage. What remained of a black sedan looked as if a bomb exploded in the front seat. Airbags were deployed, every window was now a gaping hole with glass splayed about. The front tires were turned inward and where the engine once was now resembled a wall of fragmented metal. It was unrecognizable.

Covington's patrol car was nearly as bad off. The rear and entire left side looked as if Wolverine clawed through it. The patrol light on top laid smashed on the ground and the front and rear hoods were blown off. The interior was simply a graveyard for glass, metal and airbag fragments.

"That's a shame," Robert said without looking at Eddy. He was still studying the scene. His heart sank as he counted the cordoned off areas where bodies clearly once sat. He was not sure if he wanted the answer to his next question. "Hey, Eddy. Who was in the car with the driver? You said it was just Covington and a medic, right? I see four total landing spots here."

"That's right. The fourth was a dead body that was in the woman's trunk, from what I've heard."

"What?" Robert wanted as much information as the boy had. Robert liked what he was hearing so far.

"Well, I don't really have too much insight, Mr. Remington. I can only say what I've overheard from the detectives out here. You may want to go talk to them. Detective Burleson's over there if you want to go hear the initial assessment. I've gotta get back to it here." Before walking away, the young patrolman turned to Robert with an exaggerated frown and said, "Mr. Remington, I'm real sorry about Detective Covington. I know you two were real close. I'll keep you in my prayers, sir."

Robert nodded sullenly as he stepped out of his parked car. He spotted Detective Burleson talking to some other officers in the midst of the sea of glass and carnage. Robert never particularly cared for Burleson, who came off as brazen and entitled due to being a fourth-generation detective in the Low Country. Robert could admit; however, his view of Burleson was skewed by the fact that he and Covington never saw eye to eye and had come to blows on at least two occasions. Though he would need to keep the look of a broken-hearted officer, devastated over the loss of a brother, Robert was sure Burleson was at least a smidge happy.

"Sorry for your loss, Robert," Burleson said, removing his hat and stepping away from the other officers. He took Robert's hand and shook it a bit too firmly.

"Sorry for your loss as well, Detective. Devastating," Robert said nodding as the men uncomfortably looked around at the scene.

"Yeah, yeah. Sad day for all boys in blue here. As you can see this asshole plowed right through everything in her path. BAC of .17, but had a healthy dose of benzos in her system too. Shouldn't have been anywhere near a steering wheel."

Robert nodded. He did not care one iota, but had to pretend to. He needed to appear as if he were only there as an inconsolable friend. Despite this, he had to fight the urge to blurt out "Have you figured out that the fourth body is my brother-in-law and have you determined it was in Covington's trunk?"

"Welp, probably shouldn't be telling you this yet, but you didn't hear it from me," Burleson mumbled in a low voice, inching closer to Robert. He was reading Robert's eyes and saw his gaze on the fourth body. "That's the body of Derrick Diamond in that tarp. I believe you know him?"

Robert hesitated for a moment. He needed to act surprised. Thank God he was a trial attorney the way Burleson was studying his face. "Holy shit. Actually?" The less words, the better. Do not let them pin you down to anything.

"Yep. Now let me ask you something, else."

Robert nodded slowly. Moment of truth. Come to Jesus moment. Where was this headed?

"Do you recognize the name Coral Sands?"

This genuinely did shock Robert. He knew the name and the woman. She was a journalist who had written a few articles on him and had become fond of his work. Or so he thought at first. He previously had to sick Covington on her paper—and others—in the past to keep her from digging into any of his clients' deaths.

"Yes. Matter of fact I do. How does she tie into all this?"

"Well, then you know she had a hardon for you. The FBI reached out today and let us know they'd been investigating her for stalking you for quite some time." Burleson let this sink in for a moment. Robert nodded as if he knew. "Robert, they think she was obsessed with you. Thought you two were married. Real mental patient who was also addicted to drugs and the drink."

"Yes, so I've been told," he lied. He was troubled by the FBI's involvement. "What does she have to do with this?"

"She was the driver here."

"Oh my. That's sad, but not surprising."

"Yeah. Well, seems she went so far as to shoot and kill your brother-in-law for you. That body over there had a full round in it. Used his own gun to do it. His body was in her car and flew out onto the road upon impact. He got run over by a tractor-trailer, but we were able to ID him from pictures we'd seen on the APBs. Had already been dead prior to the accident from the gun shots, obviously."

Robert felt as if a tremendous weight had just been lifted from his shoulders. This was all too perfect. It seemed too good to be true. He needed to tell Caroline and Rose as soon as possible. They were off the hook on this one. All he had left to do was quietly get rid of the remnants in his Bronco.

"Wow. That's…I don't even know what to say."

"I know it must be a lot to process. But you didn't hear it from me. Someone will formally reach out to you in the next day or so about it. FBI might before then." Before turning away, Burleson sported a toothy grin and said, "From what I understand, two pains in your ass may have just been handled for you in one swoop."

Robert returned a wry smirk and walked back to the Bronco. He had to talk to his girls.

CHAPTER 52

Rose was sitting in a Tommy Bahama beach chair perched under a matching umbrella, her rear slung inches from the cool, shadowed sand. The sound of waves crashing just in front of her and whipping wind filled her ears. The smells of salt, sunscreen and sweat all mixing together percolated in her nostrils. She had been to the beach a handful of times with her mother and Derrick, usually farther north than Sullivan's Island where the beaches were more crowded and overweight tourists piled on top of each other like sardines. She would usually sit in the sand and read alone while Derrick and her mother did whatever adults do. In hindsight, probably drugs, she thought, taking a break from her book. She could not quite explain it, but Rose felt a weightlessness sitting on the Sullivan's Island beach; a sensation she had never felt before. She had been trying for the last hour to put her finger on it, but was unable to pinpoint the root cause until it hit her: she now had no cares or fears in the world. It was normalcy. This had to be the sensation. Though she was still without a mother, which broke her soul in a way that agonized, she had also lost a wretched, evil "stepfather" who would have spent his life chasing after her. If Derrick were alive, Rose would have spent the rest of her life looking over her shoulder, peaking around corners and in a constant state of mental torment. This feathery, emancipating consciousness was acceptance of her new life. The last few weeks had forced her to both mature and relax at a rapid pace.

"I'm going to head up to the house and grab a bag of pretzels and some water. Do you want anything?" Nurse Blanchard's voice cut through the wind and over the waves, snapping Rose out of her trance of daydreams. The nurse was lying on a beach towel soaking in the sun a few feet from Rose. They had been out for only a couple of hours and the Nurse was already sporting a smooth, even tan.

"I'm good, thanks."

Nurse Blanchard nodded as she jumped to her feet and began a slovenly march through the thick sand to Sully's. They ended up a quarter mile down the beach in an open plot of sand, few other beachgoers even visible. The seclusion was selected to nap, read and drown out the world, with barely a word spoken since they arrived. Rose thought the nurse perceived something was different about her, but assumed she was overthinking it.

Less than two minutes after Nurse Blanchard departed, Rose's seclusion and peace were interrupted.

"Rose Shelby," an unfamiliar voice jolted the girl upright in her chair. It came from behind her and was a deep baritone. Rose turned around and saw two men in bathing suits and tank tops approaching. She had spotted them earlier and presumed they were a gay couple sunbathing up the beach.

"Rose, we don't have much time. My name is Special Agent Chase and this is Special Agent Sandler. We're here to show you some things, tell you some things and then we'll be out of your hair. We'd like to keep this meeting between us for now, so I'll do the talking and Sandler here will be on the lookout for your nurse. If she spots us chatting, just say we noticed your book and happen to know the author. A former white shoe attorney who became a novelist. Baldacci. Nod if you understand, Rose. This is important."

Rose nodded deliberately with hesitation. Her buoyancy had disappeared and anxiety returned. This was her true normalcy.

"Good," the agent continued with his eyes hidden behind dark sunglasses. He was kneeling beside her chair as his partner stood behind him. "Look at this photo. Do you recognize the people in it?"

Rose raised a hand to her brow blocking the sun from her eyes as she peered at the agent's phone. It showed two men carrying a large object in the dark. The agent swiped and then showed her a picture of herself and a man walking in front of the same building. Her heart sank. She recognized the second picture immediately; it had been replaying in her mind the entire day. The second picture showed her and Robert from the previous night. The first picture must have been Robert and Detective Covington carrying a very dead Derrick Diamond out to Covington's car just a moment before the second shot was snapped. Rose felt as if she was going to be sick.

"That's right. It's you, your uncle and Detective Covington. Now you're a smart girl and you know exactly what this means. Despite the fact that your stepdaddy deserved whatever he got in there last night, you know damned well a murder is a murder. The FBI doesn't take too kindly to murder, regardless of the circumstances, but hear us out. Now we know your uncle is a killer. You may very well have not known before last night, but now you sure as hell do. And, Rose, with these pictures right here, we could charge you right now as an accessory after the fact."

The agent let his last sentence settle in the air. Rose was mortified and rendered speechless. She realized that the agents believed Robert killed Derrick, which was somewhat settling to her stomach, but not much. She had read about accessories after the fact at least a dozen times. If they were trying to pin her with that, then these agents thought she merely helped hide the body and that was it; they had no idea she was the murderer. She had pulled that trigger numerous times and taken Derrick's life, but they were none the wiser. She was sweating bullets.

She quickly rifled through her memory and recalled characters in her books getting a few years in maximum security, Federal prison for as little as driving the getaway car in a murder. The nausea returned with vengeance as the sweat doubled.

"Rose, we need your help. In return, we'll make sure you never see the inside of a prison cell for your hand in the murder of Derrick Diamond."

"Wh—what?" was all Rose could manage to sputter out.

"You see, Rose, Detective Covington is dead. He was hit by a drunk driver this morning. Highly coincidental, but leaves us, the FBI, with fewer options here. Seeing as how we've got you in the crosshairs in these pictures, we're going to give you twenty-four hours to get us the information we want before we arrest you. If you give us what we want, we'll drop all charges. Kick it all under the rug. However, if you don't cooperate with us and don't get us what we need, then, Rose, you'll be in just as much trouble as your Uncle Robert."

"I—I don't understand. What has Uncle Robert done wrong? Derrick was a horrible man," she said, fighting back tears.

"We agree with you there, Rose. We read the reports and are sorry to hear about your mother. But, you see, the law is the law and it isn't really up to you, me, Sandler or anyone else to decide when a law should be enforced and when it shouldn't. And murder, you see, is at the tippy-top of the worst type of crime. Your uncle, however, is what we may deem a serial killer. He's killed quite a few times in his life, beyond Derrick. Now I'll agree, in my humble opinion, Robert only seemed to kill Derrick-types: killers, rapists and the like. The issue is, we believe he killed a sitting United States Senator a few decades back. We can't prove it—nor can we really prove any of the other murders thus far—but we only care about that particular murder."

"What? I wasn't even alive two decades ago," Rose practically groaned.

"Right. But we have reason to believe that your uncle did kill one Senator Arthur McDonough in cold blood. We're talking execution-style, bullet through the skull."

"Where do I come in here? What do I have to do?"

"We want Robert to admit to you that he killed that Senator. All while you're wearing this." The agent reached into his pocket and pulled out a pen and clicked it. "This here pen isn't just a pen. It's a recording device. When you click the top like you want to write something here, it starts recording. When you click it again, it stops. Now if you forget to click it off, it'll stop automatically after five minutes and will buzz silently to let you know. If that happens, but you're still recording, just give it another click. You got all that?"

Rose stared blankly from the pen to the agent and back. She was at a loss for words. She was fairly certain she should have a lawyer with her at that moment, but the only lawyer she knew was apparently a murderer. She took the pen with a trembling hand and inspected it. It looked like a regular pen. Were they playing a trick on her?

"Chase, the nurse has left the house," the agent on lookout said. Agent Chase stood up and took the girls shoulder in his hand.

"You record it and meet us right back here in twenty-four hours. Two o'clock on this beach. Now I've got to go."

As quickly as the men appeared, they vanished from the beach. Rose sat in disbelief at the events that had taken place in the last twelve hours. Moments ago, she thought her life trajectory had finally taken an upward swing. Now, she was not so sure.

Less than a tenth of a mile away, in bright red Mini Cooper, Agent Chase talked through the speaker phone to an elated Agent McGovern.

"Now we wait," he said before ending the call.

CHAPTER 53

Robert raced home from the scene of Covington's last breath. He somehow felt bad for *not* feeling bad about his colleague's untimely passing. He was, he thought *understandably*, being selfish as he tried to shake his conscience on the drive. Covington would be feeling the same, selfish thoughts if the roles were reversed, he resolved.

Once inside, he looked for Rose and the nurse. He hoped one would be there and the other was gone, though he knew it unlikely. They had become inseparable and justifiably so. One had lost the only woman near to her and the other was alone in a stranger's home in a new town. After searching their rooms, he circled the house back to find Caroline, who was in the living room. She was watching the local news with tears rolling down her cheeks. Coverage of the fatal wreck was playing and Covington's police department headshot was side by side with the headshot of a young medic in the top right-hand corner of the television.

"Robert. I just saw. That's terrible. We just saw him the other day. He was at your party. He told us about my sister and Rose in the hospital. Oh my God," Caroline managed to squeak through sobs. She was clutching a pillow in one hand and a soiled ball of tissues in the other. The dogs surrounded her like an emotional support kennel club. She looked up at her husband longingly, searching for comfort in his eyes. She quickly understood he had none to offer as he stared back with a look of forced pity. "What's wrong?"

"Where is everyone, Caroline?"

"The girls are down the beach a ways and I don't know where the boys are. Off at their own places. Working, I guess. What is it, Robert?"

Robert sat down in a matching recliner to his wife's and recounted the last few hours. He left out the fact that Covington was with him the previous evening when filling his wife in in the wee hours earlier that morning. The discussion then had focused more on Rose and her role and how Robert was a fool as opposed to the detective taking her brother-in-law's body away in a squad car. Covington's presence did not seem significant then.

He told of Burleson's mentioning of the FBI, the wrong conclusion that Derrick's body was in the journalist's car—a journalist that the FBI claimed was hot on Robert's tail. Caroline listened intently and lit up at the statement of the journalist.

"Wait, that's great then, Robert! They're off you. They're off Rose. Derrick's still dead. We can move past it. They think that damned journalist did it!"

"Not quite, Caroline," Robert started. "The FBI never spoke to me and they apparently told Burleson they had."

"I'm confused."

"So was I—at first. We don't have much time. The FBI is bound to contact me soon. I mean, the FBI is clearly tailing me after all of these years. They'd contacted me over the years, but nothing serious. I always assumed they were watching, I just remained vigilant. I was careful. Annoyingly careful. More cautious and thorough than Covington or Mosby ever thought I needed to be. But it seems that the FBI knew more than I'd admitted to myself. They had to have known I'd go after

Derrick. He was the bait. And somehow they concluded I'd target him. Frankly, he fit my M.O. but he also didn't. Besides the point; I'm rambling. They were already onto me. I'm not sure how the journalist fits in, though. I recognize her name and know she had written some puff pieces about me. Nothing beyond that." Robert stopped abruptly. "Wait. Back to Derrick. Caroline, who told you that Rose was raped and sexually assaulted by Derrick?"

"Nurse Blanchard, why?" Caroline responded in a muddled tone. She was not following the web Robert was currently spinning. Before Robert could continue, he heard the sliding glass door open to the back porch. The Roses had returned from the beach.

"Rose, you weren't raped by Derrick, were you?" Robert blurted out before the girls had time to close the sliding glass door.

"Robert!" Caroline scolded.

"What?" the girl shrieked in disgust. "No!"

Nurse Blanchard's face reddened as she said, "I should go. This sounds like a family conversation." The nurse hurried into her room and closed the door abruptly.

"Robert! Why would you do that?" Caroline said, squeezing her husband's forearm. Max and Louie got up from their naps as Caroline gripped Robert. Max began to growl.

"Hold on, Caroline," Robert said, shaking his forearm free. The growling stopped. "Rose, he didn't, did he?"

"No! I swear! I would've fought back," the girl demanded. She was trying to convince herself of the last sentence more so than anyone else in the room. She was adamant and stern, but was being truthful and wanted to convey it.

"Robert! What the fuck are you doing? Having an inquisition into the worst part of this girl's existence in front of everyone? What's wrong with you? The nurse said she wouldn't remember!"

"What? Aunt Caroline, I would remember something like that. I swear on my Mother's grave that didn't happen!"

"Sweetie, the psychiatrist said you've suppressed it."

"Psychiatrist? I never saw a psychiatrist, Aunt Caroline."

There was a stunned silence that hung about the air. Caroline was attempting to recount the story Nurse Blanchard had told her earlier in her stay. Rose strained to read what exactly her aunt and uncle were getting at, while, for a brief moment, feeling so angry and humiliated that she had managed to forget all about the pen in her pocket and the agents that had just harassed her. Robert ran calculations in his head, staring at the ceiling in deep concentration.

"Rose, you're positive you never saw a psychiatrist in Florence? And Derrick never tried to touch you? You were never told anything about a baby?" Robert pressed. He was onto something. He needed his newfound suspicions confirmed.

"Robert, what the hell are you talking about?" The girl had never called him by his first name. "I never saw a psychiatrist period. *Never in my life.* And if you are insinuating I was impregnated by Derrick, that is disgusting and not scientifically possible. I'm not ignorant, I know how sex works and we didn't do anything. He wouldn't dare under my Mother's roof."

"What's happening, Robert?" Caroline begged.

The sound of tires screeching out front stopped the conversation. Robert ran to the door and saw the rear bumper of Nurse Blanchard's Volkswagen skid around a corner of palm trees and out of sight.

"Caroline, Rose, I don't think Nurse Blanchard was a nurse at all," Robert called back at the stupefied women.

CHAPTER 54

Her uncle was rattling her. Rose knew with every fiber in her being that Derrick had never touched her like that. She had no clue what he was getting at and after hearing from the FBI agents on the beach that her uncle was a cold-blooded killer—of a Senator, nonetheless! —she was becoming frightened. Mix in the shock of her aunt, the last connection she had to her deceased mother, Rose was ready to bolt for the door and turn state's witness. The Witness Protection Program sounded pretty good right about now, she thought.

"Let me explain. Come take a seat, Rose," Robert said, offering the recliner as he grabbed a barstool from the kitchen for himself. The recliner swiveled to face him, startling Louie who scurried to Robert's feet. Rose took a seat with caution and timidly readied herself.

"Caroline, I'm afraid I don't want to say all of this in front of you. I'll say a little then Rose and I will go on a walk down the beach." Before his wife could protest, Robert held up a hand and changed his tone. "Caroline. I am not arguing with you over this. I will *not* make you an accessory after the fact, okay?" Rose felt a shiver go down her spine at his words.

She was an accessory after the fact in the eyes of the Federal Bureau of Investigations.

"Nurse Blanchard was an FBI plant. I don't know how I didn't see it sooner. Remember Addie? Bobby's girlfriend—or whatever the hell he called it—who broke up with him out of the blue after breakfast the other day? She was an FBI plant. I had suspicions when she decided to come to your sister's funeral and let her know I knew. She waved the white flag and moved along. Regardless, the FBI tends to tail me. They think I should be implicated in the death of certain people and therefore have been trying—and failing—to infiltrate my firm, the court and this family for years. I felt so bad for you, Rose, and all that had happened that I *naively* gave Blanchard the benefit of the doubt."

"How did you figure this out? I wouldn't have believed you if she hadn't just run off that fast," Caroline inquired. She was dumbfounded at the story of Addie. Now the nurse?

"I think the FBI was afraid I'd leave Derrick alone unless I had a certain nexus to his crime. No offense, Rose, but they rightly guessed that Derrick's mere domestic violence, although fatal, was not enough for me to risk my retirement and my freedom for. They had to add something else."

"They planted the rape and the baby story," Caroline mumbled in disbelief.

"That's right." Robert turned to his niece. "Rose, would you mind taking a walk on the beach with me? I know this is all a lot to take in about an uncle you practically just met two weeks ago, but there's plenty of people on the beach and you'll be safe. I'm obviously not going to do anything to hurt you, but I'm offering up a public walk to make you feel safe. As I said, there are certain things my wife may want to hear, but she will not be hearing from me today. In fact, if she ever hears them, they'll likely be from you on a witness stand at my trial. Should you choose to take that route. I am going to lay it all out and let you decide."

Rose was stupefied. She had no clue what to say or do in this situation. She now knew her uncle was at the house to kill her "stepfather" and she took that opportunity from him. She also now knew—from the FBI—that he was a murderer. Could she trust him? She did not think so. She gazed at her aunt who looked back and nodded. Rose remembered the pen in her pocket and her twenty-four-hour deadline. This may be her only chance. Wind up killed by her murdering uncle or spend years in a Federal prison. She would take her chances on the beach.

"I'll do it. I'm going to trust someone for once in my life," the girl fibbed. Robert nodded and motioned for the beach. After a moment or two of silent walking, he broke it.

"Make sure you click the recorder on if you haven't already. I'd prefer if you hadn't recorded any of that in the house where my wife was listening and clearly present, but if you have I suppose it's too late."

Rose stopped dead in her tracks and looked at her uncle, who was solemnly nodding with a look of defeat. "What are you talking about?"

"No need for that, Rose. I told you I am not going to hurt you. I don't hurt the innocent. You're family and I am not a monster. You'll understand me better in a bit. I'll tell you anything and everything. Once I'm done explaining, I'll answer any questions you have. I promise. I actually haven't been able to do this a single time in my life, so it might feel nice." Robert nodded his head and motioned for them to continue walking. "After the accident earlier with Covington, what Burleson said about the FBI rang a bell in my head. Then, once I figured out Blanchard was a plant—or whatever her real name is—I knew they'd have gotten to you. If not before last night, then definitely now."

Rose stared back in dazed muteness, much the same as she had done an hour earlier with Agent Chase and Agent Sandler.

"You're not the first person they tried to flip. And I'm up on their latest tech as a defense attorney—they use it against my clients in court all the time. You'd either have a Bluetooth headphone, a fake pen or some sort of belt with a recorder in it." Robert paused. "By the way you hesitated there, you were given a pen. Alright. Put it on. You're going to want to get this. I've had a good life but you've got much more to live. I may run for it before you give the recording over to the Feds, though maybe not. I think I'm too old for that. It may be a relief to actually stop living life in the rearview. With Covington gone, I've got one less comrade to do it all with. And I'm sure they think I killed Derrick—which we're going to go with, Rose, for the recording and for our lives—but they're trying to threaten you as an accessory. You play their game, record me, submit it and I'll get you a good defense attorney. You'll get off with no time at all. You've done nothing wrong. In fact, they'll probably sweep Derrick under the rug, let the lady reporter take the fall and focus on the Senator."

Rose was becoming convinced her uncle was a sociopathic genius. The type of Ted Bundy killer who was personable, intelligent and sadistic. She was almost certain she would end up dead in the surf before the end of the day. After all she had been through so far, she was ready for whatever came her way.

"Come on, Rose. Take it out and click it. At least record it and decide what you want to do next afterward. This is going to be therapeutic for me, honestly." Robert had removed the sunglasses he threw on for their walk to look at Rose. He motioned for her to lift the pen from her pocket and made a clicking gesture. She did as she was told. Robert nodded, smiled and proceeded.

CHAPTER 55

"Rose, this won't make much sense at the beginning of the story, so just stick with me and it'll all come together. I'm sure the FBI gave you their version, but I'll give you—and that pen of yours—the firsthand account," Robert said as she looked out at the half-empty beach in front of them. There were children splashing in the water as parents watched on from ankle deep in the surf. Elderly couples stretched out in chairs hiding under umbrellas speckled about the sands. Robert and Rose looked like a standard father and daughter going for an easy walk to discuss and enjoy life. None of their fellow beachgoers could know they were focusing more on death than life.

When Rose had taken the pen from her pocket and clicked the top as her uncle instructed, it lit up briefly, buzzing in her hand. Robert had eased into a slow walking pace, burying each set of toes deep into the cool sand below.

"Alright, so it began when I was stationed in the Middle East with the Army. Have you heard of the Gulf War?" Rose shook her head. "I figured. Before your time. Long story short, at the time, we thought we were just going over there as peacekeepers to settle down a toxic regime in Iraq led by Saddam Hussein. I see you nodding. Yes, that same Saddam Hussein, but this was a full decade earlier in the 1990s. Anyway, I was over there and got a taste of what it felt like to kill someone. I was a young man, fresh off taking over the family law firm and successfully driving it into the ground. So, while pushing thirty, I decided to give up the law and join the Army. It was a gamble, but I didn't see any other route my life could take. The Cold War with the Soviet Union was on the down slope and the U.S. was a dominant superpower. I wanted to have a job where I made sure I could help keep it that way. I don't know. Young, dumb ambition and blind loyalty.

"Anyway, I'm over in Saudi Arabia and I've killed a few dozen of the enemy at this point. It felt good. Like I was making a positive difference by taking the life of another man, somehow. It was an adrenaline I've never felt through anything else in my life. The problem was, the Gulf War quickly came to a close and I came home. Deployment was over and there weren't really any active combat zones around the world; nowhere I could go to kill and feed my inner adrenaline junky. I tried skydiving and horseback riding and even had a motorcycle for a bit. Nothing worked. I couldn't match that feeling after I left the Army. So I tried my hand again at law, but with a twist. Through certain contacts I made in the military, I was given contracts to kill bad people. Here, in the United States. I won't go into all of the details because it's not important for what you need to know or what the FBI wants to know, but wealthy people would be put in contact with me through middle men and I would be able to make their problems go away. I was called a professional exterminator. However, to keep up appearances, I continued to run my law firm. Soon, when I had more money than I knew what to do with, I began taking on some of these sick people as clients. I was—well, I am still—a damned good trial lawyer and that's the only thing that gave me at least a fraction of a fraction of a tiny percent of the adrenaline I got from killing. So I'd get these men—always men—acquitted at trial, then I'd find them later and kill them. I'd make them suffer the way they made their victims suffer. Because, you see, Rose, our justice system ain't all it's cracked up to be. There are flaws. The wheels of justice churn slowly—too slowly. And, quite frankly, it's an inefficient mess. So I'd rather take justice into my own hands when I can and deliver swift, *southern justice*, as I like to call it."

The girl nodded, still unsure of where the story was going. But she was hooked on every word the lunatic was spewing her way.

"Now, what the FBI is interested in and I'm sure they at least mentioned to you, is the death of Senator McDonough. Well, I knew Senator McDonough back during my Army days. Back when I went by Big Country and he went by Sweet Carolina," Robert said with a chuckle. He was playing the age-old game of remember when with himself; his audience was lost and could not appreciate the humor he found in his young nickname. "Carolina and I were fast friends. He was also from South Carolina and we ended up in the same little group. One morning, over in the Middle East, he came back in a panic. A gleeful panic. He was hysterical, yet pleased with himself I can now say with the benefit of hindsight. Said he'd killed a group of kids. Innocent Saudi Arabian kids playing in the street just a few blocks from their homes. He mowed them down with his gun, hid their bodies then came back and told me about it. That day I'll remember for the rest of my life. My life took a turn that day and I hadn't a clue at the time. I decided to help who I thought was a good person in a tough spot. I disposed of the shell casings he left at the scene. If I didn't do that, he'd probably have rotted in a military prison for years. Decades, even. Never would've been Senator and we wouldn't be having this little talk. Biggest mistake of my life."

"Why'd you help him?" The girl spoke up boldly. Robert paused and thought for a moment. He had more than three decades to think this question over and never thought he would have the opportunity to answer to another soul about it.

"Well, Rose. I think it's just what anyone would have done in that situation. I was helping a friend in a strange land who I thought had a good heart. I was sadly mistaken, but I didn't want to see my fellow soldier—someone who I felt was a brother to me—locked up abroad for a mistake. We were all a little gun shy at first. We didn't know if an IED was going to explode with the next step we took. We weren't sure if a kid had a bomb strapped to his chest. The uncertainty was excruciating at times. Mix that with the hot sun, desert heat and homesickness, and a man could about go insane. Lose himself. And Carolina did. I couldn't undo what he had done, I just hid the shell casings. I wish I never did it and I'll regret it until my last breath. I've killed dozens of men and I don't regret a single one. But hiding those shell casings…."

Robert pondered somberly then let his response sink in before he proceeded. Under his glasses, he had tears in the corner of his eyes recounting the story that had haunted him all these years.

"Fast-forward a few months and my buddy Carolina only got worse. He started losing himself over there. He was drinking heavily—but then again all of us were when we weren't on patrol. He rarely slept. When he did, he'd wake in the middle of the night screaming. He became prone to confrontation. He'd pick a fight with anyone and was always angry. He'd spend nights at brothels. A brothel—well, it's—"

"I know what a brothel is, Robert."

"Okay. Yeah, he'd spend nights there and refuse to pay. He'd harass the workers and flash his gun or knives. He was court martialed multiple times. In hindsight, what he did was akin to rape. He raped women in the uniform and in the name of the United States Army. I didn't know at the time, of course. None of us did. But he had become a full-fledged monster."

"Is all of this true? How'd he become a Senator?" Rose was skeptical.

"To this day, I truly don't understand how. I do and I don't. He came from a well-connected family in South Carolina, which, at the time, I didn't know. None of us did. That's why he'd always get off when he was court martialed. In the end, he took a bullet in the leg, got a Purple Heart and rode back to the states like a war hero. Really he went AWOL, but that's not important. His family, you see, were multi-millionaires. Nothing to get them in *Forbes* or anything like that, but wealthy enough and well-connected enough to have generational wealth and lives of ease. They were large donors to both sides of the political aisle and ran a private, family investment office for some of the larger names in D.C. So, Carolina came back, ran for the House after a couple years of private law practice, won easily and then was elected Senator. At the same time, I'm taking contracts to kill criminals all across the South and keeping an eye on the Senator. I'd lost touch with him after our time in the Gulf, but I monitored. He'd reached out once, trying to get me to sign some NDA or confidentiality agreement about our time in the war, but I refused. Everyone else we served with happily signed it—for a price. They redacted his military records, too. Me? No, I couldn't be bought. I had enough money by the time he was Senator and I didn't want his blood money. If I wanted to talk, I would. But I'm a man of action, so I stayed silent and waited for a misstep. And I almost missed it. I waited too long, though, I guess. Well, maybe not—I've been thinking a lot about fate these last two weeks or so. I think I let him live as long as he did for a reason."

Rose checked the pen to make sure it was still recording. She was not sure so she clicked it twice until she knew for certain it was.

"The way I'd find out about these scumbags that I'd represent was from people like Detective Covington. Well, from Detective Covington only, really." Robert had to be careful here. He did not want to implicate anyone else. Covington was dead, so he saw no issue with implicating his deceased friend. "He'd put me onto some case, give me the facts and I'd pop up as the attorney. One day, we're having lunch outside the courthouse in Columbia. He's a witness in my case and he was set to take the stand after. We're talking about this and that; just life and family and what not. Then he switches gears and starts to tell me about a big case he's working. It's--," Robert pauses to clear his throat. He began to seethe with anger at the story he was about to tell. Even Caroline did not know about it, despite the fact it impacted her directly. "It was an investigation into a human trafficking ring. Right here in South Carolina. Covington had gotten a tip from an informant he frequently worked with in the Low Country that some girls—girls as young as thirteen—were being run across the border of Mexico and up into the Deep South. They were brought from all countries and kept as prisoners in warehouses, cargo vans, and mobile homes. They'd be chained to the beds in some circumstances. Others," Robert cleared his throat again. "Others were drugged. Drugged with such high doses that they didn't even try to fight. Those girls didn't need to be chained."

Rose noticed Robert wipe a tear from his eye before he continued. "Covington told me his informant said the trafficking ring implicated people high up in the state. All the way up to the top. He knew I'd be interested so he slid me a file. I thanked him and said I'd take a look that night after the trial was done for the day.

"Later that night, I'm in the Lexington house reading the file and I see it in bold letters. Among a few other notable names was Senator Arthur McDonough. He was one of the main masterminds of the human trafficking ring. The informant estimated that he'd helped smuggle two thousand girls into the U.S. and keep them locked up as slaves between 1995 and 2007. I quickly called Covington and asked him who else had this information. He said only himself, the informant and now me. I told him to keep it that way and to put McDonough under 24/7 surveillance. I wanted proof. Once I had proof, I'd confront him.

"Fast-forward a week and Covington and I were back together at a diner in Mount Pleasant. I wanted to hear what he had so far. He showed me photos of the Senator with the girls, showed me pictures of the girls locked up, showed the living conditions—it was all so sick. I wanted to vomit. It was the worst case I'd ever looked into. It was just so inhumane. He said that worst part of it all was the Senator himself had a woman locked up in his own house. Essentially a slave he kept in his attic. They couldn't get inside his house to get pictures, but they had a name. Apparently, she wasn't even locked up or anything, but anytime she tried to fight back, he'd drug her. Kept her so high she couldn't think straight.

"Rose, it was your mother. And this was 2007. The Senator I killed was your father."

CHAPTER 56

Rose stood in the same motel room Coral had stood in two nights prior. Instead of the full slew of agents interrogating her as she had feared, it was merely a singular female agent named Darlene McGovern who sat opposite Rose. McGovern had met Rose on the beach exactly twenty-four hours after she spoke to the two male agents at the same spot. Rose was pleasantly surprised by the agent's demeanor: McGovern was much friendlier and less threatening than the male agents, though Rose assumed this very well could have been because Rose confirmed she already had what the agent wanted, a recording. After brief introductions, the agent explained that her colleagues were needed on other, official FBI matters that took them from the Low Country. Rose had no clue what this meant so merely nodded along, afraid for the rampage that might follow.

It had been a long night and excruciating morning since the girl was given the rundown of Robert's life, indiscretions, and all. She had listened intently, asked no further questions, and, after returning to Sully's had laid in her bed staring at the white, popcorn ceiling most of the sleepless night. Before settling in under the blanket and creaking ceiling fan, however, she had bolted her bedroom door and pushed a rickety rocking chair in front of the knob, unsure if Robert would come in and attack her regretting the knowledge he had shared that day. Rose did not know what to think and by the time the morning rolled around, she had refused to come out of her room, silently staging a locked-in hunger strike out of fear and insecurity. At one thirty in the afternoon, she finally emerged and headed for the beach in search of the agents, her pen in tow, before finding McGovern waiting in a black pants-suit. Rose, torn on what she had heard about her mother, father and uncle the day before, needed the FBI to verify what she had heard, though she had a feeling the FBI was running blind as well.

The previous day on the beach, Robert had admitted to Rose—with the pen switched off—that he fully intended on torturing and killing Derrick that night. He explained that the reason he was telling her this was that he hoped that the knowledge that Derrick was set to die that night regardless eased the girl's burdened conscience. He, of course, said it with such an expression as to remind the girl she was being recorded once the pen clicked back on and to go along with the story that *he* actually did torture and kill Derrick and she, of course, was an innocent bystander. Back on the record, he explained that when he found out his addict of a sister-in-law (though he said it much more delicately to the deceased woman's teenage daughter) was drugged and practically enslaved by a man he once helped keep out of prison, Robert became physically ill with rage. After a few moments of blind anger and sickness, he confirmed with Covington that the Senator had no live-in Secret Service and Robert wasted no time, striking that very night. He told Rose that he never wanted anyone to know about her mother's predicament and certainly never wanted the Senator's child—Rose, who Robert found out about months after murdering the Senator—to know anything about her mother and father's transgressions. Robert had ordered Covington to leave the Senator and Jenny out of any reports he logged and the detective reluctantly obliged. But now, Rose's life was at stake and Robert believed Rose had a right to know. He hoped she would forgive him, forgive her mother and live a life dedicated to being twice the woman her mother was and a hundred times the person her father was.

A day after the life-altering explanations, Rose sat in shock as the recordings from the pen played through a computer on the desk. Robert's voice reverberated off the thin, mildew-stained walls of the motel room as McGovern stared at the computer screen as if a video accompanied the words. Rose chose instead to glower at the purple and green faded rug below her feet. Hearing the words for the second time, she listened more intently and she felt it all sink in a bit further as if she was watching a movie for the second time. She began to believe Robert. Everything he told her was more than plausible and she accepted it as fact, but she had made the decision to show the FBI entirely out of fear for her own life. And at Robert's urging: he appeared genuinely guilt-ridden that Rose was brought into the situation and had to find out her father's identity this way.

When the recording clicked off, McGovern sat in silence for a dramatic moment. She leaned back in a folding chair and massaged her temples, closing her eyes. Rose watched intently as the agent appeared somewhere between stricken with grief and ill with food poisoning. After a moment, mounting all her might, the lead agent abruptly leaned forward as if she was going to squeeze the desk to sawdust between her fingers.

"Fuck!" the woman yelled. She yanked the USB that held the contents of the pen from the laptop and snapped it in half. She stood up and snatched the laptop from the desk, raising it over her head and launching it to the floor. She stomped on the laptop and broken USB drive with her black Nikes until nothing remained but fragments of glass and metal. Keys were strewn about the floor and the "Enter" button hit Rose in the leg.

Rose slowed inched to the opposite end of the room during the onslaught, fearing for her life, just as she did the day prior with her uncle on the beach. The agent before her was acting like a lunatic all from the recording and Rose had no clue why. McGovern seemed amiable and relaxed when Rose first met her, but now she was nothing like the serious FBI agents in the novels she read. She was totally unprofessional and unhinged, in young Rose's inexperienced opinion.

"I'm sorry, Rose," McGovern said as she rubbed her temples and retook her seat at the desk after a few deep breaths. "I shouldn't have reacted that way. You have to understand, though, I've risked my career and spent an ungodly number of hours—amounting to months or years of my life—on this case. And to hear I'm way off? It's absolutely gut-wrenching."

"So…do you believe him?" Rose timidly asked, her voice trembling.

The agent looked Rose in the eyes solemnly. For a long moment, a heavy silence filled the air until McGovern sighed and nodded. "I know exactly what trafficking ring he's talking about. I worked the case years back. There were rumblings that the Senator could have been involved, but just rumors; practically every member of congress in the southeast was being accused in closed door meetings. We'll have a DNA test run on you and quietly run this down with local resources, but that story you just heard from Remington was the fucking truth. That fits Remington's M.O., too. I'm afraid I'd been so wrapped up in nabbing your uncle that I missed what was right in front of my eyes the whole time."

"I don't understand," Rose with a break in her voice.

"I believe what your uncle is saying is the God's honest truth. Now, because this isn't an FBI official investigation I don't need to run this down with others. I am the arbiter of justice and decision-maker on this one and I'm telling you that Senator got what was coming to him if this is all true. If he's connected in any way to that trafficking ring."

"Am I off the hook? What about Mr. Remington? I mean, he killed people."

"Yes, yes and yes, still." McGovern paced the length of the room, hands on her head. "Rose, I'm going to tell you something not many people in this world know. No one else on this 'case' knows, at least. My very own sister was in that ring. Nineteen-year-old little Emily. She got mixed up in the wrong crowd, drugs, the works, and was found drugged out during the raid. Tied up, drugged out and blindfolded. She didn't remember all the things they did to her and it was probably for the best because I'd read the stories. We called it *Operation Savior* because we were saving these girls from *unspeakable* horrors."

Rose nodded, still not comprehending; she felt like it was too good to be true. "So Mr. Remington and I are free to go?"

"Rose, I'd like to shake Remington's hand for what he did to the Senator," McGovern stated as she began tearing up, nodding. "I'll need to quietly and independently verify some of this somehow, but once I do, yes. You see, Rose, I was particularly close to this case. Operation Savior. Because of my sister Emily, so I remember every detail about it. And it all sounded like an operation with numerous underlings and no true head. No leader. But this is all coming full circle now. You see, my sister, she swore to me—*swore* to me—that the one thing she remembers from her time locked up with this ring of sick fucks was that the son of a bitch that used to do those things to her when she was blindfolded made her call him Carolina. Sweet Carolina. That's why I believe him. That's why I know Remington is telling the truth. That information is highly classified and I didn't even put it in my report. The Carolina part, only Emily and I know."

McGovern walked over to Rose, stood her up and hugged her. "What your mother had to go through—along with my sister—is something no human being should ever have to endure. *Ever.* It illustrates the true depravity that man is capable of. I'm sorry, Rose. And I'm sorry for your mother.

And if I can verify all of this, then I'm going to bury any misgivings of yours or Remington's so far under the dirt that you'll both be spotless for life.

"Now I have an idea," McGovern said strongly, looking at the Rose with a smile.

CHAPTER 57

The rain fell loudly on the umbrella overhead. Rose had not gotten to attend her mother's own funeral a few weeks prior and she was secretly glad for her absence. As she stood in the Charleston graveyard, raining pummeling down, she felt pity for Detective Covington's wife and three young children. The youngest child, a girl who could not be more than seven, hugged her mother's leg tightly and shook with great, heaving sobs. The other two children stared blankly with the faces of sullen adults who had seen too much and had no tears left to cry. The widow was statuesque in a modest black dress, a black hat that, if any other color, belonged at Churchill Downs, and oversized black sunglasses. She resembled a resolute Jackie O and had more in common with the former First Lady than she wished; namely, that she was now a young widow and that her deceased husband, though loving, was a known adulterer. The children would not find out for years, but the marriage had been irrevocably broken for a while, with no trust or honesty left. Still, despite the flaws of the deceased, she had cried and would cry over Detective Covington more than she would cry over any other loss in her life. He was her soulmate and, though she could not know it at the time, she would never take another husband.

The umbrella Rose was under was held by Agent Gibson, or as Rose still called her, Nurse Blanchard. It had been a week since Covington's passing and the funeral was a poetically beautiful and depressive sight to behold. In that time, McGovern, through Gibson, informed Rose that her uncle was telling the truth and her father was in fact the Senator. Robert and Rose were free and their records were clean. No one else at the FBI knew about the investigation or Robert, Agent Gibson had informed Rose. They were free to carry on as if the whole ordeal never happened. Rose wondered if that would change if the agents found out she pulled the trigger on Derrick, though she doubted it would. Agent Gibson let the girl know they had disbanded all work on the Senator's case, though Rose had already figured as much given the fanfare at the funeral and all over the news. The week had been filled with Covington's picture on every newspaper, every report on television and across billboards in the Low Country and throughout the state. The *Low Country Ledger* ran the following piece:

> *SENATOR MCDONOUGH MURDER: SOLVED*
> *by Rose Shelby*
>
> *It took nearly two decades, but the execution-style murder of South Carolina Senator Arthur McDonough has finally been solved, with a sick twist that has some asking: was this good old-fashioned Southern Justice?*
>
> *The Federal Bureau of Investigations held a press conference today during which Special Agent Darlene*

McGovern issued the following statement: "After years of work and countless man hours, we are happy to report that we have closed the case on the homicide of Senator Arthur McDonough in his Lexington mansion from 2007. A Detective Joseph Covington of North Charleston was found to be in possession of the firearm that was used to kill the Senator. After searching Detective Covington's home following his tragic death by a drunk driver this past week, we were able to locate the gun and other evidence that linked him to the scene. Upon further review, however, Detective Covington appears to have killed the Senator due to his involvement in a human/sex-trafficking ring he was investigating at the time. It appears from his own notes that Detective Covington purposely left the Senator's name from the investigation in order to shoot and kill the Senator himself. Based on information we have gathered thus far, the Senator was responsible for the trafficking of over two thousand girls from 1995 through his death in 2007, roughly a quarter of which we estimate to have been underage. Given the depravity described in Detective Covington's notes, photographs and other first-hand accounts involving actions by the Senator during that time period, we

> *have decided not to further any investigation into Detective Covington's motives or actions. In fact, the FBI has posthumously nominated Detective Covington for the FBI Medal of Honor. I will not be taking further questions at this time."*

As Rose stood with Agent Gibson and watched Detective Covington's casket fall into the muddy abyss, she could not help but smile, knowing her mother was off the hamster wheel that was her desolate life. She knew her mother would be happy that Rose would be raised a Shelby in the Low Country. In the previous week, Rose had come to grips with the actions of her newfound uncle and learned to love him for them. He made the world a better place by taking people like the Senator and Derrick—two men who should have protected her mother throughout life and failed, even doing the exact opposite—out of it. She would be forever grateful to him and now to her Aunt Caroline, who would grow to become her mother figure.

Robert solemnly straightened his tie, careful to keep his umbrella steady and his wife beside him dry. Watching his beloved colleague be lowered into the ground, he yearned to take the life of those responsible for the horrors and atrocities of the world. After seeing the reception Covington received nationally for "his" work, Robert began to believe in the good of man again; he was encouraged that his own silent campaign for southern justice was all for something.
And thought about taking out the worst of mankind once more. Maybe retirement could wait.

CHAPTER 58

It had been the perfect summer morning, before turning dark and cloudy for a mid-day humidity shower. Ricky was spending his off-day shopping in downtown Greenville when his phone had begun lighting up. Reports from the Low Country had begun trickling in along with texts, emails and calls from his editor telling him to keep his ear to the ground; something about a fatal car crash involving police and a drunk driver.

At first, Ricky tried to ignore it all and enjoy his time away from work, searching for a new pair of shoes and whatever else tickled his fancy. But when the raucous thunderstorm storm forced him to take shelter back in his car, he turned to his numerous notifications. With rain beating down his windshield, no one outside the vehicle had been able to hear his gargled cries. His sweet Coral was the drunk driver. All Ricky read appeared to insinuate that she had died at the scene, but nothing definitive was being reported about the "alleged murderer." Ricky had sat in the parking garage, shrieking for over an hour before heading home. He was both furious and broken-hearted; Coral should have heeded his countless warnings about her drinking and driving habits. It was only a matter of time. Nothing he could do now.

Two days had passed since Coral's accident and still no word on her status. Ricky's boss refused to let him travel to the Low Country to find out about the status of "a drunk murderer of a friend" as he put it, so Ricky was using contacts along the coast to provide him with any information at all. Nothing was all he heard.

Ricky had spent the last forty-eight hours honoring Coral as he knew she would want to be honored if she was in fact dead: by drinking heavily. When a pounding at his door woke him from a drunken slumber, her emerged from his cave, fended off the mid-afternoon sunlight and spotted a FedEx driver at his door with a thick envelope. Ricky signed for it with a sputter of hope after seeing it was from Coral and dated the morning of her accident. He tore it open and spent the rest of the day reading and re-reading its contents before deciding he needed to defy his boss and speed for the Low Country.

About the Author

R. W. M. Flynn has always had the silent dream of becoming a published author, so for reading this book (or even picking it up off the shelf to read this blurb and give it a chance): he thanks you sincerely. Flynn lives in South Carolina with his dogs, practices law and writes daily.

Made in the USA
Columbia, SC
23 July 2025

5d165702-a1ad-46e5-867a-1d997111bcacR01